THE ROYAL TREATMENT

MELANIE SUMMERS

Indigo Group

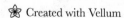

Praise and Awards

- Two-time bronze medal winner at the Reader's Favorite Awards, Chick-lit category for *The Royal Treatment* and *Whisked Away.*
- Silver medalist at the Reader's Favorite Awards, Women's Fiction category for *The After Wife.*

"A fun, often humorous, escapist tale that will have readers blushing, laughing and rooting for its characters."

~ *Kirkus Reviews*

"A gorgeously funny, romantic and seductive modern fairy tale…"

~ *MammieBabbie Book Club*

"…perfect for someone that needs a break from this world and wants to delve into a modern-day fairy tale that will keep them laughing and rooting for the main characters throughout the story.

~ *ChickLit Café*

"I was totally gripped to this story. For the first time ever the Kindle came into the bath with me. This book is unputdownable. I absolutely loved it."

~ Philomena (Two Friends, Read Along with Us)

"Very rarely does a book make me literally hold my breath or has me feeling that actual ache in my heart for a character, but I did both."

~ Three Chicks Review for Net galley

Books by Melanie Summers

ROMANTIC COMEDIES
The Crown Jewels Series

The Royal Treatment

The Royal Wedding

The Royal Delivery

Paradise Bay Series

The Honeymooner

Whisked Away

The Suite Life

Resting Beach Face (Coming Soon)

Crazy Royal Love Series

Royally Crushed

Royally Wild

Royally Tied (Coming Soon)

WOMEN'S FICTION

The After Wife

The Deep End (Coming Soon)

Dedication

To every woman who will read this book,
and to the little girl inside of you who played dress up on a rainy day,
and danced on your dad's feet.
I hope you laugh.
I hope you love.
I hope you believe in yourself because you are enough.

Author's Note

Dear Reader,

I wrote this book because I needed to laugh. I need to escape. I needed to sigh happily.

The phone rang on Halloween morning (one of my very favourite days of the year), and by the time I hung up, everything had changed. Suddenly, my tough-as-nails dad was fighting stage three cancer in his lungs and lymph nodes. News no one wants to hear. News that knocks a person on her ass.

I was faced with the very real possibility of losing my father—the man who raised me (alongside my mom) and who had the wisdom to stand back and let me be frustrated and let me fail (sometimes spectacularly), then helped pick me up, dust myself off and keep going. He's the kind of dad I can always call when life's getting me down or when I have something to celebrate, whether big or small. What would I do if I didn't have him to chat with about nothing for hours at a time? Who would I laugh with about the absurdities of life?

It's funny how the brain works. In only a few minutes, I was rendered incapable of writing the very serious women's fiction book I'd been working on. But a writer's mind must create. It cannot stop.

And so, the flood gates of humour opened up wide, and Tessa and Arthur's story came pouring out.

I wrote and wrote and, at times, laughed so hard, my cheeks hurt. And at the same time, my dad fought with everything he has. On Easter Monday, he called, and just as quickly as the crisis started, it ended. He's in full remission, and we've been given the incredible gift of more time, more phone calls, more celebrations.

Some of you will be facing your own crisis when you pick up this book. I hope that your story will end as happily as mine.

My greatest wish as a writer is to make you laugh, and let you escape, and cause you to sigh happily.

With much love and gratitude,
Melanie

A Special Note from Prince Arthur, Duke of Wellingbourne

I HATE to tell you this, ladies, but if you've ever watched a Hollywood film—or even worse—a made-for-TV movie about a royal family, you've been served up a steaming plate of horseshit. I know, because I am the Crown Prince of Avonia, but I'm not just speaking for myself. Several of my closest friends are also princes or dukes from various countries around the world. We've discussed it, and we all agree—the film and romance book industries have done us all a great disservice by setting up unrealistic expectations of what it means to date and/or marry a member of the Royal Family.

For example, if we met at a party and you lost your shoe, I can tell you with one hundred percent certainty that I will not be going door-to-door trying to return it to you, no matter how beautiful you are. First of all, it's a shoe, so you can easily slip over to the store for another pair. Second, if you're too stupid to realize you're only wearing one shoe, you and I aren't going to exactly be long-term. I might shag you if the opportunity arises, but beyond that, we're done.

If you were previously under the impression that I would chase you down with your sweaty high heel on a pillow, then you may also be under several other falsely held beliefs, such as the following:

That I wake to the sound of birds singing at my windowsill, am fed breakfast in bed by a maid with a little white cap tied to her head (what are those caps for, anyway?), then I lie about in the drawing room reading books all morning whilst my sister, Princess Arabella, plays harp. I spend my afternoons on a hunt with a gaggle of dukes, then dine on eight-course dinners with women in glittery gowns and elbow-length gloves, after which I retire to the library to smoke cigars and drink bourbon with other blue bloods.

Other than the part about having crowns locked away in a vault, servants sidling around all the time (who, by the way, provide enough jump scares to make my life the reboot of Stephen King's *IT*), and the stretch limos, the movies have it dead wrong.

Here is my typical day: an alarm clock wakes me at precisely six o'clock every morning except Sunday, when I am able to sleep in until seven-thirty (lucky me). I then dress in gym clothes and do a one-hour mixed martial arts training session with my head of security, Ollie, to keep my body in top princely condition. I shower, eat breakfast at the kitchen counter while I am briefed on my itinerary by my senior adviser, Vincent Hendriks, who, most of the time, smells like blue cheese for reasons I do not wish to uncover. I spend the rest of the day either attending incredibly tedious meetings or visiting ghastly depressing places such as the children's hospital. If I am lucky, I dine alone, downing a few beers to help me forget the sallow faces of those brave, sick kids. If I am not lucky enough to have the evening to myself, I must soldier on with my best Prince Charming smile while dining with visiting dignitaries and their blushing wives.

I'm a bit of a hit with the wives, by the way. The husbands? Not so much.

If the world were run by women (which it probably should be—I mean, look at how quickly those ladies running Iceland got the country out of bankruptcy a few years back? No pissing around. They quickly threw the bankers in jail and pulled the economy up by its bootstraps – and BOOM! Back on track) ... anyway, if the world were run by women—in particular the wives with whom I dine—our little kingdom would be the international leader in trade. And I wouldn't be in the middle of the shitstorm that has descended upon me today...

Good Men, Payphones & Other Things That No Longer Exist

Tessa

"OH, BUGGER!" The car speeds off while laughter spills from the open windows.

"You little… tramps!" I holler, which only makes them laugh harder. I'm only twenty-eight, but to them I'm a dripping wet, middle-aged hag, and my use of the word 'tramps' only confirms it for them. But I will not swear. There are children standing nearby. Oh, I did say bugger, didn't I? Shit.

My new white jeans and favourite suede boots are now soaked and covered in mud. This is literally the third time in two years that I have been the victim of the 'bowling for losers' game that has been held at this spot for, oh, I don't know, forever. There's a dip in the pavement all the way along the front of the bus transfer station, and because the station is backed by an eight-foot brick wall, there's nowhere to hide. After any big rain, teenagers appear out of nowhere to play.

To be honest, it *is* kind of fun if you're one of the teenagers crammed into the car with your friends. I'm ashamed to say I did it once, and it was a bit of a thrill, in a scary, exciting, let's-do-something-really-naughty-that-will-bond-us-forever sort of way. *Oh, my God! What if we get caught?*

But then, as soon as it was over, I looked back at our victim. She was dressed for a party, and even the wrapping paper on the fancy silver box she was holding was dripping wet. We totally killed her day for a few seconds of entertainment. I begged my friends to turn back so we could give her a ride, but, as it turns out, teenagers don't like to have their fun spoiled, and after that I had a few less friends. But it didn't really matter. I had already grown accustomed to being an outcast long before puberty hit.

I'm currently on the way to my childhood home for yet another dreaded family dinner. Being the only girl of five children, I've always had plenty of reasons that I didn't fit in—lack of penis, lack of testicles, lack of interest in football. Things have only gotten worse over the years instead of better, with my brilliant brothers moving up in the world, while I have recently dropped down a few rungs on the job ladder. These days, my brothers tease me relentlessly about being 'the dullest sharp in the Sharpe family.' Ha. Ha. Ha.

As the bus barrels toward Abbott Lane, I shrink from a relatively confident, reasonably intelligent woman to an awkward, horribly insecure fourteen-year-old. I'll spend the next twenty-three minutes hoping the bus breaks down or is hijacked by terrorists (but only if Keanu Reeves gets on first), then the next several hours wishing I had managed to dream up the perfect excuse to skip this evening's dinner.

In the past two years, I've already used horrible cramps (tried and true, especially if my dad answers the phone), raging fever, raging diarrhea—anything raging is quite effective, really—tight deadline at work (which they don't believe), bus broke down, and bronchitis (which is harder than you think to pull off when you're perfectly healthy). But today I can't bring myself to lie. Today we celebrate what would have been my grandfather's eighty-fifth birthday, and since he was the only person in my family to believe I had any potential at all, I owe it to him to be here.

———

I stand on the wet sidewalk staring at my parents' house with the mishmash of dark green-panelled additions jutting out on top of what was once a one-storey brick home. Even though my legs are damp and freezing, I take a moment to drink in the silence before I am bombarded by the chaos and cooking smells that wait for me. A light rain starts, urging me to go in and get it over with already. There are much worse fates than a family dinner. I can't think of what they are at the moment, but I know they exist.

Hoping not to be noticed when I walk through the door, I keep my voice whisper-quiet as I say, "Hi, everyone!"

My mother's head whips out of the kitchen down the narrow hall. Mum has highly-attuned ears. She can manage two conversations at the same time, all while listening for a sleeping baby and making sure the potatoes don't boil over.

"Tessa! There you are! I thought you'd never get here." She dodges my nieces, who are too busy chasing the cat around with a tiara to notice me.

"Poor Mr. Whiskers. Mum, you're not letting them dress him up again." I hand her the wine I brought for 'everyone' (and by everyone, I mean me) and give her a kiss on the cheek.

"He'll let them know if he doesn't want to play dress up." She pulls me in for a hug, and the familiar scent of Chanel No. 5 wafts into my nostrils.

A hiss and a yowl says Mum was right about Mr. Whiskers. All three of the girls come screaming back down the hall, then make a right and thunder up the stairs.

Mum looks me up and down. "Splashed at the transfer station again?"

"Yup."

"You should really think about getting a car. They have those electric ones now, so you won't be ruining the Earth like the rest of us."

"Yes, you've mentioned that before."

As much as I'd love to cruise around in my own car, I can't exactly afford one, which is a bit of stomach-tightening information that I keep to myself. So instead, I use public transit under the pretense that I have turned into a real environmentalist. While I definitely care about the earth, I also fantasize about one day pulling up in a shiny, sporty little car so that I can roar off when I have had enough 'family time.'

What I'd really like to do is to find some nice, stable, eco-conscious man who will drive me to my parents' house in a hybrid with heated leather seats. I'm sure if I found him, my 'worthiness of respect' rating would triple. But since finding a single, dependable, decent man is as likely as finding a payphone these days, I will forever remain a very single entrepreneur who gets to buy expensive footwear (on sale) without hearing complaints from someone who will later leave up the toilet seat.

Oh, that sounded horribly negative. I know there *are* good men out there, but they are for *other* women. Not for me. If there is a lying, cheating sack of crap within a ten-mile radius, I'll find him and fall for him.

My niece, Poppy, is the first of the children to notice me. Her eyes light up, and she screams, "Auntie Tessa is here!"

And so begins the onslaught of kids rushing for the packages of Jelly Babies they know I've brought. Poppy runs down the stairs and straight into my arms for a big hug. I squeeze her tightly and give her a sloppy kiss on the cheek, just so I can watch her wipe it off. That always cracks me up. I'm the old spinster aunt, except without the hairs growing out of a mole on my chin—yet. "Oh, I've missed my silly beans niece."

I crouch down and dig around in my coat pocket. "Let's see if I've got anything for you."

She grins expectantly.

"Oh, here it is. One package of Jelly Babies, world's finest candy." I hand her the package.

"Thank you, Auntie!" She gives me another hug, while the lineup of children forms not so neatly behind her.

"You're welcome, peanut," I whisper in her ear. "Don't forget, you're my favourite Poppy in the whole world."

Poppy beams as her little brother, Clarke, cuts in-between us.

I go through this routine another six times, then tell the brood of them what I always do. "Save them for *after* dinner, or your mums will be very cross with me."

By the time the words are out of my mouth, they're already gone, presumably to hide and eat the candies. I toss my wool coat onto the teetering pile of jackets on the old wooden bench and head toward the TV room to say hello to my dad and brothers.

When I poke my head into the room, my eyes are immediately assaulted by the pink flashing 'Sheepshagger Beer' sign, which clashes horribly with the red and green plaid couch and love seat. My dad is standing behind the 'bar,' which is really just a TV tray with a twelve pack of beers on it. His gaze is glued to the giant television screen.

"Hi, guys." My voice is drowned out by their cheers.

Football is pretty much their only shared passion. Well, that and beer. Oh, and making fun of me. So, I guess they have a lot in common when I think about it.

Dad notices me out of the corner of his eye and gives me a quick wave and half a grin. "Hey there, Tess… AAAHHHH!!!"

His head swivels to the screen again, and he looks like he's about to have a stroke because someone almost scored a goal. The football match is a bit of a godsend actually. It means a delay of game in the next round of 'let's pick on Tessa for not having a man, or a real job, or a man with a real job.' Now, where did my mum go with that wine?

I find her in the kitchen with my two sisters-in-law, Isa and Nina. They're too engrossed in a heated discussion about the new school uniform policy to bother with me.

"I know!" Nina, who is starting her second trimester, pops an olive in her mouth, then keeps right on talking. "I was told they weren't going to do this again this year, but you know you can't ever trust them. It's a money grab."

"A *total* money grab." Isa's head is bobbing so fast, I'm afraid it might fall right off. Wouldn't be too much of a loss for her. She tends to use it mainly for displaying her hair and makeup skills anyway. Oh, that was bitchy, wasn't it? I wonder if I'm getting PMS?

My mum takes her position in front of the stove, her hands a blur of activity, and she stirs, spices, and sautés dinner for sixteen. "So, Tessa, how's the *blogging* going?" She emphasizes the word blogging so as to prove she's finally remembered the name of my current profession.

"Really well, thanks. Steady increase in subscribers, so that's always good."

Her face pinches in confusion, and I know what's coming. "I still don't understand *how* you make money."

"It's, um, ads, mostly. Some of the companies that I review for also pay me a fee for testing their products." I wash my hands and start to slice some pickles that will be served with the stew.

Mum nods. "Right. Companies pay you to advertise on your sites."

We go over this every time, but I don't mind. It means she cares. "Yes, sort of. I get paid for the ads indirectly. They pay Google. Google pays me."

"And you *really* get enough people reading your blog to pay your bills?"

She must know that I'm exaggerating about how well I'm doing, but in my defense, I only do it because I don't want them to worry. Okay, also because I would die if my brothers found out.

"I do." I make just enough to get by. Real money. Not Bitcoins, which will be her next question.

"Real money, or those Bitcoins I keep hearing about?"

"Real money, Mum. It goes in my bank account and everything."

"Good, because Grace next door told me that those Bitcoin people are going bankrupt."

"Oh, really? Well, then I'm glad I opted for being paid in real money."

The doorbell rings, indicating that Bram has arrived. Unlike me, Bram likes to have everyone's full attention at all times. Something about being born in the middle of a pack of boys that is apparently still affecting him.

"Hello? Where is everybody?" he bellows. "I want you to meet my new girlfriend."

"Another one?" Nina purses her lips at Isa, setting off a wave of head-shaking and eye-rolling as they go in search of Bram's catch of the day.

My mum wipes her hands on a tea towel and bustles in the direction of the front door. I take the opportunity to gulp back the rest of my wine and top up my glass before going to greet his latest squeeze.

———

We sit down to eat at exactly six o'clock. The adults squish in at the dining room table, while the kids are at a precariously tippy card table filling the entrance between the TV room and dining room. The television blares in the background so my father won't miss an all-important goal. My mum cracks the window, as within a few minutes it will be stifling hot in here. She shimmies past the buffet, which proudly displays her Royal Family commemorative plate and mug collection, then is just about to sit down at the head of the table when she pops back up. "Nearly forgot the fancy napkins!"

"Now don't fuss, Mum. It's not like we're hosting the King." My dad, who likes to get through dinners almost as fast as I do, says this every time.

Mum waves off his comment as she hurries back into the kitchen, returning a moment later with a pile of thick paper napkins with a spring motif. She's big on theme napkins.

Everyone marvels at how my mother has managed to once again pull together such a fine feast. She pretends she doesn't need the praise, and then the mayhem of dishing up begins. Noah, Isa, and Nina carry plates around the table, loading up food for their children. My brother, Lars, sits on his skinny arse and loads up his own plate before his pregnant wife barks at him to get up and help her. He jumps up as though shocked to find out that four of the children at the kiddie table belong to him.

I'm positioned across from the new girlfriend, Irene, who is exactly what I expected. Young, pretty, big hair and even bigger breasts. Finn, who was hasty to grab the empty chair next to our brother's new girl, glances down her deep V every time he hands her a dish, while Bram, who is on her other side, does the same thing when she hands each dish to him.

My dad stands, clears his throat, and holds up his glass of beer.

"We're here together today to celebrate the life of a very special man who would have turned eighty-five today. He was a hell of a gardener, a kind soul, and the best father-in-law a man could ask for. To Grandpa Seth."

We all raise our glasses and toast. Tears fill my eyes. After fifteen years, I still miss Grandpa Seth so much, it hurts sometimes. He moved in with us when I was six, right after our grandmum passed on. He and I used to sneak out to the yard every chance we got. We'd talk while he worked in the garden. Well, actually, I would do all the talking, and he would do the listening. He was the only person in my family who treated me like a grownup, even when I was a little girl. He understood me like no one has since, and there's been a hollow spot in my soul ever since we lost him.

My brothers, who believed Grandpa Seth favoured me—which he *totally* did—didn't have much use for him. They've all started eating while I fiddle with my tulip-stamped napkin and wait for the lump in my throat to clear.

"So, Tess, how's the blogging going?" Noah asks, now that he is finally seated and is piling his own plate with food. *Let the games begin.*

"Tessa's a blogger," Bram tells Irene. "She used to be a real reporter until she got fired for shagging her boss."

"Bram Devon Sharpe!" my mum spits out. "We agreed not to bring that up anymore."

My face flames with humiliation. "It wasn't just shagging. We were together for almost a year."

"What's shagging, Mummy?" Poppy pipes up from the card table. "And why was Auntie doing it to her boss?"

Isa's shoulders drop, and she gives Noah a glare that tells him to handle this if he ever wants to get any you-know-what again. (I'm not guessing about that. She once told me she controls him by doling out sex on a reward-system basis. He doesn't know this, of course, and I wish to hell that I didn't, either.) Noah snaps into action.

"Thanks *a lot*, Bram," Noah mutters. "Nothing, luv, it's just a made-up thing that Uncle Bram is talking about. From the movies."

Irene smiles at me. "So, you blog?"

My mum answers for me. "Tessa's quite the entrepreneur. She's getting new subscribers every month." Her expression says, 'Isn't that surprisingly good for our little Tessa, from whom we expected so little?' To be fair, though, I am the least impressive one of the family. Noah is a structural engineer. Lars is a professor of astrophysics, so in our house, instead of saying someone is 'not exactly a rocket scientist,' we say, they're 'not exactly a Lars.' Finn is finishing architecture school, and Bram is a dentist. And I blog.

"What type of blog do you have?" Irene asks.

"I run a few different sites. Photography, running, a site about the Royals..."

My mum stiffens at the mention of my royal blog. As a huge royal watcher, it's been a bitter disappointment to have her daughter become openly anti-royal. She's such a fan, I actually think she would have preferred that I was an open polygamist.

Irene's eyes light up. "I just *love* the Royal Family! Especially Prince Arthur—yum!" She giggles, then stares at me, clearly expecting me to agree with her on the yumminess of our nation's crown prince.

"Yes, he's very popular." I smile politely.

She gasps. "I wonder if I follow your blog."

"Not if you love the Royal Family," Lars quips.

Her face falls. Mine turns red. "It's less of a fan site and more of a critical look at the necessity of having a monarchy in this day and age."

"Tessa wants to oust the whole bunch," Finn says to Irene's breasts.

"Off with their heads!" the voice of my nephew, Josh, rings out. Or is that one Geoffrey? I can't tell them apart, but it's really not my fault. They're twins, and they never stop moving long enough to get a good look at them.

"I don't want anyone to be beheaded—"

Irene is glaring at me now as though I just told her she has an ugly baby. Bram cuts me off and tells Irene's boobs that I want to see the Royal Family turn everything over to the people and get honest jobs for once instead of stealing from the commoners of Avonia, like they've been doing for centuries.

While her breasts seem neutral on the topic, their owner—and I say owner because I'm fairly sure she paid a lot for them—clearly is not. But this is to be expected—her anger, not the fake boobs. It's a polarizing topic, and if I couldn't handle people's negative reactions, I would have no business blogging about it. If there's one thing that I learned growing up with four brothers, it's how to fight, and how to let criticism bounce off me. Oh, I guess that was two things. Good thing I don't run a site about math.

I reach for the wine bottle, but when I lift it, my heart sinks to discover it's already empty. "I have nothing against the Royal Family personally. It's more of a political and philosophical question."

"If it's not personal, why did you call them 'a pack of dishonest, inbred leeches' last week?" Nina purses her lips and folds her arms over her belly.

"Oh, so you've been reading my work." I can't help but be flattered, even though I know after she read it, she probably called Lars at work and bitched at him for ten minutes about what an awful human being his sister is.

"It would be hard to miss," Finn says, his mouth full of carrots. "That line was retweeted over fifty thousand times."

Noah almost chokes on his beer. "Fifty thousand retweets? Not bad, Tess."

"What the hell's a retweet?" my dad asks.

"Do you actually believe all those terrible things about our Royal Family? Or are you just saying that to get attention?" Isa asks.

"What—"

"Not *attention*, Isa. Subscribers," Noah says. The guilty expression on his face tells me that they have clearly said this behind my back, probably on many an occasion.

"Auntie Tessa," my niece, Tabitha, is standing right behind me, her hot breath going directly into my ear, "my mum and dad said it's not nice to say mean things about other people, so why is it okay when you do it?"

"Uh, well, it's just that, the people I'm writing about aren't going to read it, so it's not really the same thing…" My entire head is hot with shame. I glance over at Isa, who gives me a smug eyebrow raise.

"So, it's okay to say bad things if the people you're talking about won't find out?" Tabitha asks.

"No, not really…" Oh, nuts, the look she's giving me makes me want to slide down off my chair and hide under the table, but somehow I think the guilt would find me there. "It's very complicated, Tabby. The people I'm writing about make choices that affect our entire country, and I believe very strongly that they're doing the wrong thing. If someone doesn't speak out, nothing will change."

She tilts her head like a confused dog. God, she's cute. "But if they'll never read what you say about them, how will they know they have to change?"

And smart. She's really fucking smart. I've been outwitted by a girl in a Hello Kitty jumper. "The thing is… well, sometimes, in politics… you need a lot of people to apply pressure to our lawmakers in order for… for…"

"Ha ha! She's got you there, Tess!" Bram laughs.

In order for what? I suddenly realize that, other than the sound from the TV, the entire room has gone silent, and everyone is waiting for an explanation that I'm not prepared to give. "You're a very wise young lady. I'm going to have to think long and hard about your questions. For now, let me say your parents are right. We shouldn't say bad things about others."

"Mum, Josh spilled his milk all over the carpet!" *Oh, thank God!*

"Shit." My dad, who couldn't care less about the carpet, is referring to the opposing team having just scored.

"Watch your language in front of the children!" My mother hurries to the kitchen for the necessary supplies.

"Grandpa just said 'shit!'"

"Geoffrey, enough!"

"I've got it, Mum. Let me clean that up."

"That's okay, dear. You eat while it's hot."

"Muuummmm, Poppy's smiling at me again!"

"Poppy, what did we say about smiling at Knox?"

"He said my bum smells like farts!"

"Well, it does smell like farts!"

"Do you have to go poop, sweetie?"

"No!"

"No talking about farts or poop at the table!"

"Hang on, what's a retweet, Finn?" My dad points a forkful of beef at me. "And more importantly, does she make any money off them?"

"You don't, but—" I start, but my dad interrupts me.

"You're not lettin' them pay you in Bitcoins, are you?"

3

A Kick to the Crown Jewels

Arthur

MY FATHER, His Serene Highness, the King of Avonia, or Winston, as my grandmother calls him, is away on a two-month diplomatic tour in Southeast Asia at the moment. Of course, this is when it would all come crashing down. Not only is the reigning monarch away, but this is the *one* time this month I was supposed to have an entire evening to myself. I had planned to spend it not-so-alone with the Duchess of Funville, who lets me play her front-nine whenever she's in town, which is not very bloody often.

She's from Scotland, and her father owns half the golf courses around Europe. She's one of very few women who is only interested in a naughty diversion, rather than hoping to end up wearing matching his and hers crowns. Since she's already got her own castle, she has no interest in mine (hers is slightly bigger, and the fact that I can admit that should indicate that I have no need to compensate for anything, wink, wink).

Instead of arriving at her hotel, like I'm supposed to be doing right now, I'm stuck dealing with what could be the final crisis that brings down our family's nearly eight-hundred-year reign. Turns out our new prime minister is secretly plotting against us. In spite of my father basically handing him the election last fall, he's going to bend us all over and give us the old 'referendum to oust the Royal Family.' Well, thank you, Jack Janssen. Wanker.

I sigh and stare longingly at the suit of armor that stands guard at the door to my office. Whatever happened to the days when a prince could say, 'Off with their heads!' and shit would get done?

I've been in a meeting with Damien Peters, my father's senior adviser and government liaison, and Mr. Blue Cheese for over an hour now. I've positioned myself behind my antique oak desk so the smell is only choking Damien, who is seated next to Vincent (but don't feel too bad for Damien. He's a complete twat). I glance out my office window at the view of the city across the river, where my naughty duchess awaits. My pants are suddenly very constrictive. Time to take control of this meeting.

I hold up my hand, interrupting Vincent, who is repeating how shocked he is. "All right, setting aside the fact that the PM is basically a lying shit, what can we do about it? If he calls for a referendum, we can't exactly stop him. We've faced these votes before, and the people haven't ousted us yet."

"Unfortunately, with the poor economy and the high unemployment rate, and your father's recent... situation... about the taxes..." Vincent pauses and clears his throat twice, which is what he does whenever he's about to drop a fucking a-bomb on me. "...the polls are showing that seventy-two percent of the population will vote to have the monarchy dissolved."

Well, isn't that a kick to the jewels?

Damien clears his throat. "There's been either no press or bad press lately, Your Highness. The people are feeling rather cut off. I'm afraid the family's private nature hasn't played out well, especially when the royal family across the pond is constantly giving interviews and photo ops—"

"They're very open with their lives. Will, Kate, Harry, all the young royals, really." Vincent gives me a look that is somehow both apologetic and accusatory.

Oh, God. If I have to hear about Mr. and Mrs. Perfect and their perfectly adorable babies one more time, I'm going to vomit. "I highly doubt that posting pics of my morning fruit plate is going to make a difference. We all know there's an ebb and flow to these things. Popularity waxes and wanes every few years. We can fix it." The words feel like sand in my mouth. I don't have the first fucking clue how to fix this. What I *do* know is that if I don't find the right combination of hopeful phrases right now, I'll never get these two out of my office, and I can pretty much forget practicing my follow through this evening.

Damien shifts in his seat—away from Vincent. "We need to win back the people, and in short order. If Janssen does call for a referendum, we'll only have a matter of weeks to convince an increasingly angry, financially-strained public that they have any use for you whatsoever."

Well, thank you, Mr. Obvious. Like I didn't know that already. Think, Arthur, think. I stand and walk across the office to the wall of windows. I look out at the city lights as they twinkle against the darkening sky. A city of critics waiting to dethrone me before I can even sit my arse down on it in the first place.

"Critics." I snap my fingers and turn to the men. "Who's my worst critic?"

"What's that got to do—"

I hold up one hand. "Worst of the worst. Who hates us the most of anyone out there?"

Vincent and Damien glance at each other and at the same time say, "Tessa Sharpe."

"Really? Never heard of her. What's up her arse?"

"Blogger. Just really hates the monarchy."

"Usual reasons? Taxes, patriarchal society, blah, blah, blah?"

Vincent pulls out his phone. A moment later, he says, "Here it is. Last week, she called the Royal Family 'a pack of dishonest, inbred leeches.'" *Ah, so we're dealing with some bitter old sea hag.*

"Ouch. That's a bit much. How's her following?"

"She has the widest reach of any anti-royal site out there at the moment," Vincent says.

"By far." Damien always needs to have the last word, no matter how trivial. I told you he was a twat.

"She seems especially fond of criticizing you, Your Highness." Vincent holds up his iPad again. "Prince Arthur is the worst of the bunch. A ridiculous man-child who spends his days loafing around and nights drinking up the people's money. I can just imagine him a few years from now, the crown tipped sideways on his drunken head, leg slung over the arm of the throne, slumped down like a petulant teenager with no fecking clue how to rule a country."

"*Loafing around?* Well, if there's anything I've never done a day in my life, it's loaf." My hackles go up at the insinuation. I walk over to Vincent, hold my fingers sideways under my nose and look over his shoulder at his screen. A picture of a lovely little blonde smiles back at me. Those long waves caressing her shoulders don't say 'bitter sea hag.' The glossy pink lips say 'good to go,' which quite frankly is my target audience. "She'll be perfect."

Both men screw up their faces in confusion. "Sir?"

I walk back to the window and suck in air that doesn't smell of feet. "We don't need to convince the entire country. That would be an impossible task, especially if a referendum is called anytime soon. We really only have to convince one critic. The harshest one." I smile confidently, hoping that this will put an end to this meeting. "I bring her into the fold, show her my best side, and get *her* to do our publicity for us."

"I don't understand."

Now, I'm really thinking on the fly. Duchess, here I come! "I shall invite this Ms. Harpy—"

"Sharpe."

"Whatever—to the palace to stay for, say…two months, during which time, I'll convince her of the necessity of the Royal Family for this great nation."

"You can't invite an unapproved member of the press to *live* at the palace."

"Of course I can. I'm allowed house guests."

"But not a tabloid journalist."

"She's not a journalist. You told me yourself. She's a blogger."

"Too risky, Your Highness. I'm sorry, but no. We can't let you make this call." Damien shakes his head as though the matter has been decided.

"You seem to be forgetting in whose house you're standing. This is the House Langdon. I am the Duke of Wellingbourne and will one day be the ruler of Avonia. This is very much my call to make."

"Your father is going to be furious." Vincent's tone is firm.

"When isn't he?" I shrug.

"You might fail miserably," Damien pipes up again.

"Or I might have a spectacular win." And a spectacular orgasm, because both of them are now gathering their things.

Vincent gives it one last shot. "Sir, if I may suggest, let's not act until we've spoken to your father."

"Tell you what. Give me the night to think about it. I'll see if I can reach him." I won't bother, but it'll be fine, really.

What's that saying about it being better to beg forgiveness than ask permission?

4

A Shocking Turn of Events

Tessa

It's nine o'clock on Monday morning. I'm standing in my kitchen next to my best friend, Nikki, who is also my camera woman for all my videos, not because she's really technically inclined, but because she's a hairdresser so she has Mondays off, and she'll work for pastries. The two of us stare silently at the latest device that I'll be testing out for my running enthusiast site. It's called the Shock Jogger. It's a thin band equipped with Bluetooth that you wear around your ribs.

"Certainly looks harmless enough, doesn't it?" Nikki takes a sip of her tea.

I pick it up off the counter. "Easy for you to say. You'll be working the camera. I'll be the one getting shocked if my pace goes below target."

She tilts her head, which this week bears intensely purple streaks. "I bet it won't hurt, though."

"I doubt it'll feel like a soft caress." I pick up the pamphlet and flip through it again. "It delivers twenty volts to your mid-section as a reminder to keep up your pace throughout your run, thus eliminating lulls that slow overall progress."

"Twenty volts? How much is that, anyway?"

"No freaking clue," I say.

"Hmm."

"Hmm." Neither of us takes our eyes off the device.

"I once read that a woman got shocked so hard that all her hair fell out."

"That can't be true." I shake my head. "Can it?"

"Doubt it. It was on the cover of *Weekly World News*."

"Then it's definitely false."

"Although they were right about that man who had a baby." Nikki takes a bit of her cheese string. "How much are they paying you to feature it?"

"Three hundred."

"How much were those Bench boots?"

"One-ninety-five during the half off sale."

"You'll have some left over."

"I could get the scarf." I take a deep breath as I pick it up. "Okay, let's do this."

Nikki picks up the camera and points it at me. I smile into the lens.

"Hi, everyone. Today, on Smart Runner, I'll be testing out the Shock Jogger by Wellbits." I hold it up to the camera. "This little guy promises to improve your running stamina and speed by nearly twenty percent in under twelve sessions by delivering a gentle reminder to pick up the pace."

After we shoot the introductory video, Nikki and I head outside to test it. I run, and she drives slowly beside me in her little Citroën. The camera is hooked in place on the driver's side door, window down, so she can keep her eyes on the road.

"The sun is shining, the birds are singing, and it's a beautiful almost-spring day for a run! Let's see if the Shock Jogger can do what it promises." I grin into the camera, pretending I'm not really freaking nervous. Deciding to save my breath, I face forward and concentrate on technique.

"So, it's been fifteen minutes," I pant into the lens. "And I haven't been shocked once yet. My pace definitely is much quicker than normal, because," *pant, pant,* "to be honest, I'm really scared," *pant,* "of the jolt this thing might give me."

When we turn back toward my apartment, I realize I've made a horrible miscalculation. My legs are already jelly, and now I have the very steep climb back home again. I explain this to Nikki, who starts to laugh. I'm now overcome by a bout of nervous laughter that is only wearing me out even faster.

"Stop it!" I shout, to myself as much as her, but it's no use. We've got a serious case of the giggles. And I'm going to get shocked. I just know it. *Giggle.* "I'll never make it up this hill!" *Pant, pant. Giggle.* "Stop laughing!"

We're about halfway up the hill when I get my first "gentle reminder." A sharp zap to my ribs has my knees jerking up to my chest at the same time that I scream in pain. "Motherfucker!"

When my feet hit the ground, they pick up the pace like they've never done before. A woman with two young children makes a *tsk*ing sound at me.

"Sorry!" I give her a wave. "I'm not really a horrible person!" *Pant, pant.*

"She's testing out the Shock Jogger," Nikki calls to them, as if her explanation will make any sense at all.

Gentle reminder? I nearly peed my pants. Now I'm running up the hill so fast that my lungs are on fire. On every inhalation, they beg me to slow down, but I can't. I reach a corner. I'm supposed to stop since I have a red light, but I can't bring myself to get shocked again.

"Oh, my God! A car! Stop, Tess!"

"I can't!" I make a dash for it. The car honks and swerves out of the way. I glance up in time to see the man behind the wheel shaking his fist. He shouts, "Arrsssssshooooollle!" through his open window.

Nikki catches up with me when she gets the green light. She's not laughing anymore. "You nearly got hit by a car!"

"I know!"

"We should edit that part out." Nikki's always the voice of reason.

"I'm," *pant,* "so," *pant,* "tired."

"Take it off!"

"What?!"

"The thingy! The Shock Jogger! It can't hurt you if you aren't wearing it."

"Right!" I strip off my shirt—modesty be damned. I *do not* want to feel that pain again. I toss the shirt through the car window, and it lands on Nikki's head.

"Eww!"

"Sorry!" Now I'm running and fiddling with the damn clasp, only in my concentration, I slow down. *ZAP!* "FUCK!!!"

"Got zapped again?"

"That time I really did pee a little." My entire body tingles (and not the good kind) with aftershocks.

"I can't get it off!" In my panic, my fingers have forgotten how to unbuckle buckles.

"Uh-oh." I hear Nikki's voice and assume she's talking about the Shock Jogger. I won't know for another two minutes why she said it.

Zap! "Fuckity-fuck! That hurts!" My knees jolt up while my torso contracts, so I'm momentarily a human sweat ball suspended in the air. "Help me! I can't get it off!"

Zap! Zap! "Son of a motherfucker!"

My hair feels like it's standing straight up with each shock. Oh, my God! What if *Weekly World News* got it right and my hair falls out? No! I can't get the boots if I have to pay for a wig.

"Not my hair!!!" I scream out as I give the band a sharp tug with both hands. It snaps and shocks my palms once more for good measure before I toss it away from me.

Unfortunately, it hits Nikki in the face. "OUCH! That really fucking hurts!" She screams as she swerves the car. It jumps the curb and stalls out in the shrubs in front of my apartment building. The airbag deploys with a loud bang, and Nikki is trapped in her seat.

"Oh, my God, Nikki!" I yell as I use the last of my strength to run to her. "Are you all right?"

"Yes. I'm fine. I might have a bleeding nose, though." Her words come out muffled.

And that's when I notice them.

The vans, the camera crews, the smartly dressed reporters holding microphones. I stop and stare. They're silent. All of them staring at me, cameras pointed in my direction.

My mouth hangs open, which really just adds to the dignity of this moment—me red-faced and dripping with sweat, in only my sports bra and running pants, having just jerked and jolted and sworn like a pirate as I ran up the hill home. Oh yeah, then caused an accident.

"Uh-oh."

"You finally noticed them?"

"Uh-huh."

———

So, let me bring you up to speed, now that things have calmed down momentarily. Nikki's nose took the brunt of the airbag force. It's broken, but she won't need surgery because the very cute doctor at the emergency clinic was able to distract her long enough to snap it back in place. (He does shifts down at the boxing ring every Saturday night for extra cash, so he pretty much has the whole thing mastered.) He got her number, too—after she showed him her gorgeous Facebook profile pic under the guise of him seeing how to set her nose. Dr. Perfect asking for her number definitely helped dial down her rage at me. He also gave her some pretty strong painkillers, which are proving immensely helpful.

While I have not had any of the pain meds, I have downed three quick glasses of white zinfandel to numb my own utter humiliation. Several camera crews remain parked outside my building. If I stretch up on my tippy toes and look out the kitchen window, I can see them on the street, five stories below.

Nikki's car has been towed to the shop, where it will cost me a little over three thousand dollars to fix the damage and reset the airbag. The building management company will be bringing by a bill to replace the hundred-year-old shrubs out front, which should wipe out the rest of my savings, so more good news there. No Bench boots for me.

Oh, and it turns out Prince Arthur, giant douche-canoe extraordinaire, made an announcement earlier this morning that has drawn the attention of every media outlet in the country and aimed it right at my head. Hence the crowd of reporters who managed to catch the entire last three minutes of the Shock Jogger experiment on film. So, the most humiliating moment of my life is now making its way around the globe via YouTube. Special thanks to Al Gore for inventing the Internet in the first place.

But back to the matter at hand. Apparently, the Crown Prince himself has offered to 'give me the keys to the castle.' He wants me—his harshest critic—to come and live with the Royal Family for the next two months, in an effort to show the good people of Avonia that he and his family have nothing to hide. He is hoping that if he can 'convince his harshest critic that his family gives more than they take, that others will soon agree, and his family will maintain their rightful place as the protectors and leaders of this great nation.'

My phone is on silent, but I can see it lighting up with calls every twenty seconds. Nikki and I are sitting on my couch, watching the Avonian Broadcast News Channel (ABNC). It's on a loop. First, his announcement, then the Shock Jogger video. One reporter has dubbed it my "Shocking Morning." Very original. *That* guy has a job at ABNC, and I don't? There is something very wrong with this world. All I can say is, thank God for whoever invented wine. Unlike Al Gore, you do not suck.

I glance over at Nikki and cringe again. "Fresh ice for your nose?" She has two black eyes, and her nose…well, I honestly had no idea a nose could swell up that much. "I am just so sorry."

"Forget about it." She can't say her 'r's now on account of the swelling, so she sounds kind of like a gangster from New Jersey. *Faggetaboutit.*

I shall not laugh. I shall not laugh.

"Go ahead and laugh. I hud it, too."

We both burst out into giggles for a second, then she groans in agony.

"Oh, shit! I'm sorry. I'll get you some more wine. I mean ice." I get up and make my way to the kitchen. I'll have more wine, though…

Nikki shuts off the television and follows me.

"So, what the hell are you going to do?"

"I have no fucking clue." I hand her a fresh towel filled with ice cubes and pour another glass of wine. "I mean, I can't just go live with the Royal Family for two months. That would be insane."

I stare out the window. I have a lovely vantage point of the entire city from here. In the distance sits the tiny, lush, green island on the other side of the Langdon River that houses the enormous palace. "I can't go live there." I point with my glass, and wine sloshes onto the floor. I sop it up with my sock and pretend it didn't happen. Yup, I'm drunk.

"Why not?"

"Because I live *here*. This is my house. I have a bed, and a TV, and...and...let's not forget about Chester." I glance over at my betta fish, who is blissfully unaware of any of this morning's horrors as he naps on his little fish hammock. I walk over to his bowl. "Hey, Chester? I can't leave you for two months. Who would feed you and change your water?"

As I turn to Nikki, the truth comes spilling out of my mouth. "Think of all of the horrible things I've written about them. Horrible, awful things. I can't go live with them. They must absolutely hate my guts."

"So what? Think of the boost this will give your career. It could give you another shot as a real reporter. Or maybe even a book deal. This could change your life, Tessa. Seriously."

She folds her arms and gives me her best school headmaster look.

"But *two months*? With people who despise me? You'd never do it."

Okay, that is totally not true. I've never met someone who cares less about what people think of her than Nikki. I once saw her literally steal a handful of Cadbury Buttons from a toddler in a stroller when she thought his parents weren't looking. But they *were* looking, and when they confronted her, she just said, "You shouldn't be feeding candy to a baby. What kind of parents are you anyway?" And when we walked away, I swear she'd already forgotten about them before we even reached the end of the block.

Nikki doesn't answer me, but just stares. I let out a long, groany-type sigh. "This is going to suck nuts!"

"Maybe. Maybe not. But it'll be totally worth it."

"What would I even wear? I obviously can't go buy a bunch of clothes now that I have to pay for the car."

"And the shrubs."

"And the shrubs, right." My shoulders slump down. "Oh, my God. The video! I can't face the Royal Family after they've seen that! In fact, I can't face *anyone*. I am never leaving my apartment again."

"You have to. You're going to be huge after this. Your blog will be *the* authority on the Royal Family."

"How is it that the biggest opportunity of my life falls into my lap at the exact same time that I become a world-famous joke?"

"Life's funny that way."

"Hilarious."

I walk back over to the couch and turn the volume back on. Veronica Platt sits behind her ABNC anchor desk with a split-screen picture behind her head. One side is me with my sweat-drenched face squished in pain and my shoulders jammed up into my ears; the other side is the ridiculously handsome Prince Arthur dressed in a tuxedo, his short, dirty blond hair looking freshly cut, wearing a shit-eating grin. The text underneath says *Love Match?*

"Oh, for God's sake…"

Veronica's smooth voice begins the next half-hour of news. "Reports from palace insiders today indicate that Prince Arthur's announcement to invite Tessa Sharpe, the so-called Royal Watchdog, to live at Valcourt for the next two months came as a complete surprise. Staff members were unaware that any such plan was being hatched until the press conference was underway. Our royal correspondent, Giles Bigly, is here with the scoop. Giles, exactly what happened this morning at Valcourt?"

The camera zooms out to include Giles sitting behind the desk. "Veronica, it's not known exactly how this bizarre turn of events came to be, but what is clear is that the Duke of Wellingbourne acted alone. This video of senior staff members during the Prince's announcement seems to say it all."

A video roll starts, the Prince is speaking, and behind him there are circles drawn in around the faces of several men and women in the background.

Giles' voice cuts in. "Watch as their mouths drop in unison, right…here!"

The video stops, and it's back to a split screen of Giles and Veronica. Veronica is nodding quickly. "Yes, Giles, they are clearly quite surprised."

"Indeed. And this has everybody asking the question, 'What exactly is Prince Arthur trying to accomplish with this?' Up until now, the entire Royal Family has been extremely standoffish with the press, Prince Arthur rarely making appearances or giving interviews. But to invite an unapproved member of the press—"

"If you could call her that." Veronica laughs.

"Bitch," Nikki says.

Giles laughs with her. "Quite so, Veronica. This is what makes it even more bizarre. We've done some digging, and it turns out she was a journalist for *The Daily Times* for almost two years but left back in twenty-fifteen to pursue her work as a blogger."

Veronica's face grows serious. "But his invitation says 'effective immediately,' which could mean she could move in tonight if she accepts. Why the rush to have her move in?"

Giles nods. "Exactly. And why the secrecy about it in the first place? Although it is quite possible that his claims should be taken at face value, one cannot help but wonder if there isn't more behind this. He stated that he is simply trying to show that the Royal Family has nothing to hide, and by inviting his harshest critic into their home, he hopes to end the current unrest about the Langdon family. But it would seem there is more here than meets the eye."

"A recent poll did show that the Royal Family is currently experiencing a nation-wide all-time low in popularity."

"Yes, seventy-two percent of people polled stated they would like to abolish the monarchy, so it is possible that the Prince's reaction is solely to do with that."

"But why the urgency?" Veronica cocks her head to the side and squints into the camera.

"That remains a mystery. One thing everybody is wondering right now is whether or not Lady Brooke Beddingfield, the woman long speculated to one day marry Prince Arthur, knows about this arrangement."

"Ooh! And if she *does* know, what does she have to say about the whole thing?"

"Good question." Giles nods.

"Any word on whether Ms. Sharpe has accepted the Prince's invitation yet?"

"Nothing yet. We have a crew outside her apartment, but no one has come out or gone in since the incident earlier today." Giles fights a bout of laughter but then gives in.

Veronica joins him. The video of the Shock Jogger test cuts in again, while the two chuckle away. I shut it off and go in search of some ice cream. A knock at the door has me jumping out of my skin.

"Should I get it?"

Nikki shakes. "I don't think so."

"Ms. Sharpe!" a muffled voice comes through the door. "It's Charles Porter. I know you're there, so please open up."

"Shit, my building manager," I mutter, then I raise my voice as I hurry to the door. "Coming!"

When I open it, I am greeted by his pinched face. Clearly, he is among the twenty-eight percent of royal fans left in the country.

"You may have noticed that we have quite the disruption outside with the reporters and camera crews."

"Yes. Sorry about that. I had no idea any of this was coming."

"Well, now there seems to be a group of protesters forming. Mainly women who are not impressed with some of your comments about the Prince and his family."

"Oh. That I did not know." This day just keeps getting better, doesn't it?

"Well, I expect you to do something about it. It's nearly dinner time, and your neighbours deserve a peaceful place to come home to."

"Agreed. I'll...figure out a way to get rid of them."

"I'll tell you how. You need to give the Prince your answer already. It's not polite to keep him waiting."

"Okay, I will." I try to shut the door, but he wedges his foot in.

"What are you going to do?"

"Right now? Make a decision." I use my foot to push his out, then shut the door in his face.

Nikki pipes up from the couch. "It's not polite to keep the Prince waiting."

"Yeah, well, it's not polite to rush a lady while she's in the middle of a crisis, either." I sigh. "There's really no way to get out of this, is there? Not if I want to keep my credibility as a hard-hitting royal watchdog."

"I think that ship has sailed."

I cringe inside again. "True."

"You have to do it. I'll stay here and watch the fish for you."

"You just want to get out of your parents' place for a while."

"I could use a little break, yes." Nikki moved back in with them when she and her last boyfriend, Todd, broke up. It's been six months, and they are driving each other crazy. "And since you broke my nose, and wrecked my car…"

"Right. I owe you."

"You do." She stares at me for a moment. "Also, two words. Book. Deal."

"All right, fine. But I'm not going out there to meet the press."

"Definitely not. You're half-drunk."

"More than half." I stand and walk over to my desk. "Might as well get some more hits while I'm at it."

———

Blog Post – March 10th

Tessa here. It's been a rather 'shocking' day for me. Wink, wink. For those of you who saw the Shock Jogger video (which is likely all of you), I apologize for the strong language and assure you that even a Tibetan monk would have likely resorted to a similarly foul-mouthed tirade given the voltage.

The second big shock for me today was Prince Arthur's open invitation for me to live at the palace for the next two months. I can honestly say, I never in a thou-

sand years would have expected such a thing. I can assure you all that in spite of media speculation (don't they have anything better to do?), the Prince and I have never met in person, spoken on the phone, texted, emailed or had any other form of communication prior to his press conference. We still haven't met, and there is not now, nor will there ever be, a romantic tie between the Prince of Laziness and myself.

As you know, he stands for everything I do not. I believe in hard work, pulling your own weight in this world, equality, and the ability for the people to elect their leaders. So, please put that ridiculous question of a possible romance aside. I'd sooner sleep with the inventor of the Shock Jogger.

I've decided to give my answer here, on my blog, because you, my loyal readers, deserve to know first. So, here's my answer:

I will accept the Prince's invitation.

I will do my best to investigate and evaluate their contributions to our society with an open mind. I suspect this will provide me with heaps of further proof as to the necessity to have them removed from power, but perhaps I will be surprised by my findings. I look forward to the challenge of bringing the truth to light.

You can count on me to remain professional, and to continue to be your voice as we attempt to bring Avonia into the twenty-first century.

5

All the King's Horses

Arthur

So, I may have gone 'off script', as they say in Hollywood. So bloody what? You'd think I'd just declared war on the Americans, the way everybody is going on about it. For years now, my father's been on me to 'show more initiative' and 'think for myself because, above all else, that's what reigning monarchs must do.'

I called him last night after spending the evening alone with a bottle of bourbon. Well, not really alone. Dexter, my constant companion, a Vietnamese pot-belly pig, was there, too. He didn't drink the bourbon, but we did share a bag of salt 'n' pepper crisps while we watched reruns of *Baywatch*. Oh, I do like the part where they run in slow motion. Reminds me of my boyhood days.

By the time last night's meeting was over, the duchess was on her way to the airport for an impromptu ski trip in the French Alps. So, I missed the one bit of fun I had planned for the entire month of March, which quite frankly has put me in a bit of a crusty mood. And before you start accusing me of only having one thing on my mind, please note that it's really frigging hard for a prince to date casually. Before I can even ask a girl out, I have to instruct Vincent to have her sign a non-disclosure agreement. And he can't even tell her who it's for, just in case she leaks it.

Not exactly a good ice-breaker. If I *do* manage to find someone I may potentially fancy and she signs the NDA without knowing who it's for, I'm sort of turned off by the fact that she signed it in the first place. Somehow it seems a little desperate, which means I immediately lose interest.

Anyway, I finally got around to calling my father just after one in the morning. Turns out it was also the middle of the night wherever in the hell he is this week. And he wasn't alone, if you get my drift (unlike me, my father has no problem asking for NDAs from any woman he meets).

I used to believe that if my mother had lived, he wouldn't be spending his nights with so many random women, and that maybe, if she were still alive, he wouldn't have turned out to be such a giant arsehole. Then, I wouldn't be in this current predicament, because the people are not as dumb as he, and all the advisers, think. The people know a rat when they smell one. And a rat he is.

I hate to say it of my own flesh and blood, but it's true. He's hurt the entire kingdom, and his family, by ignoring the economic troubles of the nation, not to mention that whole sketchy tax-dodging business. He's cooked his own goose, and probably mine as well.

So, back to my phone call with His Serene Sleaziness last night. When I started to explain our current dilemma, these were his words: "Oh, for Christ's sake! Be decisive, boy. You need balls of steel to do this job, so you better grow a pair before I kick off."

I heard the distinct sound of giggling in the background right before he hung up. I decided right then and there to hold a press conference first thing this morning to announce my plan. It seemed like a good idea at the time. I stumbled over to my computer and immediately wrote an email to my favourite reporter, Veronica Platt of ABNC, to ask her to tell all her friends. Veronica. The legs on that one. Mmm. Okay, so I may have been drunk when I wrote her, but not so drunk that I asked if she'd fancy a weekend-for-two up at our north castle. Well done, drunk me.

Veronica apparently did as I asked because by eight in the morning, our front lawn was lined with reporters and camera crews, waiting with bated breath for the big announcement. I showered, sucked down a vat of coffee, and threw on my casual 'man-of-the-people' sweater and slacks.

I know what they were thinking. You could see it in their beady little eyes— 'Oh, please let it be a royal wedding! Please!' They were looking around for Brooke Beddingfield, the woman everyone assumes I'm destined to marry. But I threw them a curveball with the whole 'I'm giving the keys to the castle to my nastiest critic' thing. By eight forty-five, the vans were peeling out of our driveway and I was tucked in bed, nursing my hangover.

Unfortunately, by nine-thirty I was back in my office—dry mouth and all—surrounded by all the king's horses and all the king's men, who, as much as they want to, will be unable to put Humpty Dumpty back together again. And by Humpty Dumpty, I mean turning back the clock so that Ms. Tessa Sharpe will not, in fact, be calling the palace home for the next two months. Well, that was a bit of a crap analogy. I really am quite hungover.

"Your Highness, we haven't even had time to do a background check."

That vein in Damien's neck is pulsing, so I know he's *really* mad. I don't care, but I don't want you to think me completely oblivious to these things.

"Well, someone better get on it, because she's arriving tomorrow. I'm sure there's some tedious paperwork that will need to be done if it turns out that I'll need extra guards posted outside my bedroom door." I stare Damien down while I tap my fingers on the cool leather arm of my chair. It's a total power move. I got it from Benedict Cumberbatch as *Sherlock*. Nice guy, by the way.

Damien doesn't answer, so I go on. "Listen, it'll be fine, I promise. In case you haven't noticed, I tend to have a way with her type."

"What's her type?"

"Female." Oh, that was arrogant, wasn't it? "I'll show her the library, the stables, I'll open up the vault and let her try on some sparkly things. She'll be putty in my hands by Friday."

"With all due respect, Your Highness, I'm not so sure we can base our entire plan on your ability to woo this woman," Vincent says. "Not that you don't have a way with the ladies, but due to the gravity of the situation, we should probably have a backup plan."

"Fine, Damien. Dig up whatever dirt you can on her, so we'll have it if we need it."

"Already on it," Damien says, and quite frankly the look on his face suggests he should be twirling his mustache right now—if he could grow one. I think he must have some pituitary disorder or something, because he doesn't have even one whisker on that pale face of his.

"Good, everything's settled, then. If you'll all clear out now, I have a raging hangover that needs attending."

The sound of laughter breaks out from the back of the room. At first I assume it's a result of my wit, but I soon discover the source of the humour is coming from one of the assistants to somebody-or-other, who is watching a video on his mobile phone. The guy next to him gasps. "Isn't that...? It's her! The Royal Watchdog!"

Everyone turns to them, and the room goes quiet. The young man blanches when he realizes that we're all staring, then he looks at me. "I really think you ought to see this, Your Highness."

And then the very best thing that I've seen in my entire thirty-one years comes onto the screen. It's Ms. Sharpe in form-fitting jogging pants and a tight shirt. My sceptre wakes up and asks if we're going somewhere, because even though I feel like shit on a stick, he'd be up for *that*. I'm trying to focus on what she's saying while she runs, but it's really no use. Those lovely, perky breasts are speaking volumes on her behalf. Suddenly, her feet leave the ground and her entire body coils up into a ball impossibly high in the air and she's screaming, "Motherfucker!"

I burst out laughing so hard that I missed most of the rest of the video, just managing to catch the part where she whips the shock-thingy at her friend, who immediately drives into some giant shrubs.

Tears stream down my face. When I finally manage to speak, all I can come up with is, "What the fuck was that?"

———

I wait all day for an answer from Ms. Sharpe, but nothing comes until dinner time. I'm just sitting down to another healthy-but-dull meal of tilapia with roast vegetables when I catch a whiff of blue cheese. We really need to get rid of these plush carpets so I'll hear him coming. "She's taken you up on your offer! Ms. Sharpe arrives tomorrow afternoon!"

My fork and knife clatter as I drop them on my plate. "Really?" A slow smile spreads across my face. I feel like a jaguar (considered the most cunning hunter in the forest, in case you didn't know) luring its prey. What? I only watch *Baywatch* when I'm drunk and lonely. Otherwise, I'm a pretty big fan of David Attenborough.

6

Big Girl Knickers

Tessa

"IT'S HERE! And it's a big one!" Nikki has been standing at the living room window for twenty minutes on limo watch.

"That's what he said." I guffaw at my own horrible joke, then feel another wave of nausea come over me. A hangover doesn't mix well with moving into a snake pit. "Oh, my God, what am *I* doing?"

"Don't start. It's too late now."

"I know, but last night, I stayed awake for hours, thinking of all the torture devices they have there…swords, cleavers, those ball thingies with the spikes. I bet they still have a rack hidden in a dungeon somewhere under the castle. What if they get me there, and then they strap me to the rack for the next eight weeks for all the mean things I've said about them?" I stand next to my open suitcase and consider unpacking.

"They are not going to torture you. They'll probably be really rude, but I am relatively sure you'll come out of there alive." She gives me a teasing grin as she sets my carry-on and laptop bag next to my suitcase.

"Oh, *relatively* sure? That makes me feel much better." I narrow my eyes at her. "You just want to get rid of me."

"Yes, I do. I'm going to spend the next several hours in the tub, then I'm going to watch the entire series of *Downton Abbey* back-to-back without having anyone snoring in the armchair next to me or interrupting me to examine another weird mole. I love you, but get the hell out."

"But...I really don't want to do this. I'm going to fuck up the whole thing, aren't I? I mean, I don't have the right clothes, I need to get my hair done—"

"You're not due for a colour and cut for weeks. You're gorgeous. So, stop fussing, pull up your big girl knickers and go!"

I shake my head vigorously. "I'm not a hard-hitting journalist. I review cameras and sports equipment for a living."

"Hey, don't say that. You were—and will be—a respected member of the press again very soon. Plus, you look like a hard-hitting jour-nalist today. Very professional in your skirt and those no-nonsense heels."

"Are they too old-ladyish?" I zip up my suitcase and lift it onto its wheels.

"You mean you weren't going for seventy-five-year-old grand-mother on her way home from morning Mass?"

I groan. "I should change again."

There's a buzz at the intercom, and Nikki gets to it first. "Yes?"

"I'm here to pick up Ms. Sharpe and take her to the palace."

"She's on her way down." Nikki turns to me. "Now there's a sentence you don't hear everyday."

"She's on her way down?"

Nikki snorts out a laugh, then winces and carefully touches her nose. "The one about being taken to the palace. I know it's going to be hard, and it's scary, but try to enjoy it. At least a little." She pulls me in for a big hug.

"That's what he said."

Now I'm feeling very teary. I'm a completely overtired, over-wrought ball of nerves. "I'm going to miss you so much," I whisper. "Two months is a very long time."

"Yes, but you can just call me in, like, twenty minutes when you get there."

I pull back and sniffle. "I could. But I won't. I'll be going on a tour of the castle or settling in, which will take at least a couple of hours."

Nikki opens the door and wheels my suitcase into the hall. I follow her like a puppy.

She pushes the lift call button. "Repeat after me: I'll be fine."

"I'll be fine."

"You know, your biggest problem is actually going to be trying not to sleep with Prince Arthur." The door opens, and Nikki pushes my things into the lift.

"What? I would *never* want to sleep with him."

She pushes me in next. "Sure you will. He's exactly your type, and he's hot as fuck."

My mouth hangs open while the doors shut.

———

When I get to the lobby of my building, I see a long black limo with two small flags flapping in the breeze. They bear the royal crest of a golden crown and sceptre with two wolves standing guard. The media has returned in full force, and I stand behind the glass wall, feeling like I may vomit. An enormous bald man with sunglasses and a black suit pulls open the door. "Ms. Sharpe. I'm Ollie. I'll escort you to the car."

"Thank you." I give him a weak smile, but his face gives nothing away.

His jaw is set, and he nods as he takes my bags. "Keep your head down, stay close to me, and say nothing."

Oh, well, that sounds a little ominous, doesn't it? I'm about to say I've changed my mind, but it's too late because he's stepping out the door with all of my clothes, and he told me to stay close. And my parents taught me to always obey strange men shaped like tanks dressed in suits. I am immediately bombarded with reporters yelling my name and asking me questions. Their words jumble together with the protesters who are booing and calling me a traitor. Ollie opens the back door, and I lurch into the safety of the creamy leather backseat. As soon as the door is shut, the noise is drowned out. I close my eyes while I shake my hands and practice Lamaze breathing. Or what I think is Lamaze breathing. It's really just what I've picked up from sitcoms depicting the hilarity of childbirth.

"Okay, Tess, get the upper hand. Establish firm boundaries. Don't fuck up." I repeat this quietly three times, starting to feel slightly less queasy.

"What don't you want to fuck up? And with whom are you establishing these boundaries?"

My eyes fly open, and my entire body flames with embarrassment. The Crown Prince of Avonia himself is sitting at the far end of the limo facing me, dressed in a dark grey suit. White shirt. No tie. He looks amused. And gorgeous. And gorgeously amused. And I completely forgot to change out of my granny shoes. Fuckity-fuck. "I thought I was alone."

"Clearly." He slides down the long U-shaped seat until he is sitting perpendicular to me, close enough that our knees could touch if either of us wanted to—which we don't, on account of how much we hate each other. But we could. I stare into the face of my enemy, waiting for his worst. Instead, he smiles and holds out his hand.

"Ms. Sharpe. A pleasure to meet you."

I hold out my hand to shake his, but he lifts it to his lips and plants a soft kiss on my knuckles instead. Well, *that* is not what I was expecting. That was lovely in a romantic, could-very-possibly-turn-my-insides-to-mush sort of way.

Wait a minute—he's just lulling me into a false sense of security before he has me beheaded, isn't he? Not on my watch! I'm keeping my head, thank you very much.

I pull my hand back quickly and cover my neck with it. "You as well, Your Highness." I nod my head in a little formal bow, as if to say, *this is my head, and it stays on.*

"So, the boundaries? The upper hand? With me, I'm assuming."

"Ummhmm," I squeak. My words come rushing back to me, and I'm suddenly so embarrassed that I am sweating. Literally sweating under my wool coat. Did I put on antiperspirant this morning? Now, I can't remember.

"Smart. I like a woman who strategizes." He smiles at me, and for one shining moment I feel like the sun is out only for me today.

Okay, I am *much* happier about that little bit of praise he's given me than I should be. I mean, seriously, Tessa, the man is your sworn enemy. You hate his entire family *and* what they stand for. Yet, one little kiss on the knuckles, and you're putty in his hands? Pull. It. Together. You're better than this.

"I'm also one for having a plan, which is why I came to pick you up myself."

"Well, you rode in the car. Your driver's the one who picked me up." *That was a little bitchy. Can you find a middle ground between giggly school girl and nasty witch?*

He tilts his head in a conciliatory gesture, then continues to talk. "I need to establish some ground rules of my own."

"Like what?" Here we go. I just knew he wasn't going to play fair.

His eyes bore into mine, and I'm just now realizing the power of ice blue irises to scare the shit out of people. "My sister, Arabella, is strictly off limits. You don't write anything more about her than you already have. Not one word, unless somehow you manage to find it in your heart to say something kind."

"Why?"

"She's more delicate than people realize. Life in the public eye has never been easy for her, and I don't want her damaged more than she already has been. So, not one word about her. If you can't agree to that, I'm afraid we'll have to turn around now and take you home."

Now, his true colours are coming out. "Maybe that would be for the best. If you weren't serious about providing me with an honest look at your family, then I'd say we're done."

He doesn't look as intimidated as I had hoped. "You'll have full access to me, I promise, and since I'm the heir to the throne, I'd think it's far more important what you uncover about me, isn't it?"

I narrow my eyes at him. I hate like hell to admit he's right. "Fine, but don't expect me to go easy on you for even a second."

"I'd be a fool to think you'd give me anything less than your worst."

"And that's exactly what you'll get. Now, I have some ground rules of my own. I want access to all meetings and functions that you attend."

"Of course, unless it's a matter of national security. I'm afraid I won't be able to bring you in on those."

I stare at him for a moment. "So long as that doesn't become an excuse to keep me out of meetings you'd rather I not attend."

"No need to worry about that. I assure you that I'm an open book, Ms. Sharpe." His voice is low and smooth, and the way he says *Ms. Sharpe* makes my traitorous knees go a little weak.

I ignore my knees and jut out my chin. "I'd also like to hold a weekly 'ask me anything' with members of the Royal Family and possibly high-level staffers. My readers can write in questions, then upvote their favourites, and the top five per week will be used in live interviews. Real answers on the fly." I'm thinking on the fly, and doing rather well at it, if I do say so myself. Tessa Sharpe, nut-cracking blogger.

He stares at me and taps his fingers on the seat arm for a long moment. "Fine."

Fine? Well, that was easy. I sit up straight and cross my legs. Locking eyes with him, I force my voice to come out anchor woman smooth. "So, Your Highness, why am I really here?"

"You didn't understand my invitation, either? I thought I made it all quite clear, and yet the press seems absolutely baffled by my motives."

"I know what you *said* your motives are. But I want the truth."

"You can't handle the truth." He does a reasonable Jack Nicholson impression that has me fighting a grin into submission.

"The truth is exactly as I said it at the press conference. I need your help." He leans across the limo and opens the door to the mini-fridge, then pulls out two bottles of water. Not Perrier or Pellegrino, either. Regular water. He hands me one and opens the other for himself. "I'm hoping to regain some of the ground our family has lost in the public opinion polls."

"Yes, but why *me*?"

"Because you hate us most."

There is something behind his eyes when he says it. If I didn't know better, I would think he might be a little bit hurt by what I've written about them. But that can't be. A man like him wouldn't care a fig what someone like me has to say.

He continues. "I have to confess that, until two days ago, I didn't know who you were. When I asked my advisers who my harshest critic was, they named you. I spent the afternoon yesterday reading everything you've written about me and my family. You have a scathing hatred for us that is rather unmatched."

My face tingles, and the back of my throat suddenly aches. It's one thing to write a highly critical commentary about a public figure, but quite another to come face to face with him.

"I find it fascinating that anyone would devote so much time and energy to discrediting people you've never met. I'm very curious about what motivates you."

Money. I stare at him for a moment while I consider my answer. I can't very well tell him the truth. How do you say, 'Nothing personal. I just realized the meaner I got, the more people read my stuff, and the more shoes I could buy'? You don't. "That brings me to my first boundary. You don't get to ask me personal questions."

He blinks in surprise. "Not even if it's about why you hate us so much?"

"Not even that. I'm here to observe and report the truth back to the people. That's it."

"Hardly seems fair," he says.

"What would make you think I was going to play fair?" My heart is pounding now. As tough as I need to be, I do not want to overplay my hand.

"Good point." He looks at me and almost grins. "But let's say I was in the market for a device that would help me increase my running stamina and pace, and I wanted to ask if you had any recommendations. Would you object to that question?"

I knew that was coming. Fucker. "You do realize that you need me more than I need you?"

"Sorry. Couldn't help myself." He gives me the look of a little boy who's been caught with his hand in the cookie jar, only he's the type to like getting caught. "Won't mention it again, I promise."

"No personal questions. Take it or leave it."

"Take it." He shrugs.

"I still don't understand why you'd want a critic to help you rather than a friend. You could have just brought in one of your lackeys and had them shoot a documentary for you."

"The people are too smart for that, and they deserve better, don't you think?" He sips his water.

"They do." My tone is firm, *very* Veronica Platt.

He gives me a satisfied grin. "Look at that. We've already found ourselves agreeing on something, and we've only just reached the palace gates."

I look out the window for the first time since getting in the limo. We are indeed driving up the long path to the palace. "Let's be clear on one more thing. We are natural enemies. That is not going to change, no matter how long I stay as your guest."

"Even better."

We pass through an opening in the palace wall that is so narrow, I cringe, thinking we're about to scrape the limo on both sides.

"Narrow, isn't it? It was built for a horse and carriage."

We arrive at the back entrance to the U-shaped palace, and the limo slows to a halt near a set of massive wooden doors. I suddenly remember his remark about it being better that we are enemies. "Why is it good for you if we remain enemies?"

His blue eyes lock on mine with an intensity that makes me want to squirm in my seat. "I believe it was Sun Tzu who said, 'Keep your friends close, but your enemies closer.'"

"It was Michael Corleone in *The Godfather*." Ha! Thank you, parents, for having four boys.

"No, it wasn't." He shakes his head, and for the first time I see him looking a little off-kilter.

"Don't feel bad. Everyone makes that mistake."

He stares at me for a second, then grins. "You just got the upper hand."

"I guess I did." Score one for Tessa Sharpe.

But…wait. He wants to keep me closer?

7

I'll Show You Mine

Arthur

"THANKS, Ollie, but I'll take Ms. Sharpe and her things to her apartment." I give him a pat on the shoulder and hope that Tessa doesn't notice the bewildered look on his face. I'm not sure I've ever carried a set of luggage, but how hard can it be, right?

I sling her laptop bag over my shoulder and pull the handle out on the huge suitcase she's brought. Yes, I'm a very all-hands-on-deck type of prince. A real down-to-earth, folksy guy.

"Shall we?" I gesture for her to go ahead. One of the footmen opens the door for us and bows deeply. I really should have told them to lighten up on the formalities. Oh, bugger, this suitcase is awkward. It was fine when we were on the pavement, but navigating this damn thing up the ten steps is not exactly going smoothly. The suitcase slams and bangs in a rather alarming fashion as I drag it up the staircase. When I glance up, I can see that the footman is trying very hard not to laugh.

"You okay there?" Tessa asks, turning back to me and wincing.

"Oh, fine, yes. One of the wheels is stuck or something."

She raises one eyebrow. "Usually, I just lift it when I'm on stairs. You might find that easier."

"Right-o, lifting. I thought this was one of those new smart suitcases that glides up stairs." I yank up the handle and drop the suitcase on the top step with a thud. I can see by the look on her face that she's not buying the smart suitcase thing.

When I pass by the footman, a line from Tessa's blog flashes through my brain about how she doubts I even know the name of the man who opens the door for me when I come home every night. She's right, of course, but there are so damn many of them all over the place. How am I supposed to know them all? I give him a hearty smile.

He nods. "Your Highness."

"Hey…mate. Great job!" Why do they not wear name tags? That's it. Tomorrow, I'll have Vincent order one for each member of the staff. Good God, I'm a nervous wreck all of a sudden. Bringing her here was a terrible idea. Note to self: Do not make decisions while drunk and/or horny.

Once inside, we start down the passageway toward the main living quarters. She is a couple of paces ahead of me, and I know what's coming when we reach the Grande Hall. Three, two, one. There it is, a little gasp escapes her mouth as she steps inside the marble and gold foyer. The domed ceiling is twenty feet above our heads and brightly lit to better show off the murals painted by Canaletto himself. She slows, her head tilted up at what truly is a magnificent sight.

"I've always loved that ceiling. I used to lie on the floor as a child and stare up at it by the hour." Where the hell did that come from? I've never tell anyone that.

Tessa turns and smiles at me. What a lovely smile. I want to see more of it, which is absurd since I absolutely hate this woman. "I'm sure my parents worried that I was rather a dullard, lying on the cold marble like that."

Her laughter fills the hall. What a lovely sound. I want to hear more of it. *What the fuckity-fuck?*

"I doubt that very much. You're many things, but dull isn't one of them."

"Really? You, who has called me a ridiculous man-child, thinks I may have more than one brain cell rattling away in my head?" *That's better. Remind yourself who she is. Don't get sucked in by her smile.*

She blushes. "I never said you were stupid."

"Only lazy."

She lifts her chin and purses her lips. Oh, those are nice lips.

"Isn't that the word for an adult who doesn't do any actual work?"

"What if that adult is still learning his trade?" My words have the effect I was hoping for. She looks confused for a moment because she was gearing up for a fight, and I'm not giving her one. And upper hand back to me! Score one for Arthur. Finally.

"Shall we?" I hold out my hand to the right and follow her toward the private residences. She walks with her head swiveling quickly from side-to-side, checking out the tapestries and paintings of my dead relatives that line the walls. Her shoes click along the marble floor, and when I glance down at them, I realize they are not sexy kitten heels at all, but rather are shoes my grandmum would wear. How very odd for a young woman. And even more surprising that I am turned on right now. Perhaps I should consider finding a therapist.

I stop in front of a set of white double doors. "I suspect you'll want to see this."

I leave her suitcase and open both doors, leading her into the library. This is a little move I picked up from *Beauty and the Beast*—the Disney version, not the horrid nineties TV series. Works every time. Why *do* chicks dig books so much? Books and horses. I'll never understand it.

Her mouth drops open as she takes in the two-storey room, filled with floor-to-ceiling bookcases.

"This is bigger than my entire apartment."

"Some of these books are over two hundred years old. Original editions. You're welcome to read anything you like." I gesture at the shelves with one hand and smile at her. She's looking around, but where are the wide eyes? Where's the mouth agape? Where is the adoring gaze? She looks…unimpressed. Almost offended, actually. "Not a reader, I take it?"

"On the contrary. I love to read." She shrugs. "It just seems such a shame to hide all these wonderful books where so few people will ever have access to them."

Huh. Well, that was an unexpected flop. I've just managed to prove we are every bit as selfish as she thought. I watch as she pulls a title off the shelf and thumbs through it. I'm both irritated by her reaction and attracted to her at the same time. On the one hand, I am absolutely hating this 'holier than thou' business, and on the other hand, I want to impress the skirt right off her.

I wonder what Sun Tzu (or Michael Corleone, for that matter) would have said about the war raging in my body right now? I want to hate her, but I also want to do very naughty things to her. Right now. On that puffy leather chair over there, for instance, or up against the wall. Ladies love that almost as much as horses for some reason. *Oh, stop that! Idiot. Your parents were right to worry that you were a dullard.*

A squealing sound from the doorway interrupts my thoughts. Dexter comes snorting and snuffing his way into the library. Dexter will save the day!

"Dexter, meet Ms. Sharpe."

He trots his big spotted body over to me and rubs his snout on my pant leg. I crouch and give him a good scratch behind his ears. His handler—well, babysitter, really—Troy chases him into the room.

"There you are, Dexter!" He spots me and straightens up. "Sorry, sir. I didn't know you had company. He just took off on me. Must've heard you come in."

"Not to worry, Troy. I'll take him from here."

"I'll be in Dexter's room if you need me."

I look up at Tessa, and she has an unreadable expression on her face as she stares at Dex. "Do you like pigs?"

"I don't know. It's really more a question of will he like me?"

"He will." I stand and walk toward her, Dexter at my heels. "Come say hello, Dex."

He sits in front of Tessa and looks up at her, like the well-mannered ungulate that he is. She bends down slightly and pats him tentatively on the head. When Dexter doesn't bite off her hand, she strokes him behind his ears, then crouches down so she can pet him with both hands.

"What a surprisingly sweet pig."

"Just like his owner."

She looks up at me and laughs, which causes Dexter to get excited and lick her right in the mouth. "Oh! God! Gross!" she sputters.

"Sorry about that." I take her hand and help her to her feet. "He tends to get a little too affectionate with the ladies."

"Just like his owner, as I understand."

I find myself blushing, which is something I don't think I've done since I was a teenager. "Come on, I'll show you to your room so you can wash the pig spit off your face."

"And disinfect the inside of my mouth." We walk side-by-side to the hall, Dexter trying to nudge his way between us.

"No need. He's really quite a clean animal."

"And yet, I still find myself wanting a bottle of Listerine."

I laugh and am yet again shocked by the fact that I could have any fun at all with this awful harpy. But somehow, I can't help it. If I'm not careful, *she's* going to end up convincing *me* to dissolve the monarchy myself.

8

Crazy Hot Leech

Tessa

"I SHOULD HAVE TAKEN your advice and become a fashion blogger," I say to Nikki. We're on the phone while I stand in front of the closet, trying desperately to figure out what to wear to a dinner with the Crown Prince, the Princess Dowager (his grandmum), and his sister, Princess Arabella. I lasted almost three hours without calling Nikki to tell her everything—all about the tour, the library, the horribly embarrassing limo ride, and the rather cold woman named Mavis who has been assigned to 'care for my every need whilst I am a guest of the Prince.' Mavis had my things catalogued and unpacked so fast, my head was spinning. Catalogued. Each item, in the order of when it came out of my luggage.

"Go with your little black dress. It's a classic."

I swipe the other clothes away from it so I can consider it. "You think? What if the ladies have elbow-length gloves?"

"What if they're in jeans?"

I'm briefly hopeful. "Do you think they might all be casual?"

"Oh yeah, sure. They're probably going to order in some pizza and swill beer from cans. Just throw on some pajamas and your bunny slippers." I hear the bath water sloshing in the background, and I am suddenly so homesick. I want to be in my tub, not here among people who probably would rather do anything than have dinner with the likes of me.

"Go with the black dress. It's sexy but respectable at the same time."

"Thank you, but I'm not really going for sexy. I need to be professional," I say.

"You fancy him!" Nikki's tone has gone from slightly bored to top-of-roller-coaster excited.

"Do not."

"You *so* do. I can hear it in your voice," she says. "I *knew* it!"

I scoff. "He's a leech on society. Why would I be interested in that?"

"Because that particular leech is crazy hot, richer than sin, and a complete charmer. He charmed the hell out of you already, didn't he?"

There's a huge smile on her face, I just know it.

"No. Not possible." Totally possible, but since I'm desperately trying to fight it, I must not admit it. "What about the tan pantsuit with the pinstripes?"

"To dinner? With the Royal Family?"

My stomach twists again at the thought. "Good point."

I grab the black dress off the rack and toss it on the bed.

———

Before I dress for dinner, I check my text messages and voicemails that I've been ignoring since yesterday.

Bram: *Oh, my God! That was the funniest fucking video I've ever seen. You must be so fucking embarrassed. What the fuck is going on with you and the Prince?*

. . .

Mum (voicemail): *Tessa, call me immediately. Your father and I are quite worried. I read in Weekly World News that you can have your hair shocked right out of your body. Do you still have your hair, darling?*

Mum (2nd voicemail): *Tessa, why aren't you answering? I hope you haven't locked yourself in the bathroom like you did when you got your period during maths class. It didn't help anything then, and it won't now. You need to call me back straight away. The neighbours won't stop ringing about you. That horrid video and the Prince's invitation in one day? I don't know what's going on with you. And when did you start swearing like a sail—"*

Text from Noah: *Ring me back now. Isa is calling me every ten minutes to find out what the hell is going on with you and the Royal Family. Plus, I want to make fun of you for that shocking video. Best. Video. Ever. Holy fuck. I've never laughed so hard in my life.*

Facebook Message from Royal Watchdog's number one fan, King-Slayer99: *Tessa, well done, you brave, beautiful woman. Finally breaching the wall of the castle of thieves. Give the Prince of Laziness a throat punch from me.*

Email from Daniel Fitzwilliam, owner of Wellbits, makers of the Shock Jogger: *Ms. Sharpe, please contact me immediately. We need to find a suitable way to mitigate the damage done by your video to our product launch.*

Dad (voicemail): *"Tessa? Where are you? Your mum has gone off her nut waiting for you to ring. You better not be living at the palace without telling your mother. I'll never hear the end of it. How's Nikki? Is her nose all right? I can't believe you threw that electric prod thingy at her. That looked very painful. I really should have spent more time working on your throw."*

. . .

Text from Finn: *Bahahahahahahahahahahahahahahahahahahahahahahaha-haha! Thanks for being such a monumental dork. BTW, what's this shit about you going to live at the palace?*

Text from Lars: *From now on, call me before you do anything. Ever. Let's start with this bit of advice: Probably don't hook yourself up to a cattle prod when you're going to get all sweaty, you dumb arse. You've screwed up all my classes today because one of my students put it together that you're my sister, and I've spent the entire day answering questions about you. Also, Nina wants to know if she can visit you at the palace if you go.*

Shit.

———

At exactly seven o'clock, there is a light rap on the door to my suite. I take a deep breath as I walk across my luxurious new digs. "Don't fuck up. Don't fuck up."

I open the door, and there he is. Prince Charming himself, dressed in a black dinner jacket, grey slacks and a tie. He gives me the once over, making me feel naked for a second, but then the smile he gives me makes me feel like I might not mind being naked in front of him. After all, it's nice to be appreciated.

"Good evening, Ms. Sharpe. You're looking rather fetching this evening."

"Your Highness." I tilt my head, and my body naturally does a little curtsy that I wasn't expecting. I must be coming down with something, because I suddenly feel all flushed again.

"I thought I'd help you find your way to the dining room."

"Thank you. That's very kind." *As long as you aren't escorting me to the dungeon to chop off my head.*

"Thank *you* for joining us."

We fall in step together down the long hall with only the sound of our shoes clicking on the floor. I have never in my life been so hyperaware of my proximity to a man as I am now. He is mere inches from me, my shoulder practically rubbing against his arm as we move.

"I thought I should give you a heads up. My grandmother, Princess Dowager Florence, doesn't know why you're really here."

Uh-oh. "Why not?"

"I thought it would be easier to keep her out of the loop. She's rather guarded with the press, and I don't think you'd get to know the real her if she knew who you were."

"Okay…"

He stops and turns to me. I do the same. His expression is suddenly very serious. "I want you to see her the way she can be when we're among friends. She's a wonderful woman. Very caring and funny as all hell."

"Really? That's not what people say about her."

"She has good reason for how she's been." He turns away and continues down the hall.

I rush my next few steps to catch up, confused about what exactly is happening and how I'm supposed to play it. "Who does she think I am?"

"An old friend from college. You live in New York but are here for a holiday for a couple of months."

"I don't like lying to people, Your Highness." Unless it's my parents about dinner plans. That I don't mind.

He glances down at me and says, "Arthur."

"What?" We stop in front of the elevator.

"Call me Arthur, or she'll know something's up."

"I don't like this. I have no respect for liars." Oh, I know I'm being a hypocrite, but please don't hold it against me. All's fair in love and war. Well, in war anyway…

The elevator doors open, and he touches the small of my back to encourage me to get on. I try to ignore the sparkly tingles going up my spine and concentrate on how pissed I am. "Did you hear me just now? I don't want to lie to the Princess Dowager."

"I don't either, but this is an unusually delicate situation. She's very old."

Ha! I've caught him talking out of both sides of his mouth.

"Which is it? Is she old, or is she going to hate me if she knows the truth?"

"Both. She's very delicate *and* she would hate you."

"She's delicate. Arabella's delicate. I'm starting to notice a theme."

"And what would that be?" He raises one eyebrow, looking amused again.

"I'm starting to think you're a bit of a chauvinist who doesn't think women can handle much more than a weak tea and some light conversation."

"On the contrary, women can be every bit as tough as men. Tougher, even. It just so happens that my sister isn't, and my grandmother is getting so old, we really won't have time for her to warm up to you once she knows who you are."

"That's no excuse." I scoff. "If she can't be decent to me knowing who I really am, then that's how the story will go out. The people deserve the *truth* about your family. After all, we are paying for your life. We should know what we're getting for our money."

He stiffens for the briefest instant, then seems to catch himself and smiles patiently. "You know, Ms. Sharpe, we are public servants in the truest of forms. My family has dedicated our lives, our very lineage, to this great nation. We provide jobs for over twelve hundred people. Honourable careers that pay well. Not to mention the two thousand-plus charitable organizations that rely on us for fundraising each year."

"Yes, thank you." I give him a sarcastic look. "I've read the brochure. Didn't really convince me."

We arrive on the first floor and the doors open. I throw back my shoulders and walk out of the lift, forgetting that I have no idea where I'm going. I take a guess and turn to the left, but a light cough from the Prince has me spinning on my heel. "This way?"

"Yes." He tries to hide his smirk. "Listen. I think we've both taken a wrong turn. I shouldn't have assumed that you would be comfortable lying to my grandmother."

"No, you shouldn't have." I point my finger in the air and wag it to increase my sassiness. "And my wrong turn would be?"

"Just now, when you got off the lift. If you'd kept going, you'd have ended up in the garage."

His tone is light, and I have to fight not to smile.

"Hardly the same thing."

"You're correct. Your transgression would have had much worse consequences. It reeks of grease and cigarette smoke in there."

His attempt at being wry doesn't work. I continue to glower.

The Prince's lips press together in a slight grimace. "Okay, Ms. Sharpe, I'm about to confirm a rumor for you, and I'm going to rely on your decency that you will not report it. My grandmum isn't well. Having a reporter among us would put undue stress on her, and I'd just as soon spare her that."

His eyes glisten, and I almost think he's about to tear up, but then he clears his throat and sets his jaw, and its business as usual. I follow him, moving slower as I digest this news.

Stopping in front of a set of imposing double doors, Arthur turns to me. "So, what shall we tell her?"

I'm about to cave, aren't I? Damn. "Which school did we go to? I forgot."

He gives me a grateful smile. "Oxford."

"Right."

I'm so thrown by this bombshell that I forget to be nervous as we walk into the dimly lit dining hall. My heels dip into a carpet so plush it feels as though I might sink into it up to my knees. It absorbs the sound of the classical music that surrounds us even though I can't see any musicians or speakers. The walls are painted a muted red and are adorned by gold crown-mouldings and sconces that hold flickering candles. A small table is set for four with so many dishes and cutlery at each place that I'm pretty sure I'll have no idea how to use most of it. I'm going to fuck this up, aren't I?

At the far end of the room, Princess Arabella and the Princess Dowager stand, sipping cocktails as we walk toward them. Arabella stops mid-sentence, her gaze drawing attention to us that I'd just as soon avoid. I wring my hands nervously as her face falls and she blinks slowly in my direction. My pace tapers off, but Arthur's hand is on my back again, gently nudging me forward.

"Arabella, you remember Tessa," Arthur says, a slight warning tone in his voice.

"Of course." She glares at me with such disdain that I feel like I've just shrunk two feet in height.

"Grandmum, good evening. You're looking well." Arthur leaves my side and gives the Princess Dowager a kiss on each cheek. "I'd like to introduce you to Tessa Sharpe. She's an old friend from Oxford."

I do my best imitation of a curtsy and stumble on my words. "Your Highness, a very good pleasure to smeet you." Dammit. "Seet you." Shit. "Meet you."

She steps forward and holds out her hands to me. I reach out, not sure what she's going to do, but then she takes hold of my fingers and holds my arms out to the sides. "Let me look at you, dear."

"Uh, okay." Yup, this seems normal. An elderly princess is slowly looking me up and down. She squints her eyes and peers up at my face. She has the same colour eyes as her grandson, icy blue that almost seem to glow against all the diamonds around her neck. And she's so tiny. I had no idea she was this small. I almost want to pick her up.

She turns and nods at Arthur. "Excellent choice, Arthur. Very lovely, good birthing hips. She's got those long legs you admire, too."

Did that just happen? I'm not sure whose face is redder now—mine or Arthur's. Wait, no, it's mine.

"It's not like that, Grandmum. We're just old friends."

"Don't play me for the fool, Arthur. I can tell by the way you walked in." She winks at him, then pats my hand. "From what I've heard, you'd do well to invite him back to your room."

"Grandmum!" Arabella gasps.

"Oh, what? You think I don't know what goes on? Nobody would stay single so long as they do these days if they weren't engaging in a little pre-marital you-know-what."

A waiter brings a tray holding flutes of champagne. Arthur takes two, handing one to me.

"I might need them both," I say under my breath.

"You'll have to fight me for it," Arthur murmurs as he lifts the glass to his lips.

"So, Tessa, Arthur tells me you work in the fitness industry? Testing out equipment?" Arabella grins triumphantly as I turn bright red. She's seen the Shock Jogger video. *For sure.*

"Yes, that's right." My mind spins desperately, trying to think of a change of topic.

"That's a strange job," Princess Dowager Florence remarks.

Arthur says, "She reviews products, Grandmum. She rates them on a scale of one to five and gives details as to the usefulness, cost value, that type of thing."

The Princess Dowager looks over at me. "How many stars would you give our Arthur here?"

"I don't know." I give her a conspiratorial smile. "I've never tested him out."

She laughs and rests her hand on my arm. "Well, let me know when the reviews are in. If it's anything less than five stars, I can sit him down and give him some tips."

Arthur pipes up. "Okay! I think we should eat."

9

Not So Divine Dining

Arthur

THIS IS QUITE POSSIBLY the most uncomfortable dinner I've ever had —and that's saying something. I once sat next to the wife of the prime minister of Malaysia, who spent the entire meal—from the amuse-bouche through dessert—trying to get her hand on my crown jewels, while her husband sat across from us, blissfully unaware, chatting with me about the Euro. If you've never tried to hold up your end of a serious, high-level financial conversation with a world leader while simultaneously fending off the attempts of a very gropey older woman… well, then, I'm happy for you. Because it sucked.

But I'd gladly be back there right now, because tonight is much worse. I knew my sister wasn't going to make this easy for me, and she hasn't disappointed. She was against this entire thing from the start, which *was* only yesterday, but still. Arabella can be a real hard-ass when she wants to be. She's doing her best to make Tessa feel very much unwelcome, whilst my grandmother continues to comment on Tessa's excellent potential for carrying my child.

It's not that Arabella doesn't grasp the concept of what I'm trying to do here. She'd already heard the whole 'keep your enemies closer' thing when I brought it up with her this morning. She's just not a very good liar. Wears her heart on her sleeve, like our mother, which is one reason that being a princess has been particularly rough for her. No matter what, she's never mastered the art of hiding her feelings and putting on a phony smile, which has been her undoing time and again with the public and the press. It's the main reason she rarely appears in an official capacity. Children's hospital—wept openly. Veteran's hospital—wept openly. Anytime she's faced with a hard-hitting reporter, she freezes up and her answers become short, making her seem very rude.

I can tell that she's spent a good part of the day reading Tessa's blog and internalizing every attack. She would see each remark as nothing short of unforgivable. Having familiarized myself with Ms. Sharpe's work, I can tell you that I've never read anything as offensive as page after page of her scornful opinion of my family.

For me, though, each reproach holds a thrilling challenge—to change her mind. There's an excitement in being presented with the extraordinary opportunity to come face to face with an intelligent adversary. I'm not accustomed to having anyone challenge me—other than my father—and for me, it's like I've found the best new game to play, one in which lies the fun of verbal sparring and strategizing. It's like a high-stakes, grownup version of Stratego. And I intend to win.

But in order for me to emerge victorious, I need backup from the rest of my family, which neither my sister nor my grandmother are providing at this moment. I carefully watch Tessa's reactions to each of them. Will she wither or stand tall? Become argumentative or remain gracious, as she has done so far this evening? She seems amused by my grandmum, rather than offended, and I find myself increasingly glad for the distraction the Princess Dowager is providing, no matter how awkward her comments make me feel. Her attempts to prove how 'hip she is to us young folk getting it on' are definitely taking some of the focus off my sister's veiled insinuations and snide remarks.

Although, the way my grandmother is going on about how

amazing I am is actually making me seem like I'm desperately seeking a wife, which could not be further from the truth. Ms. Sharpe is going to think I'm some pathetic loser who lives in his parents' basement and needs an eighty-four-year-old woman to help him score.

Is that...? Yes, I have a trickle of sweat coming down my forehead now. Oh, for Christ's sake.

Tessa is the only one in the room who seems to be conducting herself with any sense of decorum. She's struggling a little with which fork to use when, but other than that, she's very polite and asks surprisingly thoughtful questions. Arabella just knocked back her fourth Moscow Mule and is openly glaring, wrinkling up her nose and shaking her head at Tessa as she sways in her seat. I'm sweating like Dexter that time I decided to bring him with me to the Spanish Riviera. And now, my grandmother is telling Tessa to come for tea tomorrow so she can show her my baby pictures.

"I'm sure you've seen some in magazines and on the telly and all that, but only I have the photos of him naked as a jay bird." Grandmum, who also has been sucking back cocktails, seems to be taking to Tessa like a Malaysian first lady to my junk.

Dear Lord, why did I do this?

10

More Importantly, Where Does She Get Her Hair Done?

Tessa

WELL, that was quite possibly the most awkward meal of my life—and that's saying something. One down, fifty-nine days left. I wish I could call Nikki, but she's on a 'phone date' with Doctor Perfect. So, I'm lying stretched out across the massive bed in my room, trying to figure out what the hell just happened.

I've been sized up and groped by a tiny Princess Dowager and sneered at by her granddaughter. On the plus side, that was the best food I've ever eaten. But still not worth it.

My phone rings, and my mum's face fills the screen.

"Hello, Mum."

"Finally! Tessa Adelaide Sharpe, you've been ignoring me for two days."

I cross the room and plunk myself down on a window seat. "I'm sorry. It's been the strangest forty-eight hours of my life."

"Which is precisely why you should have *called me*." She huffs. "You have no idea what it's been like for me, having to find out everything via the telly! The phone's been ringing off the hook, and all I can say is what everyone *already knows*. It's been horrible for me."

"Sorry. I know, I just didn't know what to even think, let alone say."

"Are you there now?"

"Yes. I got here this afternoon. We just had dinner." This ought to distract her. She'll want to know all about the meal.

"What did you eat?"

"*Foie gras*, salad, little red potatoes with a light dill sauce, and some tiramisu."

"Oh, my God! My daughter had little potatoes at the palace." She laughs, seeming to have forgotten she's mad at me. "Who did you eat with?"

"The Princess Dowager, Princess Arabella, and Prince Arthur."

"Tell me *everything*. What are they like?"

I have to be careful what I say, because it will most definitely be broadcast all over Abbott Lane by lunch time tomorrow. "They're very...gracious hosts."

"Really? Even the dowager? Everyone says she's absolutely awful."

"She actually was very welcoming. And funny." The only reason is because she thinks she's buttering me up to be her granddaughter-in-law, but I won't mention that.

"I always knew she was full of spunk, that one!"

"You could say that."

"And Arabella? Is she as beautiful in person?"

"Yes. She's very pretty." Nasty as all hell, though. I stare out the window at the moonlit garden below. My stomach tightens thinking about Arabella's scowl, and I find myself wishing I were home again.

"And what about Arthur?"

"What about him?"

"What's he like?" The toilet flushes, and I cringe. I hate it when she calls me from the bathroom.

"It's hard to put it into words, really. He's not exactly what I was expecting..."

"In what way?"

"In a way that I can't quite sort out. He's been kind, but of course, it's all for show."

"Pish! He's a wonderful man. You know my cousin Rose met him once at a charity luncheon. She said he was an absolute charmer."

"Yes, she told me." Several times. "But being charming and being a good person aren't exactly the same thing."

"What are you talking about? He's involved with literally hundreds of charities."

"He mentioned that," I say in a flat tone.

"You're not even going to give them a chance, are you?"

"It's not about *them*, Mum. It's the concept of a monarchy that I don't agree with."

"But, maybe now that you're living with them, you'll see things in a different light?" Her voice rises on each word.

"Doubt it. Getting to know them as people won't change the facts. There is no place for a monarchy in a modern society."

"Then why are you there?"

"Honestly? I'm hoping this will be my way to get back on at a newspaper, or maybe I'll get a book deal so I can buy my own place."

"Oh." Her tone drops two octaves.

"Mum, whatever you were imagining would come from this, you need to stop now. I'm here to observe them for two months—like Dian Fossey with the gorillas. Then I'll go home, hopefully get another shot at one of the big papers, or maybe even a news channel."

"So, you won't even let us meet them?"

"I can't invite you over. This isn't a holiday. I'm here for work." My tone is more curt than I intend.

"Oh, of course. Silly me." She sounds so embarrassed that I now feel like a very bad daughter in the vein of Lizzie Borden.

"I'll see what I can do. Maybe I can bring you in for a tour of the palace in a few weeks," I say. "If they'll allow it."

"Only if it won't be too much trouble." She's playing the martyr now. Pile on the guilt.

"Never too much trouble, Mum. It just may not be possible. I'm not exactly an honoured guest."

"All right. I should let you go. You probably have work to do."

"Yes, I do."

"Are you coming over next Sunday to celebrate Geoffrey and Joshie's birthday?"

"I'll see what I can do."

"That usually means no."

"It means I'll see what I can do."

"Fine. I guess that's all a mother can hope for once her kids are grown and gone. That they'll answer the phone once in a while and pop over a few times a year to let you look at them."

"Mum, I promise I'll do my best to be there."

"Excellent. Goodnight, Twinkle! Have a great first sleep in the palace!" Her voice has gone back up to dog-whistle high. "Can you believe it? My daughter, sleeping in the royal palace, of all places!"

We talk for another ten minutes. Well, in actual fact, she peppers me with questions about the room I'm staying in, the linens, closet size, etc. while my father pipes up every couple of minutes, needing to find out about the brand of faucets in the bathrooms (Perrin and Rowe, in case you also are wondering), or if I've seen the lawn tractors they use on the grounds yet. Apparently, he has a bet with his friend, Hal, down at the pub, that they use John Deere, and if I don't find out, he'll be made to look a fool at *The Frog and Keg*.

So, by the time I get off the phone, I have a surprisingly long list of very important facts to uncover for the men at the pub, as well as a mission to find out who does Arabella's hair (because Nina and Isa simply *have* to know). Well, as a former-journalist-turned-blogger, I should at least be able to manage that. Although, I can't imagine asking Arabella anything at this point, let alone that.

"So, who does your hair? It's quite fetching."

"Feck off."

"Right-o."

————

Blog Post – March 11 – My First Day at the Palace & a Special Announcement
Tessa here, live from my home for the next two months. I've been given an

apartment at the palace that faces the meadow and woods behind the castle. It is exactly as you would expect—an enormous space that has only the most lavish of furnishings. An en suite the size of the living room in my flat, all in marble with white, heated floors. The bed is of course a king, with sheets so soft, I wouldn't doubt they're made from actual babies' bottoms. Just kidding about the baby's bottom thing. Probably spun from the fur of a two-day-old Karakul lamb.

Dinner likely cost the taxpayers in the thousands when you add up the outrageously expensive wine, the organically-sourced food, the chefs, the servers, and the clothing/jewels worn by Princess Arabella and the Princess Dowager.

Earlier when I arrived, Prince Arthur made a rather transparent attempt to bring in my luggage, proving only that he has never handled a suitcase before. He then showed me to the library, a two-storey room filled with first editions and two-hundred-year-old books for the exclusive use of the Royal Family and guests. If I had to guess, I'd say he was hoping for a Beauty and the Beast moment, but in all honesty, the hoarding of such treasures is, of course, offensive to me, as it should be to us all.

I met Dexter the pig, and I have to say, he rather won me over. That is, until he licked inside my mouth. I won't hold it against him, though. He is a pig, after all, and I was chewing gum, so I suspect he wanted a taste.

Now to the special announcement:

I've managed to secure an "Ask Me Anything" each week with the Royal Family (and perhaps some senior staff members, if there's interest).

So, send your best, most hard-hitting questions to the Reddit forum (link below). And make sure to vote on your favourites, as the five most upvoted questions will be used in an interview! I'll be conducting live interviews every Thursday at ten am. This is your chance to finally put their royal feet to the fire, so make sure to be tough!

———

It's now well after midnight, and there is no way I'm going to fall asleep. Ever. I spent two hours making notes on my first day at the palace, and by the time I finished, I was so wound up, I think I could give the Shock Jogger another whirl without getting 'gently reminded' to hurry up. I know what's keeping me awake, even though I will never admit it out loud, even to Nikki, or Chester, who will keep all of my secrets until he goes to his watery grave.

Deep down, in a place I don't even want to know exists, I am disgustingly attracted to Arthur. Of course, this is to be expected, I suppose. He's gorgeous and charming and a complete arse. He wouldn't be the first powerful flame to which I've played the part of the moth. There was my former boss at *The Daily Times*, Barrett Richfield, Avonia's most eligible young mogul who took over most of the publishing industry here and in Belgium about ten years ago. The moment Barrett laid eyes on me, I fell for him. Hard. After ten glorious shag-filled months, he announced his engagement to ABNC's evening weathergirl at the time, Helena Jones. I was quietly let go the next day, with the head of HR hinting strongly that trying to sue for sexual harassment would result in public humiliation for me. *Not him.* Not fair, but such is life. The powerful can do as they please, while the little people must do what will please them.

But not anymore. No matter how high Prince Arthur turns up the charm, I am keeping a respectable distance.

After tossing and turning for a good hour, I throw off the covers. I won't get a moment's rest until I have something salty. Maybe followed by something sweet. I really won't know until I'm eating. Unfortunately for me, there is nothing but a fridge filled with water bottles and a cart of various types of liquor in my room. And that simply won't do when a woman is trying very hard not to be attracted to a certain someone who is sleeping ten doors down the hall. Yes, ten. He pointed out which apartment was his when he walked me back to my room. And I can tell you, knowing where he is sleeping is *so much worse* than not knowing, because my salt-and sex-deprived self is hitting that late-night booty call hour, and there is a very hot man so nearby I can smell the pheromones he's giving off.

I'm pretty sure it was all that stuff Princess Florence said that did me in. I could have kept my attraction at bay, but she put the entire thing out front and center. The sex thing, I mean. Her comments cranked up the heat about two thousand degrees, and now I'll have to work extra hard to be indifferent to His Highness. But the very fact that I'm even attracted to him should send off warning bells. I don't know that I've ever had the hots for a good guy, and the fact that my ovaries are warming up to release extra eggs should tell me that he's definitely bad news. Well-dressed, devilishly handsome bad news.

Nobody will be up now, right? I can sneak down to the family's kitchen and find a snack unseen and unheard. It's so late, and they're all probably out cold on some magical sleeping potion only given to royalty so as to ensure they get their beauty sleep.

I briefly consider changing out of my fleece Sponge Bob pajama bottoms but then decide to go for it. I pull on my coziest light green hoodie and some flipflops and creep out the door.

Flipflops? Really, Tessa? The world's noisiest shoe for sneaking around a castle in the dead of night? I shuffle my feet as I make my way down the long hall. Arthur pointed out the family kitchen to me on the tour earlier, and I made a special point of noting its location in proximity to my room. I take the lift down to the main level, then turn left, and it's the third door on the right.

The halls are lit by rope lighting along the bottoms of the wall. I suppose this is meant to save energy. It's really rather dim, though. And a little bit scary. I periodically come across mounted weapons or suits of armor, and each time I can't help but imagine someone is inside the suit ready to slice me in two. I find myself holding my breath while I inch my way along, sliding my feet. Oh, yes, I am the height of sophistication.

I am almost at the kitchen when a door opens and I am almost knocked over by a very beautifully sculpted, naked, wet torso that disappears into some low slung sweat pants. The torso belongs to Arthur, of course. We both make 'ooff' sounds, and he catches me by my arms as I start to tip backward toward the floor. My hands land on his abs, and they are momentarily in heaven. I want to knead those abs between my fingers, sweat and all. Only they're too hard to knead. Nothing doughy about this man.

Well, hello, Prince. Nice to see you.

"Ms. Sharpe. What are you doing up?"

I freeze up, suddenly realizing that sneaking around in the middle of the night could be interpreted in a variety of ways, one of which is that I'm doing covert research for my blog. Or perhaps I'm planning to steal some priceless piece of art. Another is that I'm looking for *him*. God, I hope he's assuming I'm a thief. "Couldn't sleep. I'm in search of something salty."

He raises one eyebrow, and his lips twitch with amusement. "Are you, now?"

Yup. Just heard it myself. "Crisps, perhaps. Or maybe some cheese and crackers. What are you doing up so late?"

"I couldn't sleep either. Thought a late-night workout would do the trick."

"So I see." My eyes roam his shirtless body without my permission, and when I force them back up to his face, he's wearing that cocky grin again. *Dammit, eyes! Did you really have to do that? We are trying to appear professional here in our Sponge Bob pajama bottoms and flipflops.*

"I'll show you to the kitchen." He turns and waits for me to join him. He walks so closely to me that I can feel the heat off his body. That must have been some workout. He could totally increase the entire family's popularity among women aged six through ninety-eight if he'd post videos of himself exercising. I won't tell him that, though. He doesn't need any more ego-stroking.

He flicks on the lights and heads for the pantry. "How spicy do you like it?" he asks, then grins back at me. "The crisps, I mean."

"Not at all spicy. Plain. Just very plain." Nice work, Tessa. That was definitely a non-sexy answer.

"Plain's good, too." He waggles his eyebrows at me before he disappears into the expansive pantry.

I take a seat on a stool at the massive island and practice my Lamaze breathing as quietly as I can, hoping it will somehow help me get my head on straight. Who knew I would be so easily distracted by a set of sculpted pecs? Oh, and a super muscly back. And the gorgeous face of a Viking god.

He returns a second later with a bag of Lay's.

"Classics. Nice." I fidget with the hem of my hoodie, feeling like a complete idiot dressed in my jammies in front of the crown friggin' prince. I should have at least thrown on some jeans. He tears open the bag and slides it across the island to me. "Something salty for the future mother of my children?"

I choke out a laugh, my entire body heating up with a mix of giddy school girl excitement and utter embarrassment. "She was rather taken with the idea of us as a couple, wasn't she?"

"Ah, yes. My apologies for all that. I didn't anticipate her reaction." He grabs a couple of tumblers out of the cupboard and opens the fridge. "Milk?"

"No, thanks. I'm more of a water girl."

"You sure? You should make sure you're getting enough calcium." He pulls out a jug of milk and sets it on the counter. "You know, for the baby."

"If you're going to be such a nag, I don't think I *do* want to have your child." *Stop flirting! You hate him! And you're wearing a T-shirt that says 'Life's Better in Bikini Bottom.'*

"Oh, so you're considering it, then?" He hands me a water and pours himself a tall glass of milk.

"Of course. Think of the book deal I could fetch as the mother of your children." I pluck a chip out of the bag and take a bite. *Oh, please stop looking at me like that, shirtless Viking god. You are turning my body to jelly and my brain to goo.*

"Aah, so it would be strictly a business deal." He has a sip of milk, his eyes never leaving mine.

"Yes."

Arthur leans back against the counter and crosses one leg over the other. He's giving me the best view of him possible. If he were to sit beside me, I wouldn't have such a good vantage point of all his royal sexiness. And he bloody well knows it. Bastard.

Gorgeous, gorgeous bastard.

He nods thoughtfully. "That actually makes a lot more sense than the whole 'falling in love' thing that seems so popular these days."

"Probably. I read a study in which they discovered that people who have arranged marriages end up happier than those who marry for love." *Oh, yes, Tessa, wow him with your knowledge of sociological studies. This is how you got to be so popular in high school.* "Apparently, they have a worse go of it for the first few years, but then they settle in better for the long term, whereas people who marry for love have unrealistic expectations going in and end up letting each other down more often than not."

Am I still talking about this? Really? "Makes sense when you think about it." Yes, I am.

Arthur tilts his head. "I'd say it makes rather a lot of sense. Most women tend to have completely unrealistic expectations of the men they love."

"Most *women?* Men are the ones who expect that their wives won't ever grow old, or to end up with stretch marks and a squishing tummy from having their children, or be too tired from looking after those children all day to have sex."

"No, you're wrong there. I think most blokes expect all that to happen. The real problem is that women marry a man they think they can change, only then to leave them because they've changed."

I fold my arms across my chest. "Or...*maybe* they leave them because they don't get their lazy butts off the couch to help out with the kids or the cleaning."

"Nope. That's not it."

"Oh, it's not?" Good God, this man is arrogant.

"They might *say* that, but it's really because most men screw up the whole romance thing. They start out with a pace they can't keep up, and once they've secured the relationship, they let it fall off." He puts down his glass of milk and holds the counter's edge with both hands. Oh, *great.* Now the muscles in his entire upper body are flexing.

Oh my, what am I mad about again? What was he just saying? The romance thing. Right. "That part I agree with. Men do get lazy."

"And women only get weary? Come on. They get lazy, too. Everybody's selling something, Ms. Sharpe. It's only once you've bought in, you'll find out what you really paid for."

"So, an arranged marriage it is, then?"

He smiles down at me. "That would be the smart choice."

"You should tell your grandmother you want her to set you up. I'm pretty sure she'd be all over that."

"Yes, she would. Although, she was so taken with you, I'd be afraid she'd pick you."

"Better not, then." I shudder and laugh, hoping it sounds authentic, because there is no way I want him to know how much that stung.

But I'm actually glad he said it. It will stop me from fantasizing about something I can never have. And definitely do NOT want. "I should get some sleep. I'm tired, and we have an early start tomorrow."

I stand and walk out of the room before he can say anything. He doesn't chase me, or apologize, or say he didn't mean it. But why should he? We are enemies using each other for what we need. Nothing more.

I'm so bothered that I take three wrong turns trying to find my room. I suppose I should be glad that I didn't let him see that he nicked my ego a bit. At least there's that. But how pathetic of me to allow him that power in the first place. By the time my head hits the pillow, I resolve to be extra perky tomorrow, so he'll realize he can't affect me in the slightest. I also promise never to give this man an inch again. No matter what he's not wearing.

11

How Do You Like Your Eggs?

Arthur

I'M BACK at the scene of the crime—Prince Arthur in the kitchen with his big mouth. The victim: any chance I had to woo Ms. Sharpe. What the hell was I thinking with the whole 'I'm afraid my grandmother would choose you' bit? *Obviously*, that would hurt her feelings. And I really can't afford to do that when the entire point of having her here is to get her to like me.

I know women, and this one'll be as cold as ice this morning. She'll be ultra-professional now. All business, no more flirting, which is such a shame, because it was rather fun. It also means I'll have to go about this the hard way—and in my opinion, doing things the hard way is merely proof of a lack of intelligence.

I cook up some scrambled eggs and fried tomatoes—Gordon Ramsay taught me the secret to the perfect morning-after breakfast, and it's really the only thing I can make. So, I'm cooking while I wait for Ms. Sharpe to arrive and feeling oddly nervous, which is not like me at all.

"Good morning." She enters the room dressed in her running clothes. *Schwing!* Good morning, Excalibur. She's all sweaty, her cheeks are red, and she's smiling. Huh. Wasn't expecting that.

"Good morning, Ms. Sharpe. How did you sleep?"

"Fast." There's a bounce in her step as she makes her way to the fridge and helps herself to a bottle of water.

"Fast?" I laugh. "I like that." I glance over at her from in front of the stove, waiting for her to comment on the fact that I'm cooking. Usually, this comes as quite a surprise to any overnight guests, but she says nothing. "Hungry?"

"Famished."

I grin over at her like a complete moron. "I was hoping you'd say that. I took the liberty of making you my specialty."

"Eggs?" She raises one eyebrow, looking completely nonplussed.

"Not just *any* eggs. These are Gord Ramsay's perfect scrambled eggs."

"I stand corrected. Special, fancy eggs." Her tone is light and warm. Not a hint of the ice queen that I was expecting.

"But don't worry. I checked, and they aren't sourced from endangered hens or anything. Unlike the sheets."

"So, you read last night's post?"

"Of course. You were spot on about the *Beauty and the Beast* thing. I was going to take you to the stables next to wow you with the horses."

"Why didn't you?"

"Because you aren't likely to be impressed with what works on the average woman."

"I don't think you know what the average woman wants. Your problem is that you've been surrounded by people who show up ready to be impressed, which is not only highly unusual, but has given you an unrealistic view of the world. Regular people have to prove their worth through their actions and words. Not just because of their title."

Well, fuck me. She's right. Why is that such a turn-on?

She takes out a mug and pours herself a coffee. "Top up?" she asks, gesturing to my mug with the pot.

"Please." I hold out the mug and take the opportunity to stare at her face while she pours. How did I not notice that she had the most brilliant green eyes yesterday? Very nice.

When she turns to replace the carafe in the coffee maker, I find myself inexplicably disappointed. I dish up for both of us and take the plates over to the table. I wait until she has seated herself before I sit down.

"Sorry, I'm a bit of a mess this morning. I wanted to get in my run before we start the day." She picks up her fork and knife, then turns the plate a quarter-turn to how I laid it down. I stare as she starts with the tomato.

"Oh, wait. Would you like a photo of the plate for your blog?" I ask.

She tilts her head to the side. "Your ability to make a pan of eggs won't be of interest to my readers. They're more interested in serious political and philosophical topics concerning the nation."

"No, of course." Well, that certainly backfired.

She slices into the tomato, and I can't help but be mesmerized as the tomato disappears between her teeth.

"Mm, very tasty. Thank you, Your Highness."

"Call me Arthur. And you're more than welcome." I have a bite. Delicious. Just the right amount of heavy cream in the eggs to make them as rich as Oprah. "Vincent will be by in about fifteen minutes to go over our itinerary. Unless it's changed, I need to start the day with paperwork. When the King is away, I manage all of the correspondence, which takes about two hours. We have a few meetings here at the palace, then a charity luncheon, then I'm to inspect the newest graduates of the naval academy over at the base, followed by a dinner with the Moroccan ambassador. You're welcome to observe any or all of today's events."

"Sounds busy."

I shrug. "Typical Wednesday."

"I see." She has a sip of her coffee, then stares out the window at the meadow below. "Your Highness, I know something must be going on for you to need my help. Why don't you tell me so we can make this much easier on ourselves?"

"I thought I did explain it."

"You started to answer me yesterday in the limo, but then you changed the subject."

"That's not how I remember it. As I recall, we arrived at the palace and the conversation naturally ended."

"The Prime Minister is going to call a referendum, isn't he?"

I hope this won't come back to bite me in the arse. "I can't say for sure, but one thing is clear. You have keen journalistic instincts."

"Don't patronize me. It won't get you anywhere." She's fixing me with a glare that could peel paint off a truck.

I give her an overtly playful grin. "Not only smart, she's also tougher than she looks."

Tessa fights a laugh, and I'm glad she seems to know that I'm making fun of myself and all my attempts at seducing her opinion. Then her smile disappears, and it's straight back to business. "When?"

"When what?"

"When is he calling for the referendum?"

"No idea." I shrug. "Could be today, or maybe never."

"So, that's why me and why now. You're desperate." She gives me a smug smile.

"Yes, well, try not to enjoy this too much. It is my life we're talking about here." I take another bite of eggs.

We finish breakfast in silence, while the weight of what's happening sits heavily on my shoulders. There's a shift in mood in the room, and I can tell by the way she glances at me every once in a while, that she might even feel a tiny bit sorry for me. As much as I hate being pitied, I'll take whatever I can get at this point.

Finally, she speaks, but when she does, it's not what I want to hear. "Isn't there a part of you that realizes the time of kings and queens needs to come to an end?" Her voice is gentle, but her words irritate me all the same.

"Not really. I know things during my father's reign have been... less than stellar, but it doesn't mean that our family doesn't have an important place in the fabric of our country."

"That's debatable. But things change, even when we don't want them to. Surely, you must know that."

I sigh. "Surely, *you* must know I'm not going to go down without a fight."

"I'm not going to be on your side of the battle. I've been waving the banner for the other army for a long time now."

"Which is precisely why I wanted to show you what we do. I was hoping that maybe you'd understand. And if you did, you might decide to show people what they won't be able to get back if they decide to vote us out."

She shakes her head. "I have to be honest, I'm not likely to change my mind."

"I thought you were all for change?" I give her a little grin, hoping to make her smile again.

It worked. She's smiling and rolling her eyes at the same time. "Walked into that one, didn't I?"

"Don't feel bad. I'm considered extremely tricky."

That earns me a laugh, and you have no idea how wonderful that sounds to me at this moment.

"I'm asking for one chance, Tessa. One last chance for someone intelligent and honest to thoughtfully and carefully examine what we do—for not only the nation, but the world as well. Then decide if what we give is worth more than what we take."

———

"Did one of the nannies drop you on your head when you were a baby?" It's my father on the phone. Apparently, he's seen the news.

"Good morning, Father." I gesture to Vincent to give me a minute and watch as he quietly slips out the door. Ahh, fresh air.

"Were you quite drunk when you came up with this little scheme?"

"A little, but I'm sure you'll see that the reasoning was sound," I say.

"And what would that be?" I can picture him looking over his reading glasses at me with disdain.

"To turn her into a fan."

"So, how's that going? Did you impress her knickers off yet?"

"Not yet, but I will."

He sighs. "Do I need to come back and do it for you?"

That thought makes me throw up in my mouth a little. "No need. Stay where you are...in Bali?"

"Thailand."

"Whatever. It's all under control."

"No, it's not. You've let a snake into the hen house. I'm making arrangements to come home early."

Click.

That went well, don't you think?

———

"I don't know, Arthur. Just because I'm a woman, doesn't mean I'd understand the likes of *her*." Arabella is at her desk, going over seating arrangements for an upcoming People for Animals luncheon she's hosting.

I flop down into a chair opposite her. "Come on, help me out here, sis. For the good of the family...and your sad little homeless animals that you worry about so much." I give her my best puppy dog eyes, knowing how well they work on her.

She sighs and drops her shoulders. "Fine. I take it the usual crap didn't work on her."

"Not even a little."

She sets down the sheet she's holding and narrows her eyes at me. "You're not going to like it."

"Father's coming home, and I need to have this situation under control before he gets here."

"Oh," she sighs. "All right. As much as I hate to admit it, Ms. Sharpe is smart and cunning. She's well-educated politically. But beyond that, she's a person who cares about other people. Not us, of course, because she can't see us as human beings. We're more like two-dimensional villains in a Bond movie to her, as unfair as that is."

"Okay, so..."

"You," she pauses and rolls her eyes, "are going to have to show her we're human. Connect with her. You'll have to be prepared to let her see the *real* you. Not the arrogant, cocky prince, but the serious and somewhat vulnerable man."

"Not possible. There really is nothing to me besides the arrogance and cockiness."

"Fine. Go ask Mr. Blue Cheese. Maybe he'll know how to handle her." She picks up her seating chart again and lifts it so I can't see her face. "You're coming to the luncheon on Sunday, right?"

"I believe so."

"Bring her. And do your best to look affected."

"I'll give it a whirl." I get up, completely disappointed to be no further ahead than I was before I came in.

"Arthur?"

I turn and see Arabella staring up at me. "You really are so much more than you let on. I know it's a huge risk to let anyone—especially her—see that side of you, but at this point I don't think you've got any other choice."

"But I should at least try taking her horseback riding first, right?"

Arabella laughs at my stupid joke. "Get out, you idiot."

12

Things I Can't Admit Out Loud

Tessa

IT'S SUNDAY MORNING, and I finally have time to myself to think. The last several days have been so busy, I've barely had time to sleep, let alone record my observations with any type of accuracy. I follow Arthur through what is now one big, confusing blur of activities, dinners, meetings, and receptions. We rush from obligation to obligation, with his day being planned down to the minute. I try to blend into the background and watch Arthur at work, but it's difficult. My fifteen minutes of Internet fame aren't quite up yet, so I find myself fielding questions about the Shock Jogger by those who don't realize that I'm also that awful Royal Watchdog woman. Those who *do* realize who I am either glare or make little comments under their breath about me.

Speaking of glaring, I haven't run into Arabella again, which has been a bit of a relief, quite frankly. Delicate, my arse! That girl is about as delicate as an elephant gun. More deadly, too. I haven't seen the Princess Dowager either, which is sort of a shame really, since at least she was fun, even if she does only like me under false pretenses.

Since our conversation in the kitchen the other morning, Arthur and I have managed to maintain a professional decorum, which is *definitely* what I want. I don't want any confusion or unwanted feelings that will cause me to lose my objectivity. There's a strange warm sensation when Arthur looks at me, but other than that, I'm doing rather well, if I do say so myself. Except when I find myself staring at him with my jaw hanging down, as happens more frequently than I'd care to admit. Like when I see him in a suit that I haven't before (which is every day, really), or when he smiles, or when he's concentrating and his eyebrows crinkle up just a bit, or when he's laughing. I bet that's why my mouth has been dry all the time.

Note to self: keep lips together whilst in presence of Arthur to avoid dry mouth.

Mavis, the housekeeper assigned to my room, has arranged for my breakfasts to be brought to me on the pretense of needing extra time to get ready in the morning. She also has stocked my room with snacks, leaving me no reason to leave my room in the middle of the night again. This allows me to avoid time alone with Arthur, which is for the best. It's bad enough that I have the image of that ripped, sweaty body rolling around in my mind every time I shut my eyes. I can't risk another similar sighting of what could very well be a body so amazing that it could be considered a mythological phenomenon. No one who hasn't seen it would believe it exists. I tried to describe it to Nikki on the phone on Friday, but I could tell she couldn't quite grasp the magnitude of the hotness. Now I know how frustrating it must be for those people who've seen the Loch Ness monster.

So far, the family and their duties are very much what I expected. Charitable work that is done in the public eye and among people who also want credit for good deeds. This morning, the family has gone out to church, and I opted to stay back and get caught up on my work. Somehow, it would seem wrong for me to observe them when they are in a house of prayer.

I'm sitting up in bed, tapping away on my laptop as the sun shines in my window. The weather has changed, almost overnight, and now brings the scents and sounds of spring. I'm planning to go for a quick run around the palace grounds, and then take a long bath before this afternoon gets busy again. I had a peek at tomorrow's itinerary, and my feet hurt already just thinking about it. The endless standing and rushing around in heels almost has me pulling out my granny shoes again, but somehow the thought of wearing them in front of Arthur makes my stomach drop. Not that I care what he thinks of me, because I don't.

The questions from readers for the Royal Family are really piling up now. It seems that since I started this "Ask the Royals Anything" forum, I'm attracting a host of royal fans to the site. So, not my usual crowd, although my regulars are still there, thank God. Today's questions are ridiculous, and I'm pretty sure, based on the time of posting, that most of them are from lonely, drunk women who were scouring the Internet for shirtless photos of Arthur last night.

"What type of underwear does His Highness, Prince Arthur wear?" Nope.

"What workout does Arthur do to stay in shape?" Okay, maybe.

"How is Dexter and can we see some videos of him with the Prince?" Not exactly hard-hitting, but not a disaster.

"What does Arthur sleep in? The nude? Boxer briefs?" I wonder...wait, no I don't.

"Why don't you all just get jobs and stop sponging off all of us poor people?" Yes! This.

"My name is Danni. I met Arabella at Tiffany's once. I sold her a set of gold earrings. Does she remember me?"

"How old is the Princess Dowager, and is she really dying? I heard she's dying, but I'm not sure if that's just a rumour or if it's just because she's so old." Poor taste.

———

Mavis has just brought in my breakfast. I really have to say, I'm going to miss her, even though she doesn't seem to like me, and I do feel guilty about allowing people to serve me while I lounge in bed. But damn, these crepes are to die for. They have the perfect amount of warm chocolate sauce drizzled along the tops so that you get a bit with every mouth-watering bite.

Now to check my personal messages, which I have yet again been neglecting for days.

Text from Lars: *Tess, Nina says she still hasn't heard back from you about that whole visit to the palace thing. Can you please call her as soon as possible? She's going to end up going into labour early if she doesn't hear soon.*

Text from Nikki: *Has the wallpaper in your bathroom always been peeling at the top? I'm worried I've been having too many baths. It was peeling before I got here, yes?*

Voicemail from Daniel Fitzwilliam, owner of Wellbits: *Ms. Sharpe, I have not yet received a reply to my three previous emails. Again, I need you to contact me immediately so we can find a way to mitigate the damage done by your video. If I don't hear back from you, I will be forced to take legal action.*

Voicemail from Mum: *Hello, Twinkle, it's Mum. Call me about Sunday. I'm heading to the shop to get groceries, and I need to know how many people I'm cooking for. Oh, and Nina said not to get the boys Lego anything this year. Apparently, they've started leaving it in strategic spots around the house to catch robbers, and Lars almost broke his ankle when he stepped on some in the middle of the night last night. Oh, and none of that Moon Putty stuff either because they keep leaving it in their pockets and Nina's had to have the repair man over twice to fix the washing mach—*

Text from Nikki: *Does super glue work on walls?*

Voicemail from Dad: *Tessa, I'm heading to The Frog and Keg tonight. Any word on those tractors?*

Text from Nikki: *have sppr glued eyelshes to eylid. headng to hosptl.*

Voicemail from Mum: *If you are coming for dinner on Sunday, can you pick up some of that cheese from that place I like? I thought I'd make a lovely fondue.*

Text from Nikki: *Back from hospital. Wearing eye patch for the next three days but am happy have not gone blind. Googling way to remove super glued wallpaper from wall. Apparently, it bubbles if you use too much. Not to worry, though. I'll have it fixed before you get home. I promise.*

———

Conversation via Facebook Messenger between myself and KingSlayer99…

KingSlayer99: *How's it going at the palace? I can't wait to see what you've got on them by now.*

Me: *So far, I'm still searching for our silver bullet, but I know it's here somewhere and you'll be the first to know.*

KingSlayer99: *It's there, and if anyone can find it, it's you, Tessa.*

Me: *Let's hope so. Failure is not an option. How's your son's earache? Is he feeling better?*

KingSlayer99: *Much better, thank you. That warm olive oil treatment you suggested worked like a charm.*

Me: *Glad to hear it. Don't thank me. My mum's the one who told me about it.*

KingSlayer99: *But you passed it along. Very thoughtful of you. BTW, you won't fail. Just make sure you don't let those bastards lull you into thinking they're decent people, because they're NOT. I know you, and deep down, you're too good a person to last long with a pack of liars like the Spoiled Family.*

Me: *Fear not. I won't be fooled. I know who they are.*

KingSlayer99: *I have every faith that you will complete the mission on behalf of us all. I was thinking maybe after you finally take them down, we should celebrate. I could come to Valcourt when it's my ex's week with Quin. I'd like to take you for dinner to celebrate your success. You're pretty much my biggest modern-day hero. You're the most beautiful and intelligent woman — no — person to ever live in Avonia.*

Me: *You're too kind. Yes, a dinner would be grand. We should invite all the members of the Facebook group and make a night of it!*

KingSlayer99: *That's not exactly what I had in mind, but it sounds fun, too.*

Oh, dear…

13

Too Many Movies

Arthur

A KNOCK at the door wakes Dexter from a dead sleep. He's on my bed—I know it's a little gross, you don't have to tell me—and grunts in irritation at being disturbed. I, however, am not irritated at all. I am hopeful that the hand that did that knocking belongs to one Ms. Tessa Sharpe.

I stride across the room and open the door, ready to say, "Is this a booty call?" but when I see who it is, my face falls.

Damien stands before me with a large yellow envelope. "Sorry to call so late, Your Highness. The investigator has returned his report on Ms. Sharpe."

"Ah, thank you." A twinge of guilt hits me. Now that I've gotten to know her a little, this seems somehow wrong. Especially after all the flirting and the fact that she's not the completely evil witch that I thought she'd be. She's a little bit goofy and vulnerable underneath that tough-girl act, and even though I shouldn't, I *like* her. "Anything interesting?"

"You'll easily be able to maneuver her in the necessary direction with what he's found out."

"Should it come to that." I take the envelope. "Let's hope it won't."

"Anyone else have copies?"

He pauses, and I can tell he's trying to figure out what I'm about. "Do you mean, have I sent this to your father?"

"No, I meant what I asked." God, Damien, I'm not an idiot. You can't lead me into one of your traps.

"The investigator keeps records of everything. I took the liberty of copying it as well, just in case." He gives me a mealy-mouthed smile. I stare at his chin for a second. Not one whisker. How?

I walk across to the living room and flop down onto the couch. Damien sits across from me on an armchair.

After a half-hour, I know everything there is to know about Tessa Adelaide Sharpe from her bra size (a very delightful 34C), first pet's name (which I shall not share with you, as she probably still uses it for passwords), to every grade she's ever gotten in school. There's a particularly useful online dating profile that she filled out almost three years ago but then deleted. It holds the cheat codes to her heart.

Tessa Sharpe

Age: Twenty-five

Occupation: Journalist at major newspaper

Interests: I love photography, running (especially on the beach), yoga, reading, dancing the night away with friends, watching romantic comedies but they must be well-done and have an excellent plot. I also enjoy a good mystery book or film. My favourite music is pop, especially Pink and U2.

People I dislike tend to: be lazy, overly critical, or sponge off others.

People I like tend to: be kind, make their own way in the world, and work hard.

Favourite Food: Jelly Babies – world's best candy. And crisps, any flavour will do.

Biggest dreams: To one day be an award-winning journalist or writer. To see the world. To find someone who will understand me and love me unconditionally.

Biggest fears: Sometimes it feels as though the world is spinning too fast and that life is going to pass me by without me having really lived or enjoyed it.

My dream date would include: Doing something active like rock-climbing, going for a long bike ride or hike, followed by great conversation over an unhurried, delicious meal. Then we could sip some wine while watching the sunset, and then who knows?

What I'm looking for in a man: Someone fun, honest, caring, energetic, and hard-working to share my life with. It matters less to me that he makes a lot of money and more that he is passionate about his work. I am hoping to find a true partnership with a man who will be supportive of my dreams—even when I fail— and who will let me do the same for him.

Huh. I don't know whether to be impressed or skeptical. What woman really wants a man who is passionate about his work but makes no money? I call bullshit. She also seems to have an obsession with finding a hard-working fellow, which makes me wonder if her father is a real deadbeat. The funniest part is the bit where she claims to dislike people who are 'overly critical.' *Ding! Ding!* Hypocrite alert! But none of that really matters in the end, does it? What matters is that I now have an excellent jumpstart on 'Operation Impress the Knickers Off the Royal Watchdog.'

I flip to the next page in the dossier that lists her former relationships.

Damien is so excited that he looks like a five-year-old who has to pee. "She had a brief affair with Barrett Richfield when she was working for *The Daily Times*. Ended with him engaged to Helena Jones and Ms. Sharpe out on her arse."

The thought of her sleeping with a bottom feeder like Richfield makes my blood turn cold. "So, she quit when he dumped her?"

"No. He *fired* her." Damien is positively radiant right now, glowing like a spring bride.

"Why didn't she sue?"

"Who knows? Couldn't stomach the humiliation, maybe."

I shrug, pretending I'm not in the least affected by this infuriating story. Because I shouldn't be, should I? "Not exactly usable information, is it?"

"It wouldn't be if it weren't for the fact that she's been trying to get on at another paper or news program since she was let go. But she's been completely out of luck, which is our gain." He rubs his little hands together. "There's nothing easier than using someone's dreams against them."

"Not *against* her. In *our* favour." My heart drops. I really don't want to do this, but all's fair in love and war, right? Although, this is low, even for us. "Damien, I'd like to make sure that no one finds out about any of this."

"No one will. I'll see to it." He stands. "It would render her completely useless to us."

He leaves, and I sit staring at everything I need to both win her over and screw her over. I should be elated, but somehow having it in my hand makes me sick. Ruining her life like that, for my own gain. Although I really shouldn't feel bad, since she has been trying to ruin mine for years now.

I gather up the papers and walk over to my bookshelf and pull out one of the books. The bookcase immediately slides open, revealing a hidden—wait, you didn't actually buy that, did you? God, you watch too many movies.

I put the envelope in a desk drawer and lock it, then pocket the key.

14

A Day in the Life

Tessa

BLOG POST – MARCH 18TH

Tessa here. It's already been a week since I've moved into the palace, and I have to admit, I may have been the slightest bit wrong about the Royal Family lazing about all day. I've been shadowing Prince Arthur for seven days now, and he keeps a schedule one could only describe as grueling. I've documented yesterday for you:

6:00 am – Workout

7:00 am – Shower & eat breakfast while being briefed on the day's events.

7:45 am – Meetings (hour after hour of poring through requests for philanthropy from new charities, planning sessions for various political and charitable events, reading over the day's speeches and making adjustments, signing congratulatory certificates for anyone celebrating special anniversaries, birthdays or other achievements. Prince Arthur is signing on behalf of his father, who is away at the current time).

11:43 am – Break to change into suit for luncheon.

12:00 pm – Greet guest for luncheon honouring the Ladies' Auxiliary Association.

12:13 pm – Speech thanking women for their hard work and dedication.

12:17 pm – Attempt to eat lunch while being interrupted repeatedly with requests for signatures/photos (he handled this graciously, I have to say).

1:00 pm – Wrap up and attempt to leave luncheon while being stopped by those who didn't interrupt his meal.

1:02 pm – Travel to naval academy via limo while preparing speech for graduating class.

1:35 pm – Arrive at naval base. Greet graduates individually. Pose for photos.

1:55 pm – Speech

2:05 pm – Travel back to palace while making congratulatory phone call to Prince Harry on the occasion of his engagement.

2:38 pm – Arrive at palace, go straight to office to prepare for meeting with Zumundan ambassador regarding trade issue with neighbouring nation of Kalubizi (I was not able to sit in on this, but they both left laughing at 3:05 pm, so I'm guessing he did his job.).

3:10 pm – After seeing ambassador to his limo, Prince Arthur was given 12 minutes of free time, which he used to check in on his sister, who is preparing for big charity event.

3:22 pm – Prep for tea honouring Avonia's recipients of the Writers' Guild awards. More speech adjustments and time to freshen up.

4:00 pm – Greeting authors. More photos. Speech. Tea. More photos.

5:30 pm – Back to office to be briefed on local and world news.

6:00 pm – Back to his apartment to get ready for dinner with Kalubizian ambassador and his wife to open discussions about trade with Zamunda.

7:00 pm – Dressed in tuxedo, Prince Arthur greets guests and spends next two and a half hours socializing and approaching trade issue.

9:35 pm – Sees guests to limo.

9:38 pm – Quick debriefing on tomorrow's events by senior adviser.

10:00 pm – Day is done.

Now, I may have been wrong about how much they do in a day, but I stand by my opinion that what they do accomplish is not at all necessary, for the most part, for the functioning of this great country. Would the new graduates of the Naval Academy still graduate were it not for the Prince showing up to salute them? Yes, they would.

Could the Ladies' Auxiliary Association still have a lunch and toast their own success? Yes, they could.

Could a member of our government hold meetings with the Kalubizian and Zamundan ambassadors to work out a trade deal? You bet they could.

So, while decidedly not lazy, I still find that the Royals are basically unnecessary.

Stay tuned, because on Thursday at 10 am will be the LIVE interview with Prince Arthur himself. He'll be facing the five most popular questions from you, so PLEASE, PLEASE, PLEASE post some tough questions (and vote for them) so we can hold his royal tootsies to the fire.

———

Once I've posted, I take another look at the questions for this Thursday's "Ask Me Anything." They have gotten so laughable now that I cannot see how I'll maintain any dignity at all by asking them.

I pick up my phone and call Nikki.

When she answers, she says, "Did you call the Shock Jogger people back yet? They sent a registered letter. I had to sign for it."

My stomach lurches. "Not yet. It's on my list. But that's not why I called. I called because I need your advice."

"You want to shag the Prince, but you're not sure if you should?"

"No! I'm having a crisis of my journalistic integrity."

"Not as exciting, but tell me anyway," she says.

"It's the 'Ask Me Anything' questions. They're all written by Arthur groupies. What kind of underwear, what's his favourite meal, is he seeing anyone…they're all crap. Unfortunately, those are the only ones that are being upvoted."

"Ah, so your attempt at allowing the people to have an unvetted voice has come back to bite you in the arse."

"And hard. I'll look like a giant idiot asking these things. I won't be taken seriously at all. But if I don't ask their questions, I won't be the voice of the people."

I hear a splashing sound. "Are you in the tub again?"

"Yes. I had a grief headache. Matthew Crawley just died. But don't worry. I really will replace the wallpaper before you get back," she says. "Okay, here's what I'd say. Are you in this to be taken seriously, or are you in it to make money? Because if it's money, mission accomplished. Your hits must be off-the-charts amazing in the last week."

"Can't I want both?"

"You can *want* both, but you're not necessarily in a position to get both. Not right now, at least. I mean, the Shock Jogger video is now making the talk show rounds without you. I'd say being taken seriously is a good six months off. Maybe a year."

"Shit. You're right." I sigh. "Hey, how's your nose?"

"Dr. Perfect says it's healing nicely."

"How is that going, by the way?"

"Orgasmicly."

"Remind me to buy new sheets when this is all over."

"Yeah, you probably should. Maybe a new couch, too."

———

Today, Arthur and I attend the christening of a naval ship, the ANS Viceroy. Who knew royals really did that? Certainly not me. Anyway, since Avonia has only three ships, this is a pretty big deal. The Prime Minister is even here to make a speech.

Arthur, who is a commander and captain, is dressed in his Royal Navy ceremonial dress uniform, and I have to say, I died a little when I saw him in it. The white hat with the gold trim, the black jacket with gold shoulder boards, the standing collar, the matching black pants and shiniest shoes I think I've ever seen. Add to that his dazzling blue eyes and those dimples that pop when he looks at me. It's all I can do not to actually bite my knuckles.

There's not a cloud in the sky as we step out of the limo. I'm happy to feel the sun on my face and breathe in the salt air. To be honest, it's a bit of a relief to be able to step away from Prince Arthur, since the entire ride from the palace was a frustrating exercise in not gawking or appearing at all impressed.

He is immediately swept up into a tide of people, and I take a moment to walk down the pier to look at the North Sea.

"Ms. Sharpe?"

I turn and am face-to-face with the Prime Minister himself. "Oh, hello, sir." I smile, even though the hairs on the back of my neck rise for some strange reason.

"What a great day for our nation." He nods toward the new ship.

"Yes, very impressive."

"I'm quite a fan of yours."

"Oh, the Shock Jogger video?"

"No, no. That looked entirely awful. Nothing funny about that, if you ask me." He shakes his head. "I'm a fan of your Royal Watchdog work. You're very insightful, and I'm not just saying that because you happen to share my opinion on everything you've written about them."

"Thank you. That's high praise, coming from you." I smile politely, but inside alarm bells are going off in my head.

"Well, I mean it. It's about time someone in Avonia started to question the sanity of a nation choosing their leaders based on being lucky enough to fall out of the right vagina. I mean, if anyone's going to be a ruler until he dies, it should at least be someone we elected in the first place, shouldn't it?"

What? Did he just say that bit about the right vagina? "I've never quite thought of it that way."

"Just a little joke. I hope I didn't offend you. My wife's always telling me not to make jokes, because people often think I'm serious."

"Oh, no. That's...fine. I get it." I nod in a 'Well, thanks for stopping by to chat, but I really should be going' sort of way.

He doesn't take the hint. "I'm guessing it was quite a dilemma to go live with them, knowing you were moving in with the very people you've been attacking for years now."

"Yes, it was."

"What made you decide to take the Prince of Laziness up on his offer?"

He's using my own words, but they feel like acid to my ears when they spill from his mouth.

"My flat was being fumigated, so I figured I might as well." I laugh at my own joke, and he goes along with it.

"But other than that, I'm sure you were hoping to get something out of this whole thing? Book deal? A position at one of the big papers, perhaps?"

"One can dream." A gust of wind tugs at the hem of my skirt, and I put my hand down to hold it in place.

"You're a very brave young woman to go live among the enemy. I'm sure you could use a powerful friend."

"I've been just fine, sir. Everyone has been very kind to me, actually."

"Call me Jack." He glances down at my lips, then back to my eyes. Eww! "I think we could help each other out, Tessa. You are in a unique position to help the anti-royal movement. And I'm in a *unique* position to help you in return."

"What do you mean?" *Quid pro quo, Clarice.*

"It just so happens that I'm on the hunt for a new speech writer. Someone with your talents and political savvy would definitely be at the top of my list." His upper lip twitches as he speaks. "Or perhaps if that isn't your thing, you'd like to be set up with a nice, cushy job at ABNC or back at *The Daily Times*. There's a lot more security in the mainstream media than you can get as a blogger."

"That's a most generous offer, sir." My mind is spinning, trying to understand what he really wants. The fact that he brought up the idea of me going 'back' to the newspaper means he's been looking into my past, which is more than a little alarming. "I hope you won't mind me asking what I would have to do to earn your friendship?"

"Just keep fighting the good fight, as you've been doing." He takes a tissue out of his pocket and blows his nose. "And if you happen to find anything of particular interest, you could let me have a look at it first."

Ah, here we go. "Were I to do that, what exactly would you gain?"

Giving me an intense gaze, he says, "When launching an attack, a good general knows that timing is every bit as important as aim."

Slippery answer. My stomach churns, and I feel hot and dizzy all of a sudden. "I'm surprised you're planning to launch an attack. They seemed to be so solidly on your side during the election."

His lips curve up in a smile. "You know, Ms. Sharpe, there was once an ancient Chinese military strategist, Sun Tzu, who said keep your friends close, but your enemies closer."

Oh, dear Lord, our prime minister is a total schmuck. "Wise words indeed, sir."

"Yes, Sun Tzu was quite the philosopher. You should read his work some time. The Royal Family has been leeching off our nation for far too long. It's long past time to put a stop to it, and since their approval ratings are at an all-time low, I'd say our timing couldn't be better, wouldn't you agree?"

Before I can respond, a woman in a grey suit taps the Prime Minister on the shoulder. "We're just about to start the speeches, sir."

He gives me a broad smile and a little nod. "It was a pleasure to speak with you, Tessa. I'll be in touch."

I watch as he walks away, my legs numb and my heart hammering against my ribs. I have a terrible feeling that he's planning to eat some liver with fava beans. Mine, Arthur's, King Winston's. I don't think he cares, as long as he gets fed.

———

It is late in the evening, and I cannot sleep. Instead, my conversation with the Prime Minister rolls around in my head and causes my stomach to churn, even though I have no idea why. We're on the same side, and I've just been offered everything I've ever wanted—serving as a speech writer to the prime minister's office would certainly bring with it a great deal of respect. Or…having a second chance as a real journalist and a steady paycheck. Yet, I can't help feeling like it would all come at a cost that I'm not willing to pay.

I consider telling Arthur about our conversation, but then think better of it. As much as I don't think I can trust Jack Janssen, I can't trust Arthur, either. The two of us are playing a dangerous game and have been literally flirting with disaster this entire time. The smart move would be to stay quiet and say nothing until I better understand the rules.

15

The World Keeps Spinning

Arthur

IT'S FRIDAY MORNING. I have just finished a meeting that Tessa could not attend, and I'm glad she wasn't in there. It was a very long and tedious discussion on the third wave of invitations for the upcoming ball. Having received R.S.V.P.s from the second set to go out, we now choose from the 'third string' guests. It's all entirely self-serving, political and, at times, quite petty.

We actually spent twenty minutes debating whether or not to invite the Count of Dunningham and his new wife, since his first wife will be attending as her sister's plus one (her sister is second string). According to Damien, this will put us over the recommended limit of divorced couples in which both parties will be in attendance. Apparently, the maximum number is one-point-four percent of the total guest list. Any more than that, and you increase your risk of an 'undesirable scene' by sixteen percent. He has some type of algorithm he uses that also takes into account age of new wife and length of time since divorce. In this case, they've only been divorced for a year, and new wife is thirty-two, while first wife is fifty-six, putting them at a category five risk of causing a scene.

It was for that very reason that I pushed so hard to invite them. I insisted on the basis of length of time both parties have had a relationship with our family, when in reality, both the former countess and the new one seem rather scrappy, and it would really liven things up if a good cat fight broke out. Horrible of me, I know.

Damien knew my underlying motives. That vein in his neck was pulsing again—it's because he can't prove it, but he both knows the real reason, and he knows that I know that he knows and can't say as much. It's rather delightful. And petty, as I mentioned before, but please don't hold it against me—I really am starved for entertainment. If Tessa knew this type of thing went on, it would only confirm for her that we have no business leading so much as a Girl Scout troop, let alone an entire kingdom.

After checking with Mavis, the maid assigned to Tessa's room, I find Tessa in the solarium, reading a book. She's curled up in one of the puffy armchairs, and something about the sight of her there makes me feel calm, for reasons that I cannot explain.

"This was my mother's favourite spot," I say as I sit down on the chair opposite Tessa and take a deep breath of the humid air.

Tessa looks up and smiles at me.

"Or so I'm told. Apparently, she had those chairs and the couch brought in. My father thought she was mad to want to sit among a bunch of dirty plants. But I think she was right." I pat the arms of the chair with both hands. "This is the perfect place to hide from the world."

"That it is."

"Do you know that these plants have come from all over the world? Some as far as the very westernmost part of South America. They've been tended to for generations right here in this building."

"I didn't realize that." She closes her book and looks around for a minute. For once, she looks mildly impressed.

I point to a palm that has stretched all the way to the glass ceiling.

"I had a nanny who used to measure me to that tree right there and tell me if I ate all my greens, I would one day be as tall. Bloody liar."

Tessa laughs. "My mum used to tell me that if I ate all my greens, I'd get my breasts quicker." She turns bright red as soon as she says it, then starts babbling, which I've noticed is what happens when she's embarrassed. It's rather adorable.

"Not sure why Mum said that, actually. It's an odd thing to tell a girl. I mean, why would you even want to have breasts early? It just makes you the center of attention for a bunch of pre-pubescent boys who can't help but stare. Not that I had any breasts at all till I was sixteen. Flat as a board until then. And tall. Too tall. I also had to wear a retainer that made me lisp and spit when I talked. And I had bad acne."

"So, very popular, then?"

"Quite," she says. "Had to beat the boys off with a stick."

"Well, better a rose should bloom late than not at all."

Her face turns a deeper pink. "So, how was your meeting?"

"It's over, so that's about the nicest thing I can say about it." I consider bringing the subject back around to her eating her greens, but I think better of it. "I finally had a chance to read your post from Monday."

"I'm sure you have something to say about it."

"Wildly inaccurate reporting. I was only given thirteen minutes to change before the luncheon, not seventeen."

She gives me a wry smile. "I'll be sure to post a retraction."

"I should hope so." I grin over at her. "Made me look like a bit of a loafer. Other than that one egregious error, I have to consider it a bit of a victory. You admitted that we're a very hard-working bunch." I emphasize hard-working in hopes that she'll realize I'm not too different from her dream man.

"I also said your work was, by and large, useless."

"Sometimes it is." Did that just come out of my mouth?

Her eyes light up. "Did you really just admit that?"

"Admit what?"

"I said your work was basically useless, and you said sometimes it is!" She laughs.

"I did not. I said, 'Some chimes are his.'"

"What? That doesn't even make sense!" Tessa bursts out laughing, and I feel unusually happy.

"Some climbs are...bizz."

She hoots, almost falling out of her chair, and I laugh along at myself, and suddenly the world seems like a very nice, simple place to live. I know it *can* be nice at times, but it is not in any way simple. Not for me. Because here I am having the most fun I've had with anyone in a very long time, and it happens to be with a woman who's made her living bashing my family. When the moment passes, I remind myself of the job at hand.

"Do you ever have moments when the world seems to be spinning so fast that it feels as though it's going to pop right off its axis and go hurtling through space?"

"Yes! I know exactly what you mean." Her eyes light up, and I feel a pang of guilt for using the information from her dating profile.

"I don't." I try to brush off the nagging guilt while she laughs. When she stops, I give her a serious look. "Most days, I just wish I could find a way to slow it all down so I can take a breath and think before my life passes by without me having really enjoyed it." Oh, I'm pushing it now, aren't I? In for a penny, in for a pound...

Tessa nods. "I can see why. You keep up a nearly impossible pace."

"It has to be possible. I've been doing it for years."

She tilts her head and stares for a moment. "Just because something's been done one way for hundreds of years, doesn't mean it should continue."

"Ah, we're back to progress versus tradition again, aren't we?"

"It would seem to me that you're unhappy about a number of things with this life. Maybe a change would be a good thing for you, too. Imagine a life where you set your own course. *You* decide what you're going to do all week." Her eyes are wild with excitement, and I have to say it's a tiny bit contagious.

I know I came in here for a reason, but at the moment I've completely forgotten what it was. "There are days when there is nothing I'd like more."

"So maybe," she says, pointing one finger in the air, "just maybe, what would be good for the country would also be good for you."

"What *you* consider good for the country, you mean. This may come as a shock, but I'm for progress, too."

"Just not the type I'm talking about."

I nod. "I don't believe that everything new is, in fact, progress. Sometimes we change simply for the sake of change, and it takes us back a few paces in our humanity. If we lost our throne, what would become of all those who depend on our help?"

"You'd still be in a position to help them."

"I suppose." As I stare at Tessa, Arabella's words about opening up come back to me. It might be worth a shot. Who knows? Maybe I'll surprise myself and find there's more to me than I think. "The thing is, I don't know what I'd do with my life if I'm not doing this. And I know that's not a reason to keep me or my family around, but if you could put yourself in my shoes for just a moment, I'm sure you could see why I would want to stop this from happening."

She gives me a sad smile. "I hate to tell you this, but everyone who's about to lose their job feels this way. It's never easy on anyone."

"Why should I be any different, right?" I do my best to keep my tone light.

"Exactly."

"Because I *am* different." I hold up my hand before she can protest. "Not because I was born to privilege or I'm more important than anyone else. But because the *very purpose* of my existence is to become the king.

"When your parents decided to have children, it was so they could have a family to love. When you were born, they didn't say, 'We will spend every day preparing Tessa so that when the time comes, she will be the best blogger this nation has ever seen.' They said, 'Here is our perfect baby girl. I wonder what she'll grow up to become? We'll give her every opportunity so that she can live out her dreams, whatever they may be.'

"Your parents got married because they fell in love. My parents got married so that my father could produce heirs. My very life itself is solely for the purpose of providing Avonia with the next in a long line of kings, to do my service for our country and one day rule in the name of my family…so, all that to say, I am different."

"I can't even imagine what that must be like, but it sounds…very sad to me." Her face softens and empathy pours from her and washes over me.

Nope. This sharing thing is too much. If I keep this up, I'll be a blubbering idiot within minutes. I shrug. "It's not all bad. There are perks."

"Don't do that. Don't make light of what must be so difficult." Her voice is so gentle, it's painful.

"I have no business feeling sorry for myself when I sleep in a palace at night and there are millions of people in the world without so much as clean water to drink."

"I don't know. I'd say you do have cause to complain. Not very loud, mind you, or to the wrong people. But it's okay to admit when you've been hurt."

Forget it. I'm done. This is too hard. "I should go get ready. I have to leave for a board meeting for the Children's Hospital Fundraising Association in a few minutes." I stand. "I actually wanted to see if you'd like to come along."

"I don't think I could be ready in time."

"All right." I turn, but her voice stops me.

"Arthur. When I lost my job, it was awful. I was a wreck, actually. I had no idea what I was going to do, but I had to pick up the pieces and get on with things fast. If it happens to you, you'll at least have time to figure it all out."

"I'll have my home and money, right?" I swallow hard. "I know that. I do. But the thing is that my *life* will have no purpose, Tessa. None at all."

Lifting her chin, Tessa says, "I disagree. I think you're getting one's life purpose and one's occupation confused."

"In my case, they are one in the same."

"We aren't defined by our occupation. We're defined by our character."

"Certainly, but character doesn't give one a purpose."

"Neither does occupation." She sighs and shakes her head. "I'm worried that you're pinning all your hopes on me, Arthur, but even if I *did* try to convince the nation that they should vote with you, should it come to that, I'm just one person. I can't stop the world from spinning."

"I suppose not." I stare at her for a moment, then decide to risk something I never thought I would. My pride. "Tessa, I need to ask you something, and as much as I hate to do it, it has to be you. You see, while you're one of very few people willing to be brutally honest with me, you are, in actual fact, the *only* one who knows the first thing about life outside this palace. So even though you've led the charge to take my family down, I'm standing here with my hat in my hand, asking for your help. If you were me, how would you turn this ship around?"

She blinks in surprise. "You want my opinion?"

"I do. As strange as it sounds, yours is the only opinion that matters right now."

Tessa watches me for a moment before she speaks, and I can tell she's struggling with whether or not to help me. Finally, she says, "Okay. Here's what I would say is your family's biggest failing. You've done a very poor job of letting the people know who you are. We have a vague idea of what you do for Avonia and the realms, but there is a human component that's missing. The public has been given the impression that none of you believe you are accountable to us, which frankly does far more damage than good.

"If it were me, I'd try to open up and share more of who you are. Not just giving yourselves pats on the back for charity done, but let people in on the little moments that make you human. At the end of the day, that's what earns trust and adoration."

"That's a very hard thing for someone like me to want to do. People can't hurt you with what they don't know."

"Sure they can. When there's a gaping hole in our collective knowledge, it's human nature to try to fill it."

I sigh. "And they don't always fill it with nice things."

"Exactly."

"Thank you, Tessa. I'm truly grateful that you would share your wisdom with me."

The door opens to the solarium, and Vincent says, "Found him" into his walkie-talkie.

I take a deep breath and follow him out. As the door closes behind me, I realize that I've just been given the last advice I want to take. To do more of this 'open up and bleed' business.

16

A Cautionary Tale from the
Camera Operator's Union

Tessa

I'M STANDING in what is known as the gold drawing room, and I can
tell you the room lives up to its name. The couches are white with
gold trim, the tables, gold. The curtains—guess what? Also, gold. The
sun pours in through the window as I set up my camera on a tripod to
tape the first in a series of crap interviews designed by idiots and
conducted by me (quite possibly an even bigger idiot, since it was my
idea in the first place).

I practice reading the questions aloud while not glaring. Then I
check my watch. Arthur is set to be here in five minutes, and the live
feed on Facebook will start in exactly seven minutes. The fact that the
interview will be live gives true transparency, since the viewers will
know we didn't edit anything out.

Although, it also means that if I fuck anything up, it's live and will
be out in the world forever. I'm cold-sweat nervous. I shake my hands
and breathe deeply. No big deal, I'm only about to have my first

exclusive interview of my career with a major, internationally known celebrity. And I'm going to ask him if he wears boxers or briefs. I take a deep breath and hear the sound of the door.

"Knock, knock." Prince Arthur strides in, dressed in a light grey suit. He's wearing a blue tie that brings out those amazing eyes of his.

I'm dumbstruck for a moment before I force my tongue into action. "Good morning. Are you all ready for the big interview?"

"Looking forward to it." He grins. "I have to confess, I peeked at the Reddit forum to get an idea of the calibre of questions I'd be facing."

"Hard-hitting stuff, I know." I roll my eyes.

"Apparently, I have a few fans out there still."

"Apparently," I say. "I know the questions aren't exactly cerebral, but I suppose it'll give you a chance to show the people your fun side."

"It seems they're more interested in seeing my backside." He points to the chair positioned across from the camera. "Right here?"

I nod. "This shouldn't take more than a few minutes."

"I have twenty-three minutes slotted for this, so we should be fine." He sits down and checks his tie, then gives his jacket a sharp tug. Unlike me, this is not his first interview. He picks up the mic that is on the table next to the chair and fastens it to his tie (which is kind of a shame, because I was sort of definitely hoping to do that for him). *God, Tessa, you're pathetic.*

"It's a live feed, so I'm going to sit next to you and control the camera via remote."

"Excellent." The smile on his face is nothing short of devious.

I stand behind the camera, focusing in on his face. His gorgeous, impossibly handsome, could-turn-a-girl-to-a-puddle-just-by-looking-at-her face. Huh, this whole camera thing could work for me. I can stare freely without seeming creepy. Yes, Tessa the pathetic stalker has a plan.

"Okay, are you ready, Your Highness?" I sit down, mic up, smooth out my skirt, and take one last deep breath.

"Yes." He nods, then says quietly, "Don't worry. You won't fuck up."

"Camera is rolling...now." My cheeks heat up at his encouragement, and now I'm all tingling and warm right when I need to be cool as a cucumber. "Good morning, Prince Arthur. I'd like to thank you for agreeing to this series of 'Ask Me Anything' interviews."

"Thank you for setting this up, Ms. Sharpe. It's a rare opportunity to face questions directly from the public like this, so I'm looking forward to what I'm sure will be a worthy challenge. I'd like to make one request, however. Everything you ask me, I'd like you to answer as well."

I freeze up and turn to him with my mouth hanging open like an idiot. Live feed. Great idea. I manage to close my mouth quickly and purse my lips together for a moment. "I'm sure your public will much rather spend the time learning about you, Your Highness."

"I beg to differ. You're quite a celebrity in your own right." He grins at me, then the camera.

I plaster a fake smile on my face, even though I'm ready to wring his royal neck. I stare at the lens, my heart now so far lodged into my throat that I am unable to speak.

Arthur can, however. "Come on, Ms. Sharpe. Show the people your fun side."

"Okay, then. We'll start with the fifth most upvoted question and make our way to number one." I glance down at the paper in my shaking hand. "Question five received three thousand two hundred and twelve votes: 'Has Prince Arthur ever considered that he might find love with a common girl, like, say a girl named Denise, who works at the One Stop over on Broadmoor Street?'"

Arthur smiles into the camera. "Seems like people are really rooting for Denise at the One Stop. Denise, I'm sure if we ever met, you'd be an absolute heartbreaker. As to the question of finding love with what you call a common girl, I find that hard to imagine, since almost every woman I've met is nothing short of a goddess."

Oh, I am not even going to hide my disgust right now. I'm just going to wear it for everyone to see. "Thank you," I say through gritted teeth. "That was nothing short of patronizing." I turn to the camera. "So, Denise, if you're out there watching this, he's all yours, love!"

Arthur cocks his head toward me with a smirk. "So, Ms. Sharpe, have you ever considered that you might find love with a common boy, or girl for that matter?"

I glare at him. "Someday I hope to find a nice fellow, yes. Preferably, someone who lacks arrogance and cares about important issues, like the environment and human rights."

"Do you mean to suggest anyone but me? Because I assure you I *do* care about important issues, both globally and locally. I sit on the board of three dozen charities, actually, and my family supports over two thousand more each year, providing millions in fundraising dollars each year. Without our work, many of them would have to shut down."

"I'm sure that's true, but you'd still not make a good candidate, as far as I'm concerned."

"Oh, the arrogance thing." He looks directly into the camera. "She's a real nut-buster, this one."

Son of a bitch. He certainly knows how to make the most of this opportunity. Glancing down at my paper, I see the only hard-hitting question on the list is next. And it's not even cleverly worded. "Question four has four thousand ninety-eight votes. 'Why don't you all just get jobs and stop sponging off all of us poor people?'"

The prince nods once, a conciliatory gesture. "I can see how some may view my family as leeches on society—I believe those were your words. But I would like to point out that my family provides very good jobs for over twelve hundred people each year. They have full benefits, nicely padded pensions, and enjoy job security that is hard to come by these days. In addition to this, and our charity work, I believe we have an important place in protecting the people through our veto power in Parliament. It's not often that the monarchy exercises it, but on the occasion that we have, we've found the people were glad to have us act on their behalf. There was that whole matter of the bill to remove a woman's right to file for divorce back in nineteen seventy-four. My grandfather stopped that in its tracks."

"Yes, but that was over forty years ago. What have you done since then?"

"While it's true that we haven't had to step in for a long time, I believe that the knowledge that we are here to do so keeps our government leaders in check in some ways."

Damn, he's smooth. He doesn't even look a bit ruffled. And that was the best thing I had.

He smiles into the camera. "I suppose I can't ask you the same question, really, since you're self-employed."

"Correct, it would make even less sense than the last one." My turn for a smug smile. "Question three has just over five thousand three hundred votes. What workout does the prince do to stay in such incredible shape?"

He grins over at me. I know my cheeks are pink, because they certainly are hot right now.

"Thank you to the author of that question. Very flattering. Six mornings a week, I train with my head bodyguard, Ollie. He's a former commando, and we do some boot camp-style stuff as well as mixed martial arts. He also makes me run. A lot. I could use something to help improve my pace, though. I'm looking to increase it by, oh, about twenty-percent or so over my next twelve runs. You wouldn't happen to know of a product that would help with that, would you, Ms. Sharpe?"

I laugh, hoping it sounds even a little bit sincere. "You're referring to the Shock Jogger, of course. Hilarious, Your Highness." I smile over a him. "You're welcome to borrow mine anytime. I'll even help you set the pace."

"You're ever too generous. Now, your turn. What workout do you do to keep yourself in such incredible shape?"

"Running, preferably not with a cattle prod tied around my ribs. I also do yoga."

"Yoga." He lifts his eyebrows. "Keeps a person bendy, I hear."

"Yes, you should try it." I can feel a cold sweat under my arms. "Okay, we're burning through these questions now. Number two is a two-parter and has fifty-five hundred votes. 'How did you decide to get a pig, when most royal families have dogs? Also, how is Dexter, and can we see some videos of him with the Prince?'"

"It's a funny story, actually. A few years ago, I was dating a certain supermodel who fell in love with Paris Hilton's teacup pig. Unfortunately, the term teacup is wildly inaccurate when it comes to pigs, unless you're referring to the cups in that ride at Disneyland. She lost interest in both of us as soon as he couldn't fit in her purse, but it all worked out in the end. He's quite happy living here, and he makes a very good companion. Do we have time for me to bring him in here?"

"Sure." Why the hell not? It's not like I have any dignity left at this point anyway. Might as well bring in the barnyard animals.

He reaches into his pocket and pulls out his phone. "I'll just ask his handler to bring him in."

Oh, but wait a minute! Upper hand, here I come! "You *pay* a handler to look after your pig? That seems like a very poor use of taxpayer money."

"Yes, it would be if the money came from the taxpayers."

The door opens and Dexter squeals, running directly to Arthur. Arthur reaches down with both hands and scratches behind his pink ears. "Troy, we're doing an interview right now. Would you like to come on and say something to the people out there? I think they'd be interested to know about the work you do."

I watch Troy walk across the room, and my stomach drops. The first time I met him, in the library, I was so distracted that I didn't actually look at him. He very clearly has some form of intellectual disability.

Troy walks over and stands beside Arthur, peering into the camera and waving. "Hello, out there."

I smile at Troy. "Troy, can you share with the people what you do here?"

He looks at me like I'm half-baked. "Right now, I'm talking into the camera. That's what Prince Arthur asked me to do."

Arthur reaches up his hand and rests it on Troy's arm. "She didn't mean right now. She's asking about your job here with Dex."

"Oh. You should have said that then," Troy says to me. "I take care of Dexter while the Prince is busy working all day. Otherwise, he'll get bored and get into a lot of trouble. He's a rascal when he's bored. Or hungry. He once chewed up a set of candlesticks, the bottoms off a set of very old curtains, and the leg off a nice couch all in one afternoon. But that was before I started here. Now, he's a happy pig. We go for long walks every day. And we watch some TV together. He loves the nature channel, but sometimes he'll sit through a bit of a football match, if I'm lucky."

"Sounds like a terrific job."

"It is. Except when I have to give Dexter a bath. He doesn't like that very much, I'll tell you." Troy laughs as he says it, and I find myself laughing with him.

Troy takes a big breath and looks down at me. "I know you don't like the Royal Family, but I want to say they're nice people. The Prince here is real good to work for. My old boss at the warehouse used to yell at me when I'd make a mistake, and I make a lot of them. But Prince Arthur is always kind, even if I do somethin' wrong."

I feel a lump in my throat and tears pricking my eyes at the thought of someone yelling at this man. *Pull it together, Softy.* I clear my throat. "Thank you, Troy."

Arthur winks at him. "Thanks, mate. We should finish the interview now."

"Yes, you should. Mr. Vincent is standing just outside the door there, pointing at his watch. Do you see him?"

Arthur tries not to laugh. "I did not. Thank you for letting me know."

"No problem, sir," he says as he walks away. "Wouldn't want you to get in trouble. That's no fun. Come on, Dexter, buddy."

Dexter trots off after Troy, and I have, once again, been proven wrong. Bugger. But nice, too, I suppose.

"Your turn. Do you have any pets, Ms. Sharpe?"

"A betta fish. Chester."

"Is it betta fish that fight to the death if you put two together?"

"Yes." *Where is he going with this?*

"A rather competitive choice in a pet, don't you think? Chester—does not work or play well with others." He grins at me. "Some say we choose a pet that is most like our own personalities."

"And you have a pig who is very naughty when he's bored or hungry. What does that say about you?"

Arthur laughs. "*Touché, Madame.*"

"This brings us to our last question." I close my eyes for a brief second. "With over six thousand upvotes, 'Which type of underwear does His Highness, Prince Arthur wear?'"

"Clean ones. You?"

"Also, clean." Am I *dripping* with sweat? I feel like I'm dripping.

Arthur wags a finger at me. "No copying off your deskmate, now, Ms. Sharpe."

Smug bastard.

"You'll have to give another answer."

"Girly ones."

He raises one eyebrow. "Oh, my favourite kind."

"To wear?" I purse my lips.

"Ha! I walked into that, didn't I?" He's speaking directly into the camera now. "I only like to see the girly ones, not wear them."

"Okay! Well, that's it for our first live interview!" I'm using that voice my mum used when the twins started asking about how babies are made. "Now that we've gotten the silly questions over with, perhaps people can put forth some more serious political questions. Please. Let's not waste this opportunity to have access to the Royal Family by only finding out about pets and underwear." I turn to Arthur. "Thank you, Your Highness, for being quite a sport today."

"It was my pleasure. I rather like the fun questions. As far as I'm concerned, keep 'em coming! Oh, and I have finally gotten into the twenty-first century. You'll find me on Twitter and Instagram as The Real Prince Arthur, so check it out because I'll be sharing all kinds of fun pictures and secrets from now on."

Twitter? Instagram? I sit, unable to move for a second, but then I finally remember to press the remote button to shut off the camera. I slump down in my chair, letting out a big sigh. "Well, that was humiliating on so many levels."

"Why? I thought you came off as quite clever. You're quick on your feet, you know. You could do television if you had the mind to." He takes off his mic. "You're certainly pretty enough. Very smooth voice."

"Thanks." I blush, and my heart patters. "I'm sorry about implying that Troy's wage was paid by taxes."

Arthur shrugs. "No problem. It would be natural for you to assume as much. I'm on the board of a group that finds work for people whom some would consider unemployable. Everyone deserves the dignity provided by a good job, don't you think?"

"Yes, of course."

"Even people like me?" he asks.

"That's different. Troy is *earning* his wage."

"And I'm not?"

"Not the wage you're getting."

He folds his arms. "And exactly how much am I getting?"

"Well, since your family has been so tight-lipped about that, I can only guess. Probably a few hundred thousand a year."

"Interesting guess. I don't get paid, actually. Instead of a wage, I am allowed to live here, and I receive a clothing allowance. The majority of my expenses are covered by a blend of our family's investments and real estate holdings. Only twenty percent of our annual income comes from tax dollars, which goes directly to pay for staff who work to promote tourism. This amounts to just over a million per year, but over the past twenty years, our family has generated over seventy million in tourism dollars. A more than beneficial investment for the people, don't you think?"

"Why isn't this made public?"

"Ahem." Vincent stands at the door. "You are overdue to meet with the ambassador to Belgium, Your Highness."

Arthur gives me a quick bow. "Thank you, Tessa. That was a hoot." He winks and walks out the door.

I stare shamelessly at his arse and lick my lips while he walks away. When the door closes behind him, I check my armpits and see that, yes, they are indeed drenched through. Then I reach down my blouse and adjust my bra so that the underwire is no longer digging into my left boob.

"Aah." Much better. I notice my cell phone blinking on the table across the room. I get up and swipe the screen.

Text from Nikki: *FEED IS STILL LIVE! SHUT OFF CAMERA!*

. . .

Seriously?

17

Just Two People Talking

Tessa

SUNDAY MORNING AGAIN, and I'm exactly where I was last week at this time—in recovery mode, even though I haven't had a Saturday night bender. I've just made the mistake of reading the latest comments on my first 'ask me anything' interview. Unfortunately, my armpit sniffing and mining for boobs act has captured more attention than the interview itself, which has proved counter-productive for my whole 'take Tessa seriously' campaign.

I have about thirty offers from creepy men willing to 'help me adjust my breasts,' a little move which has made Arthur stifle a laugh every time he's seen me since Thursday. He also stops me before we head into any meetings or ribbon cutting ceremonies and asks, "Do you need to do a last-minute knocker-check? Now's your chance."

Grrrr. Princes, am I right?

A tap at the door interrupts my work. Assuming it's Mavis to collect my breakfast tray, I call to her to come in. Only it's not Mavis. It's Arthur. And I'm in bed still with my bedhead and morning breath, which I'm pretty sure he can smell from over there. I yank the duvet up to my neck. "Oh, I thought you were Mavis."

"Nope. Just me." He's dressed in jeans and a white T-shirt, and oh, my Lord, does he wear this look well. "I was wondering if you'd like to go for a walk."

A walk? With his royal sexiness? Sounds dangerous. "I thought you were at church."

"I rarely make it to church. I usually have important business to attend to. Well, that's my excuse anyway." He grins. "I like to sleep in sometimes."

"So, kind of like a regular person." I smile.

"Kind of, only on a much higher thread count." His dimples pop as he smiles at his own joke. "So, are you coming or not, Sharpe?"

"Give me about twenty minutes to eat and get dressed."

"Sure."

As soon as he leaves, I hop out of bed and glance in the mirror. I definitely require more than twenty minutes' worth of grooming to look halfway decent, but since he already saw me like this, anything will be an improvement.

By the time Arthur knocks on my door, I'm dressed in a light knit pale pink sweater with a white infinity scarf, and skinny jeans that are tucked into tall brown suede boots. My hair is back in a low pony and topped with a brown cap to hide the fact that it needs some attention. I swipe my lips with some gloss as I hurry to the door. *This is not a date. This is not a date.*

When I open the door, he's leaning against the door jamb, which means that we're so close, I can smell his aftershave. Let me tell you, that is some manly, sexy aftershave. I don't know which brand it is, but it should be called 'Spontaneous Orgasm.'

"All ready?"

I nod, because my mouth doesn't seem to work when he's standing this close to me.

"Let's go."

We make our way out the back of the castle, then down a long gravel path that leads around the perimeter of the grounds. The sun shines, warming the skin on my face, and I feel more relaxed than I have since I got here. Arthur seems somehow calmer, as well.

"I hope you don't mind if I pay you a compliment," he says.

"Depends on what it is."

"Setting boundaries again?" He raises one eyebrow and gives me a half-smile.

"Maintaining them." I laugh. "Boundaries are very important."

"As is getting the upper hand."

"That, too."

"I'll risk it, then, and hope that I don't cross your boundary or risk losing the upper hand."

"Ha! You're mistaken. I took the upper hand in the limo on the first day, and I don't intend to give it back."

"Well, you're entitled to be wrong." He bumps my shoulder with his, and I do it right back.

Then he stops and turns to me, and I do the same. His eyes search mine for a moment, and his expression is so intense that I'm reminded of why I was avoiding being alone with him.

"I wanted to say that, over the past two weeks, I've been very impressed with how you've conducted yourself. You've been living among a rather odd group of strangers, whilst under a lot of scrutiny, and you've really managed it all with an unusual amount of grace."

"Oh, well, thank you." I stammer on the words, trying to quash the swell of pride in my chest at his words. *An unusual amount of grace.* No one has *ever* described me that way in my entire life. "What about the on-air boob adjustment?"

"Especially that." He keeps walking, and I'm glad to not be face-to-face with him anymore. Because if we stayed like that too long, I'm pretty sure that my expression would give me away.

"You're not what I was expecting, Tessa Sharpe."

Uh-oh. Here it comes.

"I assumed you'd be an absolute harpy, but you've turned out to be rather lovely. In every sense of the word."

Rather lovely. Nikki is going to die when she hears that one. I look up at him with an impish expression. "You're just trying to butter me up."

"Of course, I am. Doesn't mean it isn't the truth, though," he says. "Did I cross your line just then?"

"I'll allow it." I put on my best regal voice.

Laughing, Arthur gives a little bow. "Oh, thank you, Madame."

"Think nothing of it."

We reach the end of the path, and Arthur takes a key out of his pocket and unlocks the wrought iron gate. It occurs to me where we are going. I've seen footage once on a documentary about Queen Cecily. We're going to her gravesite.

He opens the gate and steps aside for me to walk through. "You're probably wondering where we're going."

"I think I know." As we press on, we find ourselves in a clearing surrounded by tall trees with the gaps filled in by thick shrubs that are just about to leaf out. In the distance, there is a pond with a small wooden bridge leading to his mother's final resting place.

"This is where I go on Sunday mornings."

"The more pressing business you need to attend to."

"You take in every word I say, don't you?" He gives a slight chuckle. "This is one of very few places where I can be truly alone with my thoughts without having to carefully gauge my next reaction."

"Is that what it's like to be you? A long string of careful reactions?"

"Not always, but a lot of the time. But isn't it like that for everyone? There are societal expectations for all people in each situation."

"I suppose that's true, but I think there are more rules for you than for most people." We cross the arched bridge, and when we reach the top, a large, ornate gravestone comes into view. It is surrounded by hundreds, if not thousands of white lilies that have bloomed now that spring has arrived.

"More people watching and waiting for me to make mistakes, anyway."

"Like me."

"And many others. Each one with a different reason to hate me, or in the very least, want to see me mess up."

"Or see you succeed. You've got plenty of those, too."

"True."

We stop and sit on a bench a few feet back from the queen's grave. Silence overtakes us. The stone reads: Cecily Rose, Beloved Mother, Wife, Daughter, Sister, and Queen. A lump forms in my throat. Arthur was five when she died. Arabella was only three months old. I sniff, then realize that my vision has become blurred by unexpected tears for someone I never knew.

"Are you all right?" His voice is gentle. "Oh, I forgot I'm not supposed to ask you anything personal."

"It's okay." My voice is unsteady, and I feel silly being the one getting emotional. "What if we say that while we're here, in this place, we can alter our agreement. Just for a few minutes."

"Go off the record, you mean?" he asks.

"Yes. Let's just be two people talking. Not a prince or a critic. Just for now. Right up until we walk through that gate."

He smiles, and this time it's different. It's not the smooth woman-izer I see. It's just Arthur, a son who lost his mother when he was only a small boy. "I'd like that very much, Tessa."

"Me, too." And it's true. I would. I look back at his mother's gravestone. "I was just thinking of all that she missed out on. I'm sure she would have given anything to see you and your sister grow up."

He makes a strangled sound and when I turn to him, the expression on his face is one of bitterness. "If only that were true." His voice is barely audible.

Before I have a chance to even try to figure out what that means, he asks, "Do you want to have children? I mean, someday, when you've found the right fellow."

"I don't know, really. I have seven nephews and nieces—soon to be eight. I love them to bits, most of the time. But the whole parenting thing seems awfully hard to do well. I have a feeling I'd mess it all up."

"You wouldn't."

"How do you know that?"

"Because you're strong enough to come live among the enemy, smart enough to make a name for yourself, and kind enough to feel sad for someone who lost his mother a very long time ago." The way he says it is so confident, that I almost think he might be right about me. He goes on, "So there you have it. Solid proof that you wouldn't mess up a child. At least not too badly."

I chuckle, then say, "I don't know about that, but I *do* know that the thought of loving someone as much as a parent loves a child terrifies me. They're so fragile, and they need you for everything. Absolutely everything for so long." I sigh under the weight of that question. "What about you? I know you're *supposed* to have children, but do you want them?"

"Very much. But I also know what type of life they'd have in store for them, and to be honest, I don't know that I can do that to a child." His gaze falls on the trees in the distance. "You've seen how busy I've been these past two weeks. It's nothing compared to what will be expected of me as king. It could be a very long time before I take over, but even now, my life is not my own. In many respects, I'll be set up to fail as a father."

"But surely you could do things differently. You'd have the power to say no to certain events so you could be with your children."

"Somewhat. But the thing is, in a way, the entire nation is mine to care for, and to protect in the way I would my own child."

"I've never thought of it that way. Is that how you see it?"

"Yes, actually. As foolish as that may sound to you." He glances down at me for a second, and our eyes meet.

The connection between us is immediate. It's like we're peering into each other's souls, but instead of wanting to run and hide, I want to see more. "It doesn't sound foolish at all. It sounds…sweet."

"And bloody terrifying." He turns again to the trees.

"Because you'd be worried about messing up the whole thing on a much grander scale?"

"Exactly."

"This is going to sound very odd coming from me, but I don't think you would mess it up. I think you'd be very good at it."

"You're right. That does sound odd."

"To no one more than me." I smile a little, then explain myself. "I think you'd be a fine king—if we needed one."

He looks down at me, and I can see there's an argument forming on the tip of his tongue, but he stops himself. "We're just two people talking."

"Right. I almost forgot. I retract that last statement," I say. "What I meant to say is that over the past two weeks, I can see how much you care about your people. I've noticed the way you make each person feel like they are the only person in the room when you are talking to them. And I don't know if they gave you lessons on how to do that in Prince Charm School or what, but I *do* know that you make people feel special, and that is a gift that most people don't have."

"Thank you, Tessa. That might be the nicest thing anyone's ever said to me."

"I doubt that."

"Maybe not, but it means so much more because it's coming from you." His gaze pierces me, causing me to feel a little weak. "There's something I need to know."

"Sure, what is it?"

His voice is gentle. "Why do you hate us so much?"

I freeze up. "Oh, God. This is going to sound so cold to you, because now that I know you, it sounds very cold to me."

"Knowing the reason would be infinitely better than having to guess."

I wince, take a deep breath and start to talk. "I don't know if you know much about blogging, but it's a surprisingly hard way to make a living. There are literally millions of people blogging every day about every single topic under the sun. Chances that you'll be able to pay your bills are slim to none. So, when I was starting out, I was desperate to find ways to separate myself from the pack." I sigh and feel my heart speed up. "I'm not sure if you can imagine what it's like to be basically broke, but it's really rather stressful. I came very close to having to sell everything and move back home with my parents…"

I pause for a second, feeling stripped naked telling a prince what it's like to be poor. "What I really wanted to do—and still do—is to find a way back to mainstream media. I thought if I wrote about national politics, it would help get me there. But I needed a fresh angle, something that would get noticed. I spent weeks researching, trying to find a gap in what was already being reported. Then one day, I realized that on a lot of sites, people commented on their dissatisfaction with the monarchy—and with our system of government—but I couldn't find a place where all of those like-minded people could come together to share their opinions."

"So, you found a gap."

Nodding, I say, "I found it and filled it."

I stare at Arthur and am surprised to see that he doesn't look upset, or hurt, or disgusted. He just looks...like he understands, which is hard to fathom considering what we're discussing.

I go on, wanting to get it all off my chest. "I do believe in having elected leaders, and I always will. But I found that the more outrageous my posts, the more traffic I would get on the site, from both sides of the argument. I know this is going to sound cliché, but it really wasn't anything personal. I was just trying to make some money and make a name for myself."

"I see. So, you were just doing business."

I groan and cover my face with my hands for a second. "Somehow, I never thought that any of you would ever read any of it. I thought of it as a space for 'the regular folk' to come to complain and ask questions and challenge the system."

"But surely you must have at least considered the possibility that we'd read some of it? As you grew more popular?"

"I had fleeting thoughts, but I always managed to justify it in my mind, telling myself that if any of you *did* read it, someone like you wouldn't care what someone like me had to say anyhow."

Arthur nods. "You're not alone in that, Tessa. I think a lot of people see us as incapable of having feelings. My sister said that maybe to you, we're like two-dimensional bad guys from a Bond movie."

"As much as I hate to admit it, I suppose that's true." My stomach twists with guilt. "I don't know if this will mean anything, but now that I know you, I can see that it was all very unfair. And I wouldn't blame you if you just lost a great deal of respect for me."

"Why would I do that?"

"Because if I had some very noble reasons for becoming the Royal

Watchdog, it would be one thing, but for it to simply be about money? That's…"

"Savvy."

"Savvy?"

"Yes. You saw a business opportunity, and you took it. I don't particularly like that you did it, but it's somehow better to know it was just about the money than had it been something more personal."

I stare at him for a minute, shocked that he could be so forgiving about the whole thing. "You're a lot more generous than I thought you'd be."

"Thank you. I'm more generous than I thought I'd be, too." He grins.

He glances down at my mouth, and I find myself desperately wanting him to kiss me. Oh, dear. This is getting complicated again. I need to put the brakes on whatever this moment is. I turn to face forward again. "Tell me about your mum."

He's quiet for a moment before he speaks. "I don't remember much, really. I can tell you what I know from watching film footage of her by the hour, but my actual memories of her are those of a five-year-old. Fuzzy and incomplete."

"I can't even imagine what you went through."

"Neither can I, really. It's like it's all some horrible dream, something that happened to someone else." His focus is on her gravestone and it's unbreakable.

"I'm sure." I wish I hadn't asked because now I want to hold him tightly to me, and there's no way I can do that. No matter how badly I want to.

"She never should have married my father." He starts talking, and I'm not sure he even knows I'm here. "She wasn't cut out for this life, for life with him. There's a necessary grit that she didn't have. It killed her in the end."

The official report suggested that she died of a suddenly ruptured aneurysm. But I think that he may have just revealed a horrible, dark secret that he's been holding onto since he was a young boy. I sit next to him in shock as the pieces start to fall into place. His overprotective-ness about Arabella and his grandmother. He's so careful to make his sister's life as easy as possible, so she won't end up buried next to her mother.

He suddenly snaps out of it and looks down at me, a bit of panic behind his eyes. "I apologize. I'm being dramatic."

"No, you weren't." My gaze hardens, but I can see he's not going any farther down that road than he already has. "You've been through hell."

"Everybody goes through some type of hell, don't they?" Arthur shrugs. "She was your age when she died, you know. So young."

"And beautiful. And much loved by the people."

"Yes, she was." He smiles. "But no one really knew her. She could be very silly. She would sing to me, all kinds of songs. I was particularly fond of her version of the *Munch Bunch* theme song."

"I remember that show." I smile, then start singing. "The munch bunch, have run away..."

He grins, then does something completely unexpected. He sings, too. "The munch bunch, are here to stay..."

I laugh, surprised at this side of him. "What's the next line? I forget."

Arthur goes on singing. "The munch bunch, have found a home..."

I pick it up from there. "With a garden..."

We both laugh for a minute at ourselves. I blush at the silliness of it all.

His face grows suddenly serious. "I don't remember much about her, but I do know she would have liked you. Very much."

Tears spring to my eyes for the second time this morning. "That's kind of you."

"It's true." He reaches up and wipes the tear from my cheek with his thumb. "You have this tough exterior, but inside, you're a person who cares very deeply about others."

"How do you know? Maybe I'm granite through and through?"

"Because you just sang with me. And now you're crying."

"Well, bugger. I gave the game away." I sniff a little and smile through my tears.

"Since we're just two people right now, and people are prone to doing stupid things, I'm going to do something very stupid." He glances at my lips again.

"What?"

"I'm going to kiss you."

"That would be stupid."

"And yet, unless you say no, I'm going to do it anyway."

"I'm not saying no, so I must be as stupid as you."

"Thank God for that." He lowers his mouth over mine and kisses me. A soft, achingly beautiful kiss that warms me from my lips to my toes and back. I've never been kissed like this before. It's so gentle, so real, that I find myself melting into him.

His hand slides over my cheek and he tilts my head, giving him better access as his tongue finds mine. Our mouths move with the perfection of a champion ice skating pair, gliding and soaring together. My hand reaches for his chest, and I instinctively cover his heart with my fingers. Now that I've seen what he's been through, I've seen him in my mind's eye as a lost little boy with no mother to love him, I want to protect him and save him from anything that could hurt him. Including myself.

We stay like this for a long time, just kissing each other, nothing more. It's not sexual, but it's the most intimate, perfect moment of my life, and I can't remember a time when I've felt so close to anyone. The world falls away, and we are no longer a prince and his harshest critic, but two flawed human beings needing to be understood. And for one brief and beautiful kiss, we give each other what we've both been missing for far too long.

When it's over, I pull back, stunned at what just happened. I look at him and he looks as shocked as I feel.

"Well, that was...unexpected."

"Yes, it was." My breath is gone.

"We should be getting back." He stands and holds his hand out to me. I take it and let him help me up.

Our fingers intertwine as we walk in silence, and there is something so natural about the feeling of his hand touching mine—something so pure and familiar.

When we step over the bridge, I stop and turn to him. "I'm so sorry about your mum." I reach up and touch his cheek. "I promise I'll never tell anyone."

"Thank you." He leans down and presses his forehead to mine. I close my eyes and just feel him here. The weight he's been carrying for so many years makes my heart want to burst with pain. He moves his face back, then kisses my forehead. "Thank you for being here with me."

"There's no place I'd rather be," I whisper because my voice has been sucked away with sorrow. His sorrow. I can't hold back any longer. I wrap my arms around him and hold his body tightly to mine, and part of me hopes I can take his burden from him. Even just a bit. After a few more minutes of holding each other and more soft kisses, we break apart and start back toward the world again.

"I don't want to walk through those gates,"

"Me either." His face is filled with regret.

"But we have to."

"So, we do."

18

Will There Be Strippers?

Arthur

THE SPELL IS BROKEN the moment the gate closes behind us. Vincent's voice cuts through the warm spring air, an unwelcome intrusion on what was possibly the best dream I've ever had (which is odd because there was no sex involved). "There you are, Prince Arthur. I've been looking for you everywhere."

"You found me," I call back.

"His Serene Highness is on his way home. His flight left an hour ago." Vincent's bearing down quickly on us, and I fear soon the fresh scent of spring buds will be overcome by pungent cheese.

"What time will he arrive home?"

"Five-thirty," he says as he reaches us.

Yup. There it is. Blue cheese. "Thank you."

"Sir, I think we should really have a plan for how to…" he glances at Tessa, "…manage the current situation."

I give him an easy smile. "No need. I've got it covered."

"Your Highness—"

"It's fine, really. I can handle it." I shoot him a warning look, and he takes the hint. "Now, how are we set for this luncheon today?"

"Everything's ready. The guests will start arriving in thirty-five minutes. Princess Arabella has asked to take the lead on the speeches, and since this is her charity, I thought we'd let her."

"That's fine. If she finds it too much, I can take over."

"The head of the program has asked if Dexter will attend, considering the topic."

"Oh, yes, he'll love it."

I turn to Tessa. "He does better at these types of things than I do. He gets any number of offers from women who want to take him home." She laughs and the sound delights my ears yet again. "You'll come today, yes?"

"I'd love to. I have a family obligation, so I'll have to duck out by three o'clock, though."

This news disappoints me slightly, and I'm surprised to find that I don't want her to go, even for a few hours. "I'll arrange for a car to take you."

"I'll see to that, sir," Vincent says. "I'd better make sure Dexter has had a bath." He hurries off, taking the walkie-talkie off his hip and calling back to the palace to give instructions.

We wait for him to be a good distance from us before either of us speaks. I sigh, then say exactly what I know she wants to hear. Funny thing is, I mean it. "It seems a shame that we have to go back to the way things were."

Tessa looks up at me, her eyes full of emotion. "It does."

"And yet we must."

"Agreed." We walk for another moment, then Tessa approaches the subject I knew was coming. "Your father doesn't want me here, does he?"

"What makes you ask that?" I'm deliberately being coy while my mind races to come up with a suitable explanation. I can't very well say, 'My father's a total dickhead. He'll be absolutely awful to you, and since I like you very much, I can't bear the thought of it.' But I should probably warn her. It's what any man who fancies a young woman would do. *Wait—do I fancy her?* I stop and turn to her. "He's not the easiest man to deal with, and I'm afraid he wasn't particularly thrilled when he learned of my plans as far as you're concerned."

"Don't worry about me." She shrugs as though she doesn't care, but at the same time, her face pales slightly. "It's not like I'm his biggest fan, either."

I stare at her for a moment. The armor is back on, for which I am glad. She'll need it. "Best case scenario is that he'll be so busy with the upcoming anniversary celebrations that he won't have time to take much notice of you."

"Ah. I see." She starts back toward the palace, more slowly now than before.

My stomach twists when I think about what I've just told her, and what we said and did a few minutes earlier. If there's one thing I've managed to avoid all my life, it's complicating things in any way, but Tessa Sharpe seems to be the exception. She could very well use everything I've just said against me and make it all public knowledge, which is why I really must double my efforts to win her over.

"Tessa, will you be back in time for the sunset?"

"I don't think so. Why?"

"There's a lovely spot on the roof of the palace that overlooks the North Sea. I thought maybe we could share a bottle of wine and watch the sunset."

"I'd love that. Maybe another time?" Her face says that this is all too good to be true, which of course, it is.

I suddenly feel like a total shit for doing this, but desperate times call for desperate measures, don't they? To be honest, when I think of sitting up there with her, sipping wine, I actually *want* to do it. It sounds rather wonderful.

Well, isn't that a shock to the system?

Just as we near the palace steps, she reaches out her hand and touches my arm, then stops. "Arthur, I promise that what happened this morning will remain our secret. I have no reason to tell anyone any of that."

"Thank you." I search her face for the truth and see her sincerity. "I appreciate that."

"And as to your father, anything you may or may not have implied right now won't make good news anyway. My observations of him will be made directly and not from hearsay. I don't run a gossip rag."

I nod, and find myself absolutely riveted by her brilliant emerald eyes.

"I'm more interested in doing the right thing than the smart thing. Maybe that makes me a fool, but I'd rather be thought a fool than be someone with low morals."

"I could never see you as either." I smile down at her beautiful face, then reach up and tuck a piece of hair behind her ear. And far too soon, we find ourselves back in the palace, surrounded by people I'd rather weren't there.

————

The entire luncheon, I find myself either keeping note of the time, or searching for Tessa among the patrons, making sure she seems happy. I had her seated at a table with some very nice animal activists, not the militant ones, but the 'give peace a chance' ones. She seems to be getting on just fine, and the fact that I care even in the slightest about her comfort and happiness should be setting off alarm bells in my head.

The truth is that I cannot, no matter what, stop thinking about her. Her smile, her voice, the warmth and taste of her kiss. I can still smell her skin even though I've showered and am in a freshly pressed suit, and I know it's my mind conjuring her scent. She looks up at me and we lock eyes, smiling like fools at each other. Dexter is sitting on the floor with his head on her lap. Smart pig. He knows a quality girl when he finds one.

Oh, fuck. This is bad, isn't it? I'm supposed to be impressing her, but instead, I think I might be falling for the one person on this planet who would like nothing more than to see my life destroyed. *Very smooth, Arthur. Highly intelligent move on your part.*

I check my watch. She's going to leave in a few minutes, and I'm about to do something very stupid for the second time today. I take my phone out of my pocket and hold it under the table.

· · ·

Me: *Any chance you want a plus one for this mysterious family obligation?*

I watch as she slides her phone off the table and discreetly reads my message. A slow smile spreads across her face and she starts typing.

Her: *Dexter?*

I chuckle to myself, hoping no one notices.

Me: *No, the other surprisingly sweet pig in the family.*
    Her: *LOL. You would hate it. It's a horridly loud birthday party for my very wild but adorable twin nephews, who are turning six.*
    Me: *Will there be strippers?*

I hear her laugh from here, and I feel like a comedy giant who could sell out Valcourt Hall (which is absolutely insane because this is only some text flirting with someone whom I'm only text flirting with so I can get into her pants. And her good graces).

Her: *Not if you don't count their three-year-old brother who hates to wear clothes.*
    Me: *He definitely does not count.*
    Her: *All I can promise is that there will be cheap store-bought cake with sickeningly sweet icing and beer.*
    Me: *You had me at sickeningly sweet icing.*
    Her: *Meet me at the front doors in fifteen?*
    Me: *I'll be there.*

She glances up at me with a little grin, and I find myself slightly excited. This is truly odd, because I've never been even remotely happy about attending a child's birthday party, even as a child. Even when it was my own.

But it's only because I really am under the gun to win her over before my father's shadow comes creeping over the castle. Not at all because of that delicious kissing business from earlier.

19

Toy Shopping with the Prince

Tessa

WELL, now, isn't life funny? Two weeks ago, I was on my way to my parents' on the bus, mud on my pants, freezing cold, and wishing I had a nice man with a little hybrid to drive me there. And now, I'm sitting in the back of a stretch limo, fantastically warm, clean and dry, next to a prince who snogged me senseless this morning, while his driver, Ben, makes his way to my parents' neighbourhood.

I finally figured out what impossibly handsome means. It's when a man is so absolutely handsome that it's impossible not to stare. He's answering emails on his phone right now, so I can gaze at him all I want and he won't see me. Just to give you a mental image, picture a crazy hot Viking sex god wearing jeans and a light blue button-down shirt that matches his eyes. And as an extra bonus, his sleeves are rolled up three-quarters so I have a view of those muscles in his forearms.

"You're being rather unproductive right now," he says without looking up.

"Should I be working?"

"That would be up to you, but it would be helpful if you weren't staring at me." He looks up and grins. "If you keep doing that, it'll mean I'll keep thinking about *why* you are staring, which will mean I'll take much longer than necessary to reply to this email, which means that it will take that much longer before I can give you my full attention."

"Well, we can't have that." I pull out my phone and text Nikki.

Me: *Guess where I am?*

Her: *On a bus on your way to your parents' place?*

Me: *In the back of a limo with Prince Arthur on the way to my parents'.*

Her: *SCREEEEAAAMMMMMM! Are you serious? Stop by here on your way! Please, please, please!*

Me: *No way. You'll chain him up and keep him like that lady in that Stephen King book.*

Her: *Maybe, but I promise not to hobble him. Please? We could share. There's definitely enough of him to go around.*

Me: *How's your nose?*

Her: *Good point. Don't bring him today. Maybe in two weeks? I should be fine by then.*

Me: *That will also allow you suitable time to purchase chains and duct tape.*

Her: *Now, you're talking. Wait a minute, he's going to your parents' with you? For the twins' birthday party?*

Me: *Yup. His idea.*

Her: *He's really pulling out all the stops to win you over.*

Me: *You have no idea.*

Her: *What?! Dish. Now!*

Me: *Nothing, he's just very accommodating.*

Her: *OMG! HOW accommodating?*

"Ben, can you stop here, please? At this store on the right?" Arthur asks.

"Yes, sir."

. . .

Me: *Gotta run. Fill you in later.*
Her: *You better.*

I toss my phone in my bag, suddenly feeling very guilty about both implying anything at all to Nikki and not telling her the whole truth. Being a woman is complicated sometimes.

The car stops, and I realize I don't know where we are. I look over at Arthur. "What are we doing?"

"I can't very well show up uninvited *and empty-handed* to a child's birthday party." I watch through the window as Ollie walks briskly into the store.

"I was just going to pop some cash in an envelope."

He looks down his nose at me. "Really? What kind of horrible auntie are you?"

"The kind that brings Jelly Babies every time I see them."

"Oh, so not so horrible, after all," he says. "Jelly Babies are the world's best candy."

"That they are." A slow smile stretches across my face. Maybe we have more in common than I think.

"You have excellent taste, Ms. Sharpe."

"I'm surprised you'd say that, since I don't really like you at all."

"Proves my point."

Ollie comes back out and nods. The driver opens the door for us.

Arthur gestures toward the shop. "Are you coming?"

We follow Ollie into the tiny, cramped toy shop. We're the only patrons, but if I had to guess, I'd say it'll fill up fast if we don't hurry. The limo with the royal flags parked out front is a dead giveaway.

An older man stands behind the till, his eyes wide. "You're... you're...Your Highness." He bows deeply.

"Good afternoon," Arthur says, his voice easy. "We're in the market for some birthday gifts. Six-year-old, very wild twin boys."

"Yes, sir!" The man hurries over to us. "We've got just the thing.

Came in last week." He walks us over to a display of neon razor scooters and gives us a quick sales pitch.

Arthur looks at me. "What do you think? Will this do?"

"Only if you want to be their favourite person for the rest of their lives."

"Excellent. That will mean two down, five million to go." Arthur turns to the shopkeeper. "We'll take two. One Gooey Green and one Blaster Blue."

The man takes two boxes and starts for the till.

"What should we get for the rest of the kids?" he asks.

"Why would we get them anything?"

"So they won't be jealous."

In the next twenty minutes, we choose gifts for all my nieces and nephews (including the one who hasn't arrived yet), Arthur poses for several pictures with the man who owns the shop, as well as his wife and mother-in-law, who happened to be in the back room having tea. We also stop at the wine store next door and pick up four bottles of very nice wine, as well as a case of beer for my dad.

When we're settled back in to the limo, we sit quietly for a moment, our hands nearly touching. I look down at my fingers next to his against the leather seat. He has big, manly hands that dwarf mine and make me feel like a child. When I look up at him, he's also staring at our hands. He slowly slides his toward mine and links his pinky finger around mine. It's the slightest of gestures, but it sets off an explosion of happiness inside my body.

"So, give me the rundown on who I'm about to meet."

"Sure. My parents are Ruben and Evi. My father is a mechanic, my mother is a stay-at-home…wife. I was going to say mum, but then I realized we've all grown up and moved out. She babysits the grand-kids a lot, though——"

"So, she's a stay-at-home grandmum."

"Exactly." I nod. "I have four brothers. I'm the only girl. The eldest is Noah. He's a structural engineer and is married to Isa, and they have three kids, Tabitha, Poppy, and little Clarkie. Watch out for Clarkie. He's going through a bit of a head-butting phase, so keep your…umm…sceptre protected at all times."

He nods. "Got it. Ruben, Evi, Noah, Isa, Tabitha, Poppy, and Clarkie, the ball-buster."

I laugh, impressed with his ability to recall everyone's names. "Okay, next in line is Lars, who is a professor of astrophysics at Valcourt Tech—"

"A total dullard, then."

"Yes. Especially when it comes to choosing women and raising kids."

"Oh, dear."

"Wife is Nina, who is pregnant with what she hopes is a girl. They already have four boys, including our birthday twins, Geoffrey and Josh, as well as Knox and Stephen, named for my brother's biggest hero, Stephen Hawking. Then there's Bram, the dentist who has never hired a hygienist he hasn't slept with."

"Ah. I see."

"Finally, there is Finn, who is finishing architecture school this spring."

"Huh. So, all rather impressive career-wise." He gives me a thoughtful look for a second, then nods once. "Now I understand."

"What?"

"You grew up with four boys, all very smart, all probably loving to torture the only girl in the house. Underachieving mother. They likely thought you were also going to be a nice little housewife, and you've spent your entire life proving them wrong."

I glare at him and slide my hand away, feeling irritation rise from my toes to my arched eyebrow. "Wow. That was offensive on so many levels."

Arthur looks taken aback. "How so?"

"First of all, calling my mother an underachiever for dedicating her life to her family. You've just insulted, like, half of the women on the planet." He opens his mouth, but I cut him off. "Second, I don't appreciate the little pop-psychology assessment."

"I'm sorry. I didn't mean to offend. I'm just trying to figure you out."

The way he says it douses almost all of the flames of anger in me, but I keep my chin out, all the same. "Well, you *did* offend."

"I wish I hadn't because you were smiling before, and now... you're not." He lifts his hand and touches my bottom lip with his thumb. "It's quite a loss for me, because I've become rather attached to your smile in a very short period of time."

Well, when he puts it that way... "I suppose your heart was in the right place."

"Forgiven?"

"Forgiven." I give him a little grin. "Plus, this gives me the upper hand again, in a very big way."

He narrows his eyes playfully. "Because I've admitted to being a Tessa's-smile-addict?"

"Because if I tweet your comment about stay-at-home mums being underachievers, you'll be totally fucked."

"Oh, bollocks. You're right."

I narrow my eyes and try for my most ominous look. "You're mine now, Your Highness."

He licks his lips. "What are you going to do with me, Ms. Sharpe?"

The car stops. I look out the window to see my parents' house to my right. "For now, force you to spend time with my family."

"I'm more interested in what you'll do to me *after* the party."

This time as I get ready to go inside, it's with a nervous excitement that I haven't felt since...well, maybe ever.

20

Cheap Cake & Royal
Commemorative Knick-knacks

Arthur

"Your Highness, please wait here so I can run a quick security assessment of the premises." Ollie stands next to the door as Tessa gets out. Why is he talking? I'm trying to enjoy her very fine arse from this vantage point.

"No need, Ollie. I'm sure it's safe," I say, following that fine arse out of the limo.

"I'm afraid I cannot allow you to go in until we know for certain."

"Oh, but it's my parents' house," Tessa says. "Who would be waiting to assassinate the Prince? No one even knows we're coming."

Tough girl. Have I mentioned that I'm really starting to like her?

Ollie ignores her. "With all due respect, Your Highness, Ms. Sharpe here isn't exactly a friendly. There's a good chance there's more like her inside."

I grit my teeth and talk through them. "Really not necessary, Ollie."

Tessa touches my arm. "It's all right. I understand. I'll go in with him."

"Sorry, Tessa," I say, searching her eyes to see if she's offended.

She smiles. "It's fine. Really. The kids'll think this is a hoot."

I wait beside the car, feeling like a complete idiot as I watch her jog up the front steps. She opens the door, then she and Ollie disappear inside. I stand and take in the sight of a perfectly normal street lined with normal houses that are filled with normal families who have normal struggles. How magnificent it must be to be unknown.

I see curious onlookers hold back front room curtains across the street. I give them a small smile and a wave. Stunned smiles and waves are my reward before the front door to the Sharpe home opens and a stream of children come pouring out like milk from a spilled jug. They scream as they head straight for the limo. Grownups follow them, barreling down the steps in my direction. Fuck me. This is a little much.

"It's a real limo!"

"I told you it was, you idiot!"

"There he is! It's Arthur!"

"Prince Arthur, hello!"

"Can we get a ride?"

"No, you can't ask for a ride, you dough head. He's a prince. He's not going to let your grubby bum in his limo."

"Tabitha! That's not nice."

"He smells like farts! We can't have him smelling up the Prince's car like farts."

I burst out laughing as mayhem ensues right out on the sidewalk. I search the crowd for Tessa, only to spot her on the top step, wincing. I wave and mouth, "It's all right."

She smiles as the children introduce themselves to me, and I shake their sticky little hands, one at time, memorizing their names as I go.

Josh, who has especially hot, gooey fingers, pipes up so he can be heard over the other children. "Can we go for a ride in your car, Your Majesty?"

"Oh, you mustn't call me Your Majesty. That title is reserved for the reigning monarch."

Josh tilts his head, looking very confused.

"Only my dad is called Your Majesty. Call me Arthur, okay?"

"Okay," he says impatiently. "Can we go for a ride, Arthur?"

"If it's okay with your par—" Before I can get the words out, the back door of the limo is swung open and all the kids pile in, followed by three men whom I assume are Tessa's brothers.

One of them calls out, "That's it. No one else can fit back here."

As the door closes, I hear one of the kids shout, "Once around the park, Jeeves."

A burst of laughter comes from inside.

Tessa is standing next to me now, her hand on her forehead. "I'm so sorry about that. Poor Ben."

"Quite all right. The privacy glass is sound-proof."

"Still." She shakes her head. "You'd think they'd never met a prince before."

"Oh, I'm nothing. It's the limo that's the real star of the show."

We are approached by the leftover adults. I smile at the older couple before me. "You must be Tessa's parents. Evi and Ruben, right?"

I give them a small bow and shake Ruben's hand. "Wonderful to meet you both."

Kissing Evi on her cheeks, I continue, "You must be very proud of Tessa. Few people manage to keep me on my toes the way she has done."

Evi blushes deeply and they both beam at me. "Yes, she's a real pistol, this one."

I move along to a younger, rather round-looking woman whom I'm afraid might pee her pants, she's so excited. "Ahh, Nina, right? There's nothing as lovely as woman with child. The perfect symbol of hope." I put both hands on her belly and lower my head a little. "Hello, in there! Come out soon so we can meet you."

Ladies love that. Except, when I look up at her face, the happy mummy is not happy at all. She looks rather pissed off. Now that I think about it, her belly doesn't have that hard quality that most pregnant bellies do. It's…squishy.

Oh, shit.

Wrong sister-in-law.

If looks could kill, she'd be tried for treason. "I'm not pregnant. And I'm not Nina. I'm Isa."

Well, fuck me. There's no coming back from that, is there? "Isa." I stifle an uncomfortable laugh and pull my hands away. "I'm not wearing my contacts today so my depth perception is very much off." That didn't even make sense, did it? Fuckity-fuck.

She glares at me and points to the woman standing behind her, who is trying very hard not to laugh. "*She's* Nina."

"Right. Sorry." Fuck. "Hello, Nina."

"Let's go inside, shall we?" Tessa says.

Oh, yes. Dear God, let's go inside where I pray they will serve a lot of booze.

———

The next hour of the party hums along without a hitch. I stand around in the kitchen with Tessa's brothers and father while we drink beer and try to stay out of the way of sugared-up children. The ladies of the family, other than Isa—who can hold a grudge with the best of them— giggle and grin at me, offering me mini sausage rolls and asking me question after question about life in the palace (it's busy, but at times it can be very quiet), who does my sister's hair (a hairdresser), do I really have my own crown (yes, but I take it off when I shower or go to bed).

Tessa smiles at me from across the room, and every once in a while, mouths an apology to me. God, she's pretty.

When we sit down to dinner, her brother Bram pipes up. "So, Tess, are you and His Highness an item now or what?"

"Not at all. He was just kind enough to join us for the party."

"Really? Because it wouldn't be the first time Tessa's overshot the mark with who she thinks will fancy her."

"Shut up, Bram," she says quietly, her eyes firing daggers at him.

He has a sip of beer. "Yeah, she once fell for her—"

"Bram! That's enough!" Evi's voice puts the sharp in Sharpe. I sit up straight in my chair in response.

"Arthur, I have to say I'm shocked that you're here." This comes from the tall, skinny one called Lars. "After everything Tessa's written about you, I'd think you would hate her."

"Far from it. If a man can't handle a little criticism, he's not much of a man, is he?" I say, slicing into the turkey with my knife and popping a forkful in my mouth.

"I wouldn't expect you'd pay much attention to anything she'd have to say, anyway. Am I right?" Bram asks.

What a little prick. "Why not?"

"She's not exactly the sharpest tool in the Sharpe family." They all start snickering.

My head snaps back, and I set my fork and knife down. "On the contrary, Tessa's one of the most brilliant people I've met. And I've met most of the top engineers at NASA."

"You must be talking about some other Tessa." Finn laughs. "This one's a disgraced journalist who got fired and ended up reviewing camera equipment and taking the piss out of the King for a living. Doesn't take a Lars over here to do that."

I stare him down for a moment, trying to regain my composure before I jump across the table and punch him in his smug face. "If you really don't know how intelligent and insightful she is, it would seem to me that you've never bothered to listen to a word she's said, or read a sentence of her writing. Quite frankly, that says a lot more about your own intellect than hers. Tessa's brilliant. And she's self-made, unlike me. I have nothing but the highest regard for her."

I glance over at her and see that Tessa is blinking back tears. She gets up and excuses herself quietly. I'm just about to get up and go after her when her mother stands.

Evi shakes her head at her sons. "Can't we just have one bloody nice family dinner with the Prince without you boys acting like donkeys?"

She gets up and follows Tessa out of the room.

"Grandmum just swore!"

"Why did she say we're acting like donkeys?"

"She didn't. She was talking about our dads."

"Can we open our presents now?"

21

Speaking of Arses...

Tessa

"WELL, THAT WAS...SOMETHING," Arthur says as soon as the limo pulls away.

"In hindsight, it was probably not such a good idea to bring you." I cringe, thinking of the many lowlights of the party.

"I disagree. That's the best time I've had in years."

The look of pure amusement on his face is contagious, and I find myself grinning back at him. "My favourite part was when you were talking to Isa's stomach."

He bursts out laughing and covers his face with one hand. "Why did I do that? I mean, seriously? With my hands on her belly and everything."

We laugh until tears are streaming down our faces.

When I recover a little, I say, "Hello in there! Come out soon so we can see you!"

He shakes his head. "That was bloody awful, wasn't it?"

"Isa will *never* forgive you."

"Are you quite sure? I thought the whole thing seemed to roll right off her back," he says, tongue in cheek.

"You may have lost one vote there. Too bad, because it was a guarantee."

"Shit. If only the kids could vote. They'd save my sorry arse." He grins. "I really did enjoy the part when they were opening our presents. That was genuinely fun."

Our presents? That has a nice, yet terrifying ring. "Your presents, you mean. And it was fun. It's my favourite part of being an aunt," I say.

"I can see why. It was much better than the bit when Lars connected his phone to the telly so he could show everyone the Shock Jogger video."

I slap my hand to my face. "Ugh. That is never going away, is it?"

Arthur tries not to laugh. "I'd say it's unlikely since the *Auto-tune The News* guys came out of retirement in your honour. I can't believe that you've already got more hits than the double rainbow guy. Rather impressive, if you think about it."

I purse my lips together and stare up at him from under my eyebrows.

"Oh, it's not so bad. You look quite fetching in just your sports bra and those tight running pants. Bouncy, yet firm."

Mental note. Make sure to jog around the palace grounds every morning. I smile up at him and glide my index finger down the center of his face. "I'm...drunk."

"Me, too." He grins. "Isn't it wonderful?"

"Yes. And quite necessary when attending a birthday party for six-year-olds."

"Agreed."

I lean my head on his shoulder again, feeling warm and safe and just the right amount of tipsy. "The kids adored you. And my parents did, too."

"I really like them. The kids, especially. They're hilarious. Your parents were very welcoming, but they really don't give you enough credit, so they lose points for that." He lazily runs his fingers down my arm, and I feel the most delicious chills.

"Your brothers are arses, though. The lot of them. Even the rocket scientist."

"Right?" I sit up and look at him. "Finally, somebody sees it."

"I could tell immediately." His face grows serious. "Speaking of arses, my father will be home when we get there."

My eyes grow wide at his statement.

"I shouldn't have said that. Too much beer. Can you please forget the last three seconds?"

"Yes, of course."

"Thank you. You're very kind for a cruel wench of a blogger."

"Aww. You're so sweet."

Arthur laughs, and I totally love that he gets me. Then his eyebrows knit together and he stares at me for a long moment. Just when I start thinking he might kiss me, he clears his throat. "About my father, things don't exactly have the same feel around the house when he's home. You'll find it considerably more formal. Some have described it as tense, even."

Uh-oh. Even my tipsy brain is picking up on the fact that we're heading into troubled waters. I suddenly feel a little more sober. "Don't worry about me. I can handle it."

"You're not as tough as you pretend to be. I saw you tear up when your brothers were embarrassing you at dinner."

I glance out the window for a second, watching the blur of lights pass by. "I didn't tear up because they were being nasty. I teared up because you were being so nice."

"Oh. I see."

I'm scared to look at him, but I do it anyway. "I'm used to them being awful to me, but having someone stand up for me was…unexpected. So, I'll be fine as long as your father isn't overly kind."

"He won't be, which is what worries me."

"Don't worry. It's not like I expected a warm reception from any of you."

"You should have a warm reception everywhere you go. When I am king, I'll make it a law. Tessa Sharpe is to be received warmly wherever she goes."

"Good God, you're horribly perfect, which is something I never thought I'd say in a million years. Not to you."

"Well, these past two weeks have been full of surprises for both of us, then."

We find ourselves staring into each other's eyes again, and again, I am mesmerized by him. I want to be looked at like this every night for the rest of my life, and if I hadn't had so much wine, I would know enough to be terrified right now. But I'm drunk on wine, and drunk on Arthur and drunk on every swirling feeling he stirs in my body, heart and soul. It's only been a few days, and I know better than to let myself feel any of these feelings, I promise I do. But have you ever been swept off your feet? Like, in such a way that you can't even feel your legs because they're weak with longing when you're around that one guy? Because that's how I feel right now. And I don't ever want this feeling to disappear.

"I need your opinion on something," Arthur says, his voice thick with lust. "I have what could quite possibly be a very bad idea, and I need to know what you think.

I swallow hard. "You've probably figured out by now that I don't mind sharing my opinion."

"I may have noticed." He glances at my lips. "What if we made the limo a 'just two people' zone?"

"That would definitely be a very bad idea."

His eyes lock on mine and heat up my entire body in an entirely magnificent way. "Agreed. We'll be in the limo a lot over the coming weeks. It would be careless."

"Completely careless." My voice has that breathy quality that only he can draw out.

He lowers his mouth over mine. "So, then we shouldn't."

"No, we definitely shouldn't." I tilt back my head and close my eyes.

Just as his lips brush against mine, Ollie's voice intrudes over the speaker. "We've arrived at the palace, Your Highness. And I believe your father's waiting for you."

22

Cockblockers & Rat Poison

Arthur

OLLIE CAN BE such a cockblocker sometimes. Like now. I know my father has likely given strict orders that he wants to see me immediately, but seriously? Couldn't he have told Ben to maybe take the long way home? Say, via France? Does no one realize how long it's been since I've had my sceptre polished?

We step out of the limo and into the dark night air. It's an unusually warm spring evening, and Tessa clearly knows not to get too close now that we're here. She's put on her broadcaster voice and is thanking Ben and Ollie for accompanying us to her parents' house. She's a real peach, by the way. She even went outside with plates of food and a beer for each of them during the party. Later, she took out a couple slabs of that sickeningly sweet birthday cake, as well. It was the simplest of gestures, but I could see the impact it had on them both. And I have to say, I'm more than a little ashamed that I've never even considered doing that myself.

"Thanks, fellows. Goodnight."

I walk up the steps with Tessa, as slowly as possible, both of us knowing that once we reach the other side of those doors, everything will change. Already, there's a space between us that wasn't there before, and it is physically painful for me not to touch her. As ridiculous as that sounds, it's true.

When we reach the top step, I turn to her. "I'm very sorry our night has come to such an abrupt end." And I am. I really and truly am.

"Me, too. It's been a wonderful day. So much more than I ever expected." Her smile doesn't reach her mossy green eyes, but I love her for trying to pretend.

"Thank you again for coming with me. Just having you there was…a once-in-a-lifetime thrill. For my mum, I mean. She's such a fan. And for me, it was lovely to have someone there to do my fighting for me for once."

"The honour was mine." There is so much I want to say at this moment, it would take me all night. But in a few seconds this door will swing open and our perfect day will come to an end.

"Can I ask you something? Why did you stick up for me, back at the house?"

"Because it was the truth. You *are* brilliant. Even though some of your arguments are misinformed, your reasoning is sound given the information on which you have based them. You've managed to articulate your beliefs with a clarity few people possess." I smile down at her. "Besides, you're rather easy on the eyes and an absolutely amazing kisser."

She grins up at me, and this time I know she's not just pretending to be happy. And for one perfect moment, things are just as I want them to be.

Then the door opens and Damien is standing on the other side with an insolent look on his face. "There you are, Your Highness. His Serene Majesty has been expecting you for some time."

We follow him inside and toward my father's office. When we reach the doors, Damien stops. "I think it's best if Prince Arthur goes in alone, Miss. His Majesty has pressing business for the Prince."

"Certainly." She nods. "Goodnight, Your Highness."

"Goodnight." I watch as she turns the wrong way and starts walking. "Tessa."

"Yes?" She looks back.

"Your room is that way." I point in the general direction of the private residence wing.

"Got it."

She spins, and I can't help but watch as she hurries down the hall. "So, the old man is pissed at me?"

"I did try to warn you. I'll be in my office if I'm needed." Damien bows, then leaves me alone to face my father.

I take a deep breath, hoping to sober up in the next ten seconds. I close my eyes and silently tell myself: *get the upper hand, set the boundaries early, don't fuck up.*

Then I open the door to my doom.

———

People will tell you my father looks like a teddy bear but has both the voice and demeanour of that bad uncle in the cartoon about the lions. You know the one, Jeremy Irons played him. I think he had a scar on his face or something. Anyway, anyone who says that about my father is not wrong. He can lure you in with his friendly smile and his thick light brown hair that never wants to lay quite flat on his head. But you'd do well to remember that if you're not careful, you could find yourself tossed off a cliff into a stampede of wildebeests. Well, not literally. But he will certainly fuck you over if the opportunity presents itself. I really should have said no to that last beer.

So far, tonight's reception is pretty much par for the course for as long as I can remember. I stand behind the chairs opposite his enormous, shiny walnut desk while my father sits in his high back leather office chair doing paperwork, a glass of whiskey in his right hand. He doesn't look up at me but continues writing. The only thing that has changed is that when this first started, I could barely see over his desk.

I stare at all of the animal heads on the wall to the left of me. All things he has shot himself, or so he claims. I find myself staring at the buck in the dead center of the wall. His black, glassy eyes reflect back my own hollow heart when I am around my father.

Finally, he speaks. "My son returns. I understand you were on urgent business on behalf of your cock."

Here we go. "Nice to see you, too, Father. Glad you had a safe journey."

He waves a hand at me but keeps working.

"I am told that you and this blogger critic person have been inseparable. Really living up to your potential as far as your intelligence goes, aren't you?"

"I know it seems unconventional, but acting according to regular protocol hasn't been serving us all that well in recent years. And I must say, things are going very much according to plan."

"Really?" He puts down the pen and has a sip of his drink. "This ought to be good."

"It *is* good. At the pace I'm going, I'll have her convinced long before the two months are up."

"And then what?"

"Then, she will do the heavy lifting on our behalf." I walk over to his drink cart and pour myself a bourbon. Fuck it. Might as well have a little nightcap at this point. "In fact, I'm certain if we were to poll the people again right now, we'd find that our approval rating has gone up just by having her here."

"And yet, I still want her out of my home immediately."

"We can't get rid of her now. It would be a PR nightmare. Besides, things really are going rather well." I can't hide my stupid grin when I think of her, which is not at all helpful right now.

"*Rather well?* You've got an idiot living here who can't manage to go more than two minutes without making a total fool of herself."

"I wouldn't say that. She's actually quite smart. Prone to embarrassing little mishaps, yes, but the people find it rather endearing." And by people, I mean me. "Plus, she does hold a lot of sway, and if you've bothered to read her blog lately, she is coming around to our side already."

"Endearing, really? Sniffing her armpits on camera?" He wrinkles up his nose. "She's making a mockery of us all. And don't think I don't know what's been going on. Arthur, Crown Prince of Avonia, Duke of Wellingbourne, idiot who's about to allow a mangy little twat to bring down the monarchy."

"Do NOT call her that."

"Oh, Christ, you are predictable." He shakes his head in disgust. "Why shouldn't I call her that? She is of no more consequence to me than a fruit fly landing on my plate."

"It's unfortunate that you see her that way, because she may be the one person in this entire kingdom who can save our sorry arses. Besides, I have a plan B tucked away, should it become necessary." I hate myself immediately when the words leave my mouth.

"Which is?"

I can tell that he already knows. This is a test of my loyalty, and there's really no point in failing. Keep your enemies closer…

"Damien's managed to dig up some dirt on her past we can use against her. But like I said, we won't need it."

My father scoffs. He's very big on scoffing, which is why I never do it. "You're going to fail, you know. Even if your plan had a hint of merit to begin with, there isn't even any time to execute it. But no matter." He swats the air with one hand. "Now that I'm here, I'll take care of things myself."

"For once, can you just allow for the possibility that someone other than you might be able to——"

"You have no idea, do you?"

"About what?" Bollocks. I probably should know what he's about to say.

"Tomorrow, the PM's office will announce the referendum. They want to dissolve our powers once and for all. The vote is to take place in ten weeks."

"Oh. I see." I drop down into a chair and glance up at the crest behind his head. It's the royal seal, carved out of wood, then dipped in gold back in the days when Robin Hood and his merry men were running around the forest in tights. The shine has dulled, and the wolves protecting the crown seem almost sinister to me at this moment ——like they're going to jump off the wall and attack me. I really shouldn't finish this bourbon.

"Yes, *now* you see. Let me make something clear to you. We will retain power by any means necessary. Do you understand that? Any means. I don't give a good Goddamn who gets hurt in the process. Not you, not your little blogger bitch. The only thing that matters is retaining our rule over this nation."He pounds his fist on his desk, causing his pen to hop then roll onto the floor. It's his signature move. Has secretaries jumping out of their skirts, and the old bastard loves it.

"So nice to know how much you care, Father. As always."

"Stop being a child. Our family has held this nation for the better part of a millennium. We will not lose it under my reign."

———

Things pretty much went downhill from there. He sniped at me for not knowing about the PM's announcement that hasn't happened yet. I sniped at him for backing the wrong horse.

He told me that should this moronic plan of mine fail, I will be single-handedly responsible for bringing down this monarchy and shall go down in history as the first heir never to take the throne.

To which I responded, "I'd say you'll go down as the king who lit the match that burned down the whole house."

"If it does all go up in flames, it might be a blessing. You would make a terrible leader. You're weak like your mother."

This is where things got really ugly, because I said something I've never said, and never thought I would say in my entire life. Certainly not to him. I said, "Perhaps you'd like it if I took the same way out that she did."

He stopped and just stared at me with his cold, dead eyes. Up until that moment, he had no idea I know she took her own life. He may have suspected I knew, but I never once said it out loud.

"What did you just say?"

"You heard me, old man."

Then he threw his glass of whiskey at me. I ducked, and it hit the floor behind me.

. . .

So, now I'm lying in bed, listening to the seconds tick by on my wall clock and waiting for morning to come. If I'm really honest, I'd tell you I hate the man. Always have. Well, not always. There was a time when I was very small that I sought his approval above and beyond anything else. But when I turned ten, I realized it would never come. And it never did. Then when I found out how my mother really died, that was it for me and him. I was fucking done.

I should have just poisoned him myself a long time ago. I could have found some untraceable liquid on that black-market Internet site with all the weapons. I wouldn't be the first in our family to do it, either—poison a king, I mean, not shop online.

About two hundred years ago, the Duke of Elderbridge poisoned his brother, King Edwin, with rat poison. He was hoping to get the entire family in one shot, but he forgot which goblet didn't have the poison and drank it himself, leaving his youngest sister alive and ready to rule. She did a bang-up job apparently. Managed to lower taxes by tossing almost all the prisoners out of the dungeons and putting them to work on the nationally-owned farms. So, at the same time she lowered taxes, she made healthy food available to everyone at a fair price. See? I told you women should run the world. Why does no one else see this?

Anyway, back to my father. The man's got another twenty years in him if he's got a day. And by the time he gets done with it, the throne won't be worth sitting on, if it's even here at all come summer.

I wish Tessa were lying next to me right now. Or under me. I should really get up and crush some water right now. I'm going to be horribly hungover again tomorrow morning.

Or on top of me. I would like her on top of me, just as well as under me.

23

No Taxes Were Used in the Making of This Dress

Tessa

TEXT FROM ME TO ARTHUR: *Any chance you're making eggs this morning?*

Arthur: *Not today. I'm afraid I'll be tied up in meetings all day. In one now, actually.*

Me: *Good. I didn't want to hang around with you anyway. I was just using you for your culinary skills.*

Arthur: *I've never been used for that before.*

Me: *Get used to it. They were damn good eggs.*

I sit at my desk and wait for an answer, but none comes. Mavis brings a tray of food. "I thought you'd want to take breakfast in your room again." She sets the tray down. "There's a note from Mr. Hendriks for you."

I pick it up, leaving the food untouched. "Thanks, Mavis."

I open the envelope and see a handwritten note.

· · ·

Ms. Sharpe,

The next days will be busy for Prince Arthur. He and his father will be in meetings that must remain private for the benefit and security of our nation. The Princess Dowager has requested that you attend her suite to choose a dress for the upcoming ball. She asks that you are there by ten o'clock sharp.

Please ring me at the number below should you need anything.

Kindest regards,

Vincent

I look at my phone again, but there's still no text from Arthur. A pang hits me. Loneliness, maybe? Longing for something I can't have and shouldn't want, is more like it. Bugger. I've really gone and messed things up.

I tear a piece off the warm blueberry scone and pop it in my mouth. Mmm. Fuck me, these really do melt in your mouth. Some secret royal recipe they hide from the public, who only get to eat very ordinary scones. Bastards.

Oh, dear, Tessa, is that all you can come up with? Delicious scones? That's not exactly going to bring down the monarchy, is it?

It's been over two weeks, and I haven't found anything to prove my point. I know what the problem is. It's that Arthur is far too good in his attempts to win me over. And my lady bits want me to let him convince me. Dear God, do they ever. I think about yesterday. The walk, the kiss, the luncheon flirty texts, toy shopping, the party…it was almost like fitting in a month's worth of dating into one day. But it wasn't, and we aren't. And I have to accept that. No matter how much I laughed or how weak my knees went when he kissed me, we are very much on opposite sides of a battle, and it's one I cannot afford to lose if I'm ever to get a second chance as a respected journalist.

I reach for my phone and dial Nikki's number.

"There you are. Finally," she says instead of 'hello.' "I saw you and Prince Charming on the news at the toy store yesterday."

"There were cameras?"

"Someone in a shop across the street with a cell phone. That looked rather cosy."

"It was fun, but don't read anything into it. He's desperate to do whatever it takes to please me, remember?"

"Well, going to your parents' for a family dinner is above and beyond. It almost makes me feel like he deserves to be king someday."

Me, too. "Ha! It'll take a lot more than a family dinner and some flirty texts to convince me."

"Flirty texts?" she asks. "Spill it, lady."

Shit. "Oh, it was nothing. He's just...exactly as charming as you thought he'd be."

Nikki laughs. "So, I was right, then. Your biggest problem is going to be not sleeping with him. Wait. You haven't slept with him, have you?"

"No, I have not slept with him. God. I'm not a complete idiot," I huff.

"But...you want to."

"Maybe a little."

I hear the water slosh, and then Nikki's muffled voice screaming. The water sloshes again and she's back. "Sorry, about that."

"Underwater scream?"

"Yes. You *totally* have to sleep with him! I mean, when in your life will you ever have the chance to shag a real prince? Think of the stories you'll have for your grandkids one day."

"I don't think those are the kind of stories you tell your grand-children."

"Maybe not, but think of the stories you'll have for all the other ladies at the nursing home someday?"

"They'd never believe me. They'll just think I've got dementia. But anyway, I called you to talk me down off the ledge, not encourage me to jump."

"Okay, you're right. You cannot sleep with him," she says firmly. "It would be a huge mistake, it could ruin your career, not to mention cause you to lose what little morsel of respect your family has for you, should they find out."

"That's better. Keep going because I'm still getting the vision of him without his shirt on flashing in my brain every time I close my eyes."

"Well, in that case, you should forget everything I just said and sleep with him."

"Nikki! Seriously. I'm having a crisis here," I say. "As my best friend, I need you to help me out here."

"Why? Would he be up for a threesome? Because I've never thought of you that way, but if Prince Charming was down for it, I'd have to consider it."

"Okay, number one, *no*! Number two, *not helping!*"

"Sorry. It's just too much. My brain is short-circuiting with every word you say right now."

"Maybe your brain has turned to liquid from living in the bath."

"Possibly."

I glance at the clock. It's already nine-forty, which means I only have twenty minutes to shower, change, dress, and find my way to the Princess Dowager's. "I have to go. I have an appointment to pick out a ball gown in a few minutes."

"A ball gown? Oh, my God! I'm so jealous, my pruned-up skin is actually turning green."

"If it's any consolation, I wish you were here with me for all of this."

"Thanks. Me, too. But if it can't be me there trying on ball gowns and ogling the Prince, I'm glad it's you and not some other bitch."

"Aww. Thanks."

———

Blog Post – March 25th

Today I did something I never in a million years thought I would do (although that seems to be my catch phrase over the last two weeks). I was fitted for a ball gown in the Princess Dowager's suite, no less.

I have been asked to attend the upcoming anniversary ball that is to be held on Saturday, May 6th. As your eyes and ears on the Royal Family, I have agreed. Naturally, I require something to wear, but had assumed I would head over to the mall like I usually do when I go to a ball (just kidding, I've never been to a ball before). Anyway, the Princess Dowager had other ideas.

To be honest, going into this, I was certain that this would provide another perfect example of the lavish, over-priced, unnecessary lifestyle of the Royals, but I came away to discover that couldn't have been further from the truth. The Princess Dowager explained to me that as a patron of the arts, and a supporter of female entrepreneurs in particular, she takes every opportunity she can find to provide opportunities for up-and-coming designers to showcase their work.

Now, before you start to think that I have been bought by a shiny dress (it's divinely sparkly, by the way), I want to make it clear that I'm paying for the dress myself. I worked out a deal with the lovely and talented designer, Olivia Paul, whereby, in addition to paying for the cost of the dress and for her time, I will help get her name out there. Therefore, no tax dollars were used for the making of this dress.

This is what Ms. Paul, who uses only cruelty-free, sustainably-sourced fabrics, had to say about the matter. "For years, I have been waiting for my big break. That's how it is in this business. It's years of hard work, toil, sewing until your fingers bleed, and praying that someday you'll have your chance to get your name out there. The Princess Dowager has given me that chance. My time has come to shine, and now it is up to me to succeed or fail."

I, for one, hope she succeeds. If she doesn't, I'm going to look horrible on May 6th (wink – just kidding, I wrote that because I'm rooting for her). She's a very hard working, talented, kind person who deserves every success.

Ms. Paul went on to tell me that she lives in the industrial loft where she works. She barely makes rent each month, but she's still living her dream. Her gratitude for this opportunity was so magnanimous that it was difficult to remain unmoved. The Princess Dowager was absolutely aglow with pride during the fitting. Their connection was something quite lovely to see, even for a hardened old soul such as myself.

For those of you who are interested in seeing the dress, the big reveal will happen on the night of the ball. And no, I won't be Prince Arthur's date, in case you were about to write in and ask.

Please visit Olivia Paul's website for more information on her work (listed below).

Stay tuned for more on Life at the Palace!
Tessa

KingSlayer99: *Tessa, what is happening between you and the Prince of Lies? I didn't like the looks of that footage at the toy shop yesterday. Has he found a way to blackmail you into making him look good? If so, tell me so I can help. I have connections.*

Me: *No need to panic. No blackmail.*

KingSlayer99: *Too bad. If you could catch him trying to blackmail or bribe you, you'd have what we need.*

Me: *I don't think he'd ever do that. He's actually not as awful as I thought he'd be. He can be surprisingly thoughtful.*

KingSlayer99: *It's all an act. He's just using you to get you to back down.*

Me: *And I'm letting him think it's working, but don't worry. I'm keeping my wits about me.*

KingSlayer99: *Good, because you're our best shot at taking them down.*

———

Voicemail from Mum: *Tessa, It's Mum. I'm still waiting to hear back from you about whether Prince Arthur would like that plate commemorating his parents' wedding. He said he'd never seen it before, and I'm sure he would want it as a keepsake. Call me back and let me know.*

Text from Nikki: *I've just solved your sex problem. Two words. Chastity belt. I'm sure they've got one laying around somewhere. Just ask his gran if you can borrow one until you leave.*

Voicemail from Dad: *Tessa, still wondering about the lawn tractor situation at the palace. Pub night's coming, and Artie didn't seem to know what kind of tractors they use either. You've sure got him fooled. The way he went on about how smart you are. Oh, and your mum wants to know about that plate. She said she can bring it by the palace on Friday on her way to that Caring for Your Bonsai seminar she's going to.*

Voicemail from Daniel Fitzwilliam, owner of Wellbits: *This is your last warning, Ms. Sharpe. Call me by end of business today or the next person you hear from will be my lawyer.*

———

"This is Giles Bigly for ABNC. I'm standing outside the steps of the parliament building among hundreds of members of the press. In just a few moments, Prime Minister Janssen will be making what we expect to be a monumental announcement. Insiders say that he's going to announce a referendum to remove the executive power function of Avonia's monarchy and place the Royal Family in a ceremonial role once and for all."

"Giles, do we know for certain that this is what the Prime Minister is going to announce?"

"It seems as though it's highly likely, Veronica."

"This will come as quite a shock to all royal fans, as well as the Royal Family themselves."

"It certainly will, although it is my understanding that they may have been given some forewarning."

"Could that possibly be the basis of the Prince's recent invitation to Tessa Sharpe to live at the palace?"

"The timing would suggest as much. It could be a last desperate attempt at turning things around for—oh, Veronica, here comes the PM now."

———

"Are you watching this?"

"I am." Nikki's voice is quiet. She sounds as stunned as I feel.

"I can't believe he really did it." I've always hoped for this moment, but now that it's here, there's something not quite right about it.

"Have you talked to anyone in the family yet?"

"No. Not yet. They're all in meetings."

"So, are you happy? I mean, this is what you wanted, isn't it?"

I don't have a response right away, and even the fact that I'm not immediately sure tells me something has changed. "Of course. Why shouldn't I be?" My voice sounds hollow, even to my own ear.

"You sure?"

"Yes, definitely. I think so." I swallow, staring out at the tranquil meadow below. If I'm really honest, I feel sick inside, knowing what this moment must be like for Arthur and Princess Florence. Even

Arabella must be in shock somewhere inside these walls. Their entire way of life could be ripped from them in a few weeks' time.

"You'll have to post about it. You're probably getting hundreds of hits. People are waiting for your reaction."

Shit. "Right. I suppose I should."

I hang up and stare at my laptop screen for a long time. I know I need to make a statement, but in my heart, this announcement terrifies me rather than giving me reason to rejoice. I'm honestly so confused right now that I don't know what to think or how to respond. My feelings for Arthur have everything to do with it. Somehow, I've allowed my judgement to become clouded again by a handsome man. I should really stick to giving product reviews and taking photos, because if there's anything more at stake, I am guaranteed to completely fuck it all up. I really am a very dull Sharpe.

KingSlayer99: *It's finally happening! Are you as excited as I am? I can't stop smiling.*

Me: *Yes! It's amazing news. Couldn't be happier. Just working on my celebratory blog post now.*

KingSlayer99: *In only a few weeks we'll be celebrating the vote and our nation will finally be free!*

Me: *Absolutely. Can't wait!*

Blog Post – Hoorah! The Time for the People to Have a Say Is Upon Us

The nation watched in shock today as Prime Minister Jack Janssen announced plans for an upcoming referendum to determine whether or not we need a royal family in addition to an elected government.

The short answer, of course, is 'no,' and if there is any justice in the world the vote will come out that way. Although my days at the palace have shown me that I was wrong about several assumptions I held regarding members of Avonia's Royal Family, the institution itself still bears no more merit than it did two weeks ago.

We are living in the twenty-first century, a time of self-determination, civil rights and freedoms. Allowing non-elected leaders to rule is simply holding on to an antiquated system when a much better alternative can, and should, be chosen.

I have not spoken with any members of the family yet today, as they are all in meetings, but I can tell you that, on a personal note, I do feel for them. This is in many ways their darkest hour.

But change is never easy, even when necessary, and should they be removed from power, at least they can take their money with them.

24

Salty or Sweet

Arthur

It's after ten in the evening, and I am finally alone for the first time today. Well, Dex is here, of course. I inhale sharply, and the air feels like knives in my chest, as it has all day. Bugger. I really should have tried harder to be 'the people's prince' long before this month. It was all fine and dandy when the referendum was just an idea, but now that it's been announced, it's like finding out that the White Walkers have breached the wall and we don't have even one dragonglass dagger among us. We're well and truly fucked.

Now with the announcement, and my father here, my time with Tessa will be significantly reduced just as the necessity of getting her onside has increased a million-fold.

I grab a glass and pour myself a scotch, letting the amber liquid glug out until there's enough to numb this awful feeling.

"Dex, we're going to have to up our game." He opens one eye and glances at me before going back to sleep. Lazy pig.

I pick up my phone. Even though I'm as worn out as a seven-hundred-year-old tapestry, I get to work.

Text from Me to Tessa: *What are you up to?*

    Tessa: *Catching up on some emails. How are you?*

    Me: *Superb. Why do you ask?*

    Tessa: *No reason. Just that there was some type of announcement today that I thought may have impacted you.*

    Me: *Oh, yes, Coldplay is going on tour again. I'll probably get tickets. Not sure, really. Are you thinking of going?*

    Tessa: *The other announcement.*

    Me: *Right. That one. I don't want tickets to that event at all. Fancy something salty?*

    Tessa: *If you mean crisps, then yes.*

    Me: *I have some for you in my room. Oh, that sounds pervy, doesn't it?*

    Tessa: *Quite. But if there really are crisps, I'll risk it.*

    Me: *Excellent. Just follow the trail of them leading to the bed.*

I hurry over to the *en suite* to brush my teeth. Can't be smelling like scotch, now can I? Catching my reflection in the mirror, I see that I look like hell. Like I just went ten rounds with Floyd Mayweather, only he didn't leave any bruises.

I'm a total shit. I should just tell Tessa the truth and send her home already. I thought it would be so easy to use her and dump her, but now, somehow, I can see it will be harder than it seems. Ditching one's morals always is, isn't it? But it's not just that. As much as I can't admit it, I have very real feelings for her. Very strong, very real feelings.

I hear a light knock at the door and hurry over, my heart picking up its pace a little. If I were to be really honest with myself—which I won't—I would say that this is the best part of my day.

I tug open the door and there she is. Lovely. I give her my best come hither smile. "Ms. Sharpe."

But she doesn't smile back. Her eyes are filled with a concern I wasn't expecting.

"How are you?" she asks.

Fuck me. Now I want to crumble and spill my guts while I lay my head on her lap and she strokes my hair. "Fine. Barbeque or plain? I have both."

"Barbeque." She follows me into the room.

"So, she wants to heat things up?" I ask, grinning over my shoulder. I pluck the bag out of the sideboard and open it.

"Arthur, I know it's been a very hard day for you. You don't have to pretend."

When I turn around, she's standing right in front of me. She puts her hand on my chest, and if that isn't the most comforting thing ever, I don't know what is. "I'm here if you need to talk."

Reality slaps me in the face. "You're the last person I should be talking to about any of this."

"I know. But what if we say we're just two regular people when we're sharing a bag of crisps?" she asks with a sad smile.

"Can we?"

"Yes, Arthur. You can trust me. I have no need to play dirty."

"You're already winning, aren't you?" I try for a light tone, but it comes out all strange.

Her soft, green eyes stare up at me. "I'm not sure if I am."

"I do have one confession to make." I watch as her eyes grew wide. "I didn't really ask you here for crisps."

She smiles up at me, then reaches her face up to mine. "Good, because I didn't come here to eat."

And then she kisses me. It's a light, soft, gentle brush of her full lips against mine, and it's the most delicious taste I've known. I drop the bag and pull her to me with both hands around her waist. I was wrong before. Having her hand on my chest was not nearly as comforting as holding her in my arms. We stay like this, our mouths blending together, our bodies pressed up against each other, both of us exploring one another with our hands.

There's a thrill to this moment that exists in no other. The thrill of someone new. But this is different, and I don't know if it's because my entire world has just been rocked, or because I shouldn't want this woman, but I do know I have never felt an explosion of urgency like I do now. I am aching to be with her.

And apparently she feels the same way, because she just tugged my T-shirt over my head rather roughly, and now she's taken hers off as well. Oh, yes. "That is a very nice pink bra, Ms. Sharpe."

"You like it?"

"It makes me want to do very naughty things to you."

"That's why they make them like that."

"Geniuses, those bra designers." My hands are now cupping her breasts, and I run my thumbs over the centre, feeling her nipples peak underneath the lacy fabric. "I especially like the clasps."

I wrap my hands behind her back and undo her bra with a quick snap that says 'This is not my first boob unveiling.' But fuck me if it's not the best. Her tits are absolute perfection. Perky. Full. And delectable.

"Mmm. Very nice. A man could lose himself right here." I lower my mouth to her breasts and choose the right one to start on. "In fact, I think I will."

We end up naked on the couch because it's the nearest soft surface, and I'll be damned if I'm going to waste time going all the way to my bedroom. I need this woman right now. She's soft and warm and wet in all the right places.

Tessa is on my lap, and the way she's moving and rubbing herself against me is the best thing I've ever felt. Then it happens.

Snort.

Dexter has woken up and is standing with his chin on the couch cushion next to us, staring. We both burst out laughing, and Tessa tucks her head into my neck to hide.

Then she does something completely surprising. She lifts her head, looks at Dex and says, "Dexter, quit beaver damming me."

Oh, I think I love this girl. "Not to worry." I pick her up and carry her to the bedroom, then slam the door shut with my foot.

"Will he be sad, all alone?"

"He'll be happy as a pig in crisps." We kiss some more while I hold her in my arms. I do like the feeling of those strong runner's legs wrapped around my waist.

Just when things are about to pass the point of no return, she pulls back a little. "Condom."

Right. Very necessary. "Of course." I drop her onto the bed, which makes her laugh, then walk over to my nightstand to retrieve an heir stopper.

Once my battle gear is in place, I hover over her for a moment so I can just look at her. "Fuck, you're beautiful."

"You'll say anything to get me to like you." She gives me a saucy grin.

"True. But you are, you know." I kiss her mouth, and it's a long, full, deep one that makes her moan.

"Arthur, I think we need to agree that this isn't going to change anything, right? We're still going to be enemies in the morning."

I feel a pang at her words, but I spread a cocky grin on my face anyway. "Of course. That's what's going to make this so much fun."

And then, much to Excalibur's delight, I find my way inside her wet, tight warmth. That feels ssoooo good. It's enough to make me forget today's shitstorm. Hell, it's enough to make me forget my own name.

We move together like we're made for each other, doing things that are both intimate and somehow acrobatic at the same time. Things I do not ever want to forget, because I cannot remember ever feeling this happy. It's a most delightful mix of 'I hope this never ends' and 'I can't wait because I'm about to have an earth-shattering orgasm.' By the end, we're a tangled, sweaty, deeply satisfied heap of humans. She's on top of me, her body pressed against mine, and I can feel her heart pounding in her luscious chest.

She sighs. "Your grandmother was right about you."

What? "That did it. I was starting to get hard again, but that definitely put the brakes on my coming erection."

She laughs. "Sorry. I didn't mean to."

"No need to apologize to me. I was about to give you another award-winning orgasm, so it's really your loss."

"Another?" She lifts her head, wearing a huge grin.

"Oh, don't pretend that wasn't magnificent. You actually meowed at the end there."

She blushes and nods a little. "True. It was very nice indeed."

"*Nice?*" My eyes grow wide.

"*Very* nice." Tessa laughs. "Oh, no. Have I bruised your giant ego?"

I flip us both so I'm on top of her. "That's it. We're doing this again until you admit the truth."

"Good. That's what I was going for this whole time."

And I won't go into any more details because I'm sleepy, but suffice it to say that after round two she was quick to admit she'd most definitely had more than one award-winning orgasm this evening. And I have to say, she wasn't the only one. I actually thought I went blind for a brief moment.

25

Pity Sex & Worm Funerals

Tessa

OH, my God. I can't believe we just did that. Three times. And so very well. And I can't believe I am now lying next to him naked, with his arm slung over me like...like I belong here. But I don't, and we both know it.

Logic and common sense are both screaming at me to sneak out of his bed this instant, but hormones and ovaries are ordering me to stay put in case he wakes up ready for round four. I hate to tell you, ovaries, but we're using protection, so whatever egg is next in line doesn't have a chance.

I need to go. I am supposed to be trying to take down his family on behalf of all my followers. Oh, right...and because I've told millions of people it's the thing I want most in the world. Isn't it?

I'll go. It's the smart thing to do.

Oh, but look at his gorgeous face. Those are ridiculously long eyelashes for a man. I can reach out and touch them. And look at all those lovely rippling muscles on his arm that's pressed against me.

Oooh, those muscles are definitely making an argument for staying, and maybe doing the old, 'My body is wiggling into you of its own accord because I'm fast asleep' thing.

Get up. Go back to your room before anyone catches you.

Arthur's eyes open and he grins at me. "Well, hello."

A smile spreads across my face before I can stop it. "Hi."

"I thought I was dreaming, but all that really did happen, didn't it?"

"It did."

"Even the part where you were upside down?"

I find myself giggling into my pillow. "Even that."

"How the fuck did we manage that anyway?"

"I have no idea."

"We should do it again so we can document the steps." He gives me a light kiss on the lips. "Not now, though. You're not in the mood."

"What makes you think that?"

"When I woke, you had that little crinkle between your eyebrows you get when you're worried about something."

How does he know that? "I was just thinking I should go before I get caught." I run a finger down his cheek. "I was also questioning my sanity, because there's no way I should have let you lure me into your bedroom."

"Lure you? You're the one who came under false pretenses. I was only planning to feed your salt addiction."

"Good point."

"I can't blame you, though. I have it on good authority that I'm irresistible."

"Says who?"

"I'm not sure, but apparently they tell my grandmum everything." He traces my collarbone with his finger, sending tingles around my body.

"I don't find you attractive at all, really," I say.

He stops his hand and raises one eyebrow in response.

I hide my smile with everything in me. "I only slept with you because I felt sorry for you."

"Oh, so that was—"

"A pity fuck, I'm afraid." I try my best to look apologetic, but he's clearly not buying it.

"Three times?"

"I felt really, really, really sorry for you."

His eyes grow wide and laughter spills from him as he tosses the covers off both of us, and rolls on top of me. "For someone who claims to be so honest, you really are a bold-faced liar."

"Am not."

And now he's working his way down my body with his tongue, and I'm pretty sure that he's about to remove me of both a confession and my wit.

Dear Ms. Sharpe,

As per the King's orders, the 'Ask Me Anything' interviews have been suspended indefinitely. He trusts you will understand that given the current situation, the family must use the utmost caution in all media appearances, and will henceforth only allow taped interviews with trusted news sources that can assure an absence of technical issues. As a guest of the palace, he further trusts that you will handle the matter with delicacy as far as your readers are concerned. In addition, he extends his regrets in not having had time to receive you.

Regards,

Damien Peters

Chief Adviser to the King

Blog Post – Interviews Canceled

Tessa here. I regret to inform you that the "Ask Me Anything" interviews have been suspended whilst the Royal Family concentrates their efforts on the upcoming referendum. I'm sorry that I didn't have a chance to get all of your questions answered, and hope that one day in the future, the opportunity will present itself again.

I've taken down the forum until such time as the interviews will be given the green light.

———

My cell phone rings. It's Nikki. "You saw the post?"

"It was because you left the camera on, wasn't it?"

"That's what the note from the King's senior adviser implied, but I think it may be more about His Serene Majesty throwing his weight around now that he's home."

"Why didn't you go after him on the blog? You should take a picture of the letter and post it."

"I have a feeling that that little move might get me kicked out of the castle."

"So? You did what you set out to do. You've built your reader base, your advertising dollars are up, and now that the referendum's been called, you could come back and lead the charge from home base."

"I can't just leave. I made a commitment," I say, hoping she won't dig any deeper.

"If the King kicks you out, it'll be out of your hands."

Sound convincing, Tessa. She cannot know you don't want to leave because you got shagged last night. Four times. "I honestly think I can be of more use from the inside. For now, I'll cooperate. That'll allow me to gather more information. I haven't found anything I can really use. Oh, crap. I'm being called to a thing. I have to run. Call you later."

I hang up before she can say anything else. Guilt clouds over me. I just lied to my best friend. I am a shameless, unprincipled woman. God should smite me down. But if he could just wait until I've had a few more rounds in bed with Arthur, that would be lovely, because up to this point in my life I've been really very good. Except for lying to my parents on occasion, and now Nikki. And for betraying my principles and my readers by sleeping with the Prince. Oh, just smite me now.

———

"I need your advice, but first you have to promise you won't say anything to anyone about this conversation."

I'm in my room and am on the phone with Bram, who has called to ask for 'tickets' for the ball. Apparently, his new hygienist will 'definitely go down on him' if he can bring her.

"Get me the tickets and you've got a deal."

"They don't sell tickets. It's not a bloody Justin Bieber concert. It's a ball, which means they send out invitations."

"So, get me an invitation."

"I'm not exactly an honoured guest, you know." I sigh. "I'll see what I can do, but no promises."

"Then no promises not to tell."

Argh. Why did I start this conversation? Oh, right. Because I slept with the Prince like a total fucking idiot, and now I'm freaking out. "I'll tell Dad you were the one who filled his ship in a bottle with Coke."

"You wouldn't."

"I would and will."

"You told me you'd never rat on me about that."

"I lied. I've been saving it for something important." Ha! So, who's the smart one now, Bram?

"Fine. What?"

Yay! Score one for Tessa! "You know how you're a total slut?"

"Did no one teach you how to ask for a favour?"

"Are you going to deny it?" I ask.

"It's called stud because I'm a man."

"Whatever. How do you do that?"

"Do what?"

"Sleep with women and not develop feelings for them?"

"I just told you. I'm a man," he says. "Wait a minute. Are you shagging the Prince?"

"No! I'm just considering it. Not with the Prince, though! Definitely not with him…and I'm just *thinking* about it."

"Not that bald bodyguard dude?"

"Not him either. None of your business. All you need to know is that it's not Arthur."

"Oh, it's him, all right!" He bursts out laughing. "Good Christ, you really have a gift for completely screwing up your life, don't you?"

"For just once, can you try not to be an arsehole?"

"But it's so much fun." He takes a bite of something crunchy and chews into the phone.

"Back to the question at hand. How do you stop yourself from getting attached?"

He has another bite and chews for a long time before answering. I pretend I don't hear it because, not unlike a third-grader, he's doing it just to get a reaction.

"I just go into it knowing what it is, I guess."

Hmph. "But doesn't it ever get complicated?"

"No. I know exactly what I want, how to get it, and how to get out without things getting complicated."

Well, this is no help at all. I shouldn't have asked.

"You'll never be able to do it, though, so if you are thinking of sleeping with him, you probably shouldn't." Bite. Chew. It's definitely an apple. "You're not built like me, Tessa."

"How are you so sure?"

"I'm going to tell you something, and if you ever tell anyone, I'll find a way to make your life a living hell, got it?"

Typical big brother threat. "Got it."

"It's because you're a nice person. You pretend to be all tough and strong, but deep down you're just like Grandpa Seth. Way too fucking nice for your own good."

"That's not true. I'm very tough. I can be ruthless, even."

"Sure, you can write mean stuff when you're hiding behind your computer screen, but you could never say it to someone's face."

"I just called you a slut, didn't I?"

"Yeah, but we're on the phone. Also, I am one." Crunch. Chew. How big is that fucking apple? "Listen, remember that time when Finn and I were burning worms with a magnifying glass? You set up a hospital and tried to revive them. You spent hours out there, and by the time Mum made you come in for supper, you were bawling. Over some worms. Then you and Grandad had the worm funeral?

175

Remember that? With the bagpipe music and the little matchbox coffins? Face it. You're a nice person. You always have been."

"Fine, I'm nice. Now how do I sleep with someone without starting to imagine it's anything more than a shag?" Well, four mind-blowing, toe-curling, I've-died-and-gone-to-heaven shags.

"I already told you. *You* can't. So, unless you and Definitely Not The Prince are going to end up riding off into the sunset in a white carriage, you better stay the hell away from him. Because you're going to get hurt."

Crap. That's what I thought.

26

A Girl Can Change Her Mind...
Can't She?

Tessa

So, I have not exactly taken Bram's advice. Instead, I have slept with Arthur every night for the last four glorious weeks. We've shagged so much, I can't even think straight. I find myself both completely exhausted and deliriously happy, probably in much the same way as a new cult member during the indoctrination phase.

I honestly don't know how he has so much energy. I've had to replace my morning run with night sex, and occasional morning sex, oh, and yesterday we did it in the middle of the day in his office. Mmm. That added thrill of getting caught seems to do something unexpected for me. Anyway, Arthur still gets up for his morning workout with Ollie, manages all of his obligations throughout the day and evening, then comes knocking on my door all freshly showered and delicious for round after round of orgasmic fun.

Almost better than the sex are the little romantic moments we've shared. We've managed to sneak away to the rooftop terrace twice now, and both times, it was wildly romantic. Arthur brought up a bottle of wine and some cheese, crackers and grapes, and we had a little picnic while the sun went down. It's something I've always wanted to do with a man—the right man, that is—and it's as perfect as I imagined it would be. The rest of the world dissolves, and it's just the two of us alone. No phones, no laptops, no money problems, no referendums, just us.

This may all sound like a dream come true, but it's clearly very wrong. And it wouldn't take a Lars to figure out that this is going to end badly for me, both emotionally when my heart is smashed to smithereens, and career-wise if anyone finds out.

The one other negative, and it's a biggie, is that now the King is back, I haven't had access to any meetings. Everything is done behind closed doors, and I find myself wandering the palace grounds half the day taking photographs of flowers and interesting architectural elements of the buildings for my photography site. Even though my Royal Watchdog site is getting a decent number of hits every day, I'm spinning my wheels instead of moving forward.

I should just go home. That would be the smart thing to do. But I'd hate to kick Nikki out when she's expecting to have two full months to herself. Also, she hasn't fixed the wallpaper yet, and I really should give her a chance to do that. It has *nothing* to do with the fact that this entire fabulously exhilarating secret affair will end the moment I walk out the door. Nothing at all.

I've been sitting at my desk all morning, making lists of the pros and cons of the monarchy. But what it really reads like is a list of all the things I was wrong about over the past two years since I started the Royal Watchdog, because most of what I thought I knew was actually a result of misinformation and assumptions made by other royal-haters like me. Turns out, I don't hate them. They neither loaf around during the day, nor drink and party all night. They're a hard-working bunch, seven days per week.

Who knew?

Their real fault is in neglecting to communicate this with the public, but they are attempting to fix this, and even if it is the eleventh hour, at least they're trying. Now that I've gotten to know them (especially Arthur, obviously), I can see that more than anything, they're so private because they've been through a horrible tragedy, and not because they all truly believe themselves to be unaccountable to the public.

I've had ample time with the recipients of the many charities they support, and not one person had anything negative to say about anyone in the family. In fact, they all said that without the family's fundraising and awareness campaigns, most of these charities would have folded long ago. Now, of course, I don't expect them to be unbiased (or even truthful) when they're the recipients of big wads of cash, but still, they wouldn't need to gush about the members of the family either.

Then there's Troy. Dexter would be lost without him. And where would Troy end up if not for Arthur? Back at some dingy warehouse, getting yelled at? Not if I have anything to say about it.

But now what? I can't very well go public and tell the world I was wrong.

Can I?

———

Text from Lars: *Would you be able to arrange for Tabitha's class to be given a tour of the palace? They're learning about our system of government, and it would be a huge deal for her if you could make that happen.*

Voicemail message from Mum: *Tessa, is that you? (Long pause.) Oh, I've got your machine again, haven't I? Grace next door said that you posted something about getting a good deal on a gown for the ball, and since her daughter is getting married this fall, she was wondering if you could introduce her to the designer for a mother-of-the-bride dress? Call me back as soon as you get this, please.*

Voicemail message from Charles Porter, building manager: *Hello, Tessa. The work has been completed on the shrubs out front. I'm sliding the bill under your door, even though I know you're still living at the palace. The board does not consider that an excuse for non-payment. You have thirty days before interest starts to accrue. I also wanted to mention that your lease is coming up for renewal at the end of May, and I would like to discuss it with you.*

Voicemail from Jack Janssen, Prime Minister: *Tessa, it's me, Jack.*

Just checking in with you to see if you've given any thought to my offer. Call me back. I'd love to have you aboard.

Message from KingSlayer99: *You haven't been online for days. What's going on? I expected that you'd be leading the charge. Avonia needs you, Tessa. Where are you?*

———

It's late at night, and Arthur and I are wrapped up in each other's arms. Despite basking in the rush of endorphins at the moment, there is a niggling feeling of unrest that is threatening to spoil my good mood. The Prime Minister's message has everything to do with it. I still haven't told Arthur that, in a vague sort of way, he's offered me a job.

I can't remember a time in my life when I've been this conflicted over anything. The very reason I'm here is to advance my career, which aligning myself with the Prime Minister would ultimately do— maybe. But when I think about Arthur, I just can't bring myself to do it. Also, I really haven't uncovered anything newsworthy to give Jack Janssen anyway. I called him back earlier and left a message to that effect, trying to sound both non-committal and definitely interested at the same time, which resulted in my tone of voice rising and falling at the strangest places and ended with me saying I was coming down with a sore throat.

Arthur sighs happily and laces his fingers through mine. I turn to face him and just stare for a long moment, taking in his perfection in this moment of contentment. God, I like him *so, so much*. I should tell him about the Prime Minister. But how can I trust him? I mean, *really trust* him? He was very plain about trying to seduce me to get me to vouch for his family, and I've bloody well let him do it. The smart thing to do is to keep the Prime Minister's offer a secret. That way, when this fantasy with Prince Arthur ends, I'll at least have a soft place to land as far as my work goes.

Or not.

It's all a big gamble. The truth is, I'm in over my head. I do not belong here in the palace, and I certainly don't belong in the middle of a feud between our nation's leaders.

"What's wrong, Ms. Sharpe?"

"What makes you think something's wrong?" I smile sweetly at him.

"Because you're making that little clicking sound with your tongue that you do when you're deep in thought."

"I don't click my tongue."

"Of course you do." He kisses me on the cheek. "Don't worry, it's endearing."

"I think I should go home," I blurt out.

"Do you mean back to your room?"

"No, back to my flat. Back to my real life."

He lifts himself onto his side and stares down at me, his face lit by the moon outside the window. "Why on Earth would you do something like that?"

"Because I'm supposed to be here in a professional capacity, and now that your father is back, I'm not accomplishing anything in that regard. Besides, sleeping with you isn't exactly smart. If word got out, it would crush any credibility that I have." I sigh. *Also, I feel very guilty every time I see you, knowing I'm entertaining a job offer from your worst enemy.*

"You agreed to give me two months. Don't go back on your word."

"I'm not. I mean, I don't want to, but things have changed since I agreed to stay."

He touches my bottom lip with his thumb. "Yes, they certainly have—in ways I don't think either of us could have anticipated."

"That's the problem. I don't know what we're doing here, and I honestly don't know what to think."

"Don't think. For once in your life, just let yourself feel, and I'll do the same." He nuzzles my neck, then plants soft kisses from my earlobe down to my collarbone. "Do you *want* to leave?"

"No."

"Then stay. I know we shouldn't be doing this, but there are few things in my life that have felt this right before. When we're together…" He stops himself from finishing the sentence, and I am dying inside to know what the last few words would have been. "It matters to me that you're here, Tessa. I need you to know who I am. Even if we lose, I could almost live with it if I felt like you understood."

I blink back tears and whisper, "I see you, Arthur."

"You may be the only person who ever has. Give me another two weeks, Tessa, before you go back to your life."

Back to my life? Huh. Well, that tells me I'm making the right choice to keep the Prime Minister's number in my contact list...

27

Cavemen & Dead Kings

Arthur

I STAND next to Tessa at the bottom of the palace steps and watch as the children disembark from the school bus. She asked me to lead her niece's fifth-year class through a tour, and I was happy to agree to it. I know the past few weeks have been rough for her, with my father shutting down her interviews, leaving her to sit by and watch as camera crews and journalists parade in and out, getting the scoops I know she wishes were hers.

I'm also hoping this will help reduce the guilt I feel when I think of the dossier I have on her. Even though I've only used a few very small bits of information from her online dating profile (and that was weeks ago, frankly), I know I really should have told her about it by now. Relationships are built on trust, and I'm afraid I've failed her in this regard. But telling her the truth now would be a disaster, especially since she's been burned so badly by men before. She would most likely turn on me in a most spectacular way, and if there's one thing I can't risk right now, it's to have a spurned anti-royal blogger on my hands. So, maybe a few little lies can be buried without consequence...

I look over at Tessa, lovely, lovely Tessa, and decide to come clean. As soon as the referendum's over.

She looks up at me. "Thank you for doing this, Arthur. I know you'd rather poke out your eyes with a bobby pin than give a tour to a bunch of nose-picking ankle-biters."

"What? Me? No." I'm joking around, but on the inside my chest feels tight.

Tabitha runs up to us and gives Tessa a vigorous hug. "Thank you, thank you, thank you, Auntie Tessa!"

"You're welcome, little peanut. I'm so happy to see you." She plants a kiss on top of her niece's head, and I can't help but think how sweet she is. "You remember Prince Arthur."

Tabitha pulls away from Tessa and grins up at me. "Hi! Thanks for letting my class come. I'm pretty sure I'm the most popular girl in fifth year now."

"What? I'm shocked that you weren't the most popular girl before. A beautiful, smart thing like you." She steps forward and gives me a big hug. I'm a bit taken aback for a second, but then I realize it's kind of nice to be on the receiving end of a hug from an ankle-biter. Besides, she doesn't look like the nose-picking type anyway.

I give Tabitha my hand, then walk over to greet the rest of the class.

Isa hurries over to introduce me to the teacher, Mrs. Glassbottom, an older woman with red glasses and a fluffy orange scarf around her neck. She does a slightly awkward looking curtsy, then turns to the students, claps her hands twice, and says, "Yoohoo!"

The kids give a long drawn out, "Yeeesss?"

"Now, I know you all know who Prince Arthur is, but I want to remind you again to address him as Your Highness, and this is your last warning—I mean you, Kyle—you must be on your very best behaviour during the *entire tour*, or I shall have to bring you back to the bus. No running, shouting, touching anything, and no second chances."

I can't help feeling amused at this warning. It takes me back to my own school days, and I'm afraid I may have been the Kyle of my class. "Hello, everyone. It's a pleasure to meet you all and take you for a look around my house. Mrs. Glassbottom has given you some wonderfully clear instructions, but who can remember one more rule?"

Hands shoot up high in the air from each student. What a rush of power. Now I know why people bother to become teachers in the first place. "The last rule is to have fun."

Predictable, I know, but also effective. The kids cheer, and I gesture for them to follow me. "Who here has ever met a pig before?"

The next hour is akin to herding puppies on speed. I feel like I'm constantly riding a line of having them learn a little something and losing their interest completely. There's an art to this—knowing how long to talk and when to get them moving again—and unfortunately, I do not have this mastered yet. Kyle and two other boys disappear from the group somewhere between the Grande Hall and the library.

"Not to worry, I'll have the security team find them." I wink at the kids, then nod at Ollie, who rolls his eyes at me—discreetly, of course—and sets off in the direction from which we came.

"We'll be in the throne room!" I call to him, which earns an 'ooooh' from the class.

We make our way down the wide hall, and I call out names of my dead relatives as we pass by each painting. I give the odd tidbit of what I hope will be interesting information, things like, 'she was beheaded on her twenty-fourth birthday,' or 'died in a fire', or 'the King of Spain tried to have him murdered in his bed, but his wire fox terrier, Bones, saved his life.' The adults in the group seem a little unsettled, but the children love it.

Then we reach the tall double doors at the end of the hall. I turn to them with wide eyes. "This, boys and girls, is a most sacred of places—the *throne room*."

A hush falls over the students as we file in to the enormous church-like hall. It's hard not to be filled with awe, even for me. The domed glass ceiling sits directly over the single throne, allowing the sun to shine directly on the ornate red and gold chair. A wide, red carpet stretches from the entrance to the steps of the throne itself. I search for Tessa in the group and find her gazing at the tall, arched walls.

Secretly, I'm filled with a smug satisfaction to see she's willing to be impressed by it all.

I lead the group toward the front and stop in front of the red rope that blocks off the throne. "Now, you may think my father, King Winston, sits here all day and greets people and makes important decisions, but he doesn't. A long time ago that would have been the case, but at some point, one of the kings, or more likely a queen—they're always so sensible—realized that they could get a lot more work done sitting behind a desk. So, most of the time you'll find the King in his office instead of here."

Kyle, who has now joined us, pipes up. "If you don't need it, can I take it home, then?"

The class titters with laughter, and Mrs. Glassbottom levels him with a hard look I know from personal experience. "I'm afraid not, young Kyle. We hold very special ceremonies here, such as the coronation of a new monarch or official photos on royal wedding days or celebrating the birth of a new member of the family. We also use it when knighthoods are given out, or when we greet government leaders from other parts of the world."

"Prince Arthur, when was the last time you used this room?" one of the parents asks.

"Well, this past fall, actually, when it was time to elect a new prime minister. My father held a ceremony in which he presented the previous prime minister a gift to commemorate his service, and then called the next election."

Mrs. Glassbottom cuts in. "That's right, boys and girls. In fact, no one else in Avonia is allowed to call for an election. It is both the king's duty and his honour. If he didn't do it, we would keep the same prime minister for many years."

Tabitha's hand shot up, and her teacher points to her. "Yes, Tabitha?"

"So, if a king liked a prime minister, he could keep him in power forever?"

"Theoretically, yes, but that has never happened because the Royal Family believes the people have the right to elect their leaders on a regular basis, which in Avonia has always been every five years."

I give Tessa a pointed look and smile when she purses her lips and shakes her head at me.

Thirty minutes later, we stand side-by-side and wave to the students as the bus pulls away.

"Thank you, Arthur," she says. "I really appreciate you taking the time to do this."

"I was happy to. It wasn't as bad as I thought it would be, actually." I look down at her and feel an overwhelming urge to pull her into my arms and kiss her hard on the mouth. But I can't, because as far as the world knows, we have nothing more than a strange professional relationship.

There's a gleam in her eye when she looks up at me. "I thought you did a wonderful job. You know, you could have a bright future as a tour guide if the vote doesn't go your way..."

"Could I, now?"

"Oh, yes. Easily. Maybe even work your way up to a double decker tour bus." She grins. "If you want, I could give you a good reference."

"Really? You would do that?" I ask. God, she's fun.

Tessa shrugs. "Maybe. I'll give you a chance to convince me later." A slow grin spreads across her face, and it's all I can do not to pick her up over my shoulder like some caveman and take her back to my room.

"That's very generous of you, Ms. Sharpe."

"I'm a generous kind of girl."

"And here I thought I was the one who just did the favour..."

"It's all how you spin it."

28

The Real Media Is in the House

Tessa

IT's after three in the morning, and I'm pretty sure there is no way I'm going to fall to sleep. I can't shake this nagging feeling that something is wrong, but I can't figure out what. I mean, I know there is a lot wrong with what I'm doing, but there's something else I can't put my finger on.

The tour today was a terrific success—well, other than losing those boys, but Ollie did find them safe and sound, dismantling a suit of armor. For once, I was able to feel like a hero in front of Tabitha and Isa. I had a very nice day overall, in fact, and this evening, well, let's just say what started out as me thanking Arthur for giving the tour, ended with him thanking me twice. Thoroughly.

I should be sound asleep. But there's something I'm forgetting, or maybe I'm supposed to do, but I can't think of what it is. I slip out of bed, careful not to wake Arthur, then make my way over to the window and stare out at the moonlit meadow. After a few minutes of coming up blank, I decide it must be because the ball is coming up, and I'm getting very nervous. That, or maybe it's because my time here at the palace will soon come to an end, and I know that will also mean the end of my time with Arthur. I look over at him, and my heart twists at the sight of him lying there.

I've never felt this close to anyone in my entire life. He's not only fun and sexy and, well, completely perfect, really, he also *gets me* in a way no one else does. For the first time, I feel like someone understands me, and not only that, *he likes me* for who I am, quirks and all.

I watch him turn over in his sleep, and it hits me like a ton of bricks. I'm going to be an absolute mess when I have to give him up.

————

It's the week-long build up to the ball, and King Winston has made good on his promise to bring in the big guns. 'Approved members of the press' (which includes my old colleagues from *The Daily Times*) seem to be everywhere. It's like high school all over again. I'm surrounded by the cool kids, wishing I could be one of them while they pretend I don't exist.

The worst of it was earlier today when Veronica Platt interviewed the entire Royal Family. They set up in the solarium, and I sat in, hoping to get a little networking. Turned out it was a horrible idea, because no one from ABNC had any interest whatsoever in even looking at me, let alone talking to me.

Veronica is not only more gorgeous in real life than she is on the telly, but she very clearly fancies Arthur. I could only stand about five minutes of her making eyes at him before I decided to sneak out. Only the door made a loud creaking sound when I opened it, and I heard the director yell, "Cut. Sorry, Your Majesty, we'll just have to wait until the Shock Jogger blogger's gone."

The sound of snickering followed me out as the door swung shut and caught the back of my ankle. Not only was I humiliated, I also lost a few layers of skin in the process, so now I'm limping around with my ankle bandaged up.

Later, they filmed a segment in which Veronica spent an hour with the head accountant, who opened up the books to show where the money comes from and where it goes. Most of their expenses are paid by land holdings, investments and an ancient grant that collects interest in the millions each year. The entire thing was like career torture for me. That was *my* story to get. Not hers. *I* should have been the one thoughtfully poring over the records and asking intelligent questions.

I'm not only considered utterly ridiculous, I've become completely redundant around here. Possibly even worse, deep down I know I have to make a decision that will deal the death blow to my 'career' once and for all. I have to tell the truth about the family and shut down my blog forever. I can't, in good conscience, continue spewing angry words that have no merit behind them. While I haven't changed my political views, I can't bear to leave all those nasty things I've written up where they can hurt Arthur. But how does one publicly admit they were so horribly, willfully wrong for so long? The thought makes my stomach ache.

So, for the past several days since I realized this, I've done what I tend to do when faced with a dilemma.

Nothing.

Instead of getting on with it, I avoid the entire thing and hope it will go away. I'm about to lose the respect of the only group of people in Avonia who think I have something of value to say—my anti-royal crowd. KingSlayer99 is never going to want to speak to me again, which in an odd way will be a real loss for me. He's been the closest thing I've had to someone who respects me until I met Arthur. But in the end, I have to disappoint him, so I might as well just get it over with rather than sit with this awful pit in my stomach for weeks before I woman-up and get the job done.

It's high time I grow a pair of ovaries already and deal with issues head-on rather than sweeping them under the rug. Yes, that's it. Starting today, I will no longer ignore problems but will face them head-on and just get them out of the way immediately, instead of allowing them to block my path to success.

Ack! My phone is ringing, and it's Daniel Fitzwilliam from Well-bits. I'll let that go to voicemail.

———

Voicemail from Daniel Fitzwilliam, owner of Wellbits: *This is your last warning, Ms. Sharpe. Call me by end of business today, or the next person you hear from will be my lawyer.*

Email from Me to Daniel Fitzwilliam, Owner of Wellbits:

Mr. Fitzwilliam,

I have just now received your rather terse message. I have been away from home on assignment since the day after the unfortunate incident (which your product caused). I am deeply disappointed with the way in which Wellbits is handling this matter. I would have thought that a reputable company would offer me some type of compensation for my pain and suffering. Rather, you have decided to lay the blame on me, the victim in this whole thing. I'm the one who was shocked repeatedly. I'm the one who has become an international humiliation, and I demand that you cease and desist all harassment on this matter or you will be hearing from my lawyer.

Regards,

Tessa Sharpe

———

The ball is in three days' time, and I am trying very hard to somehow convince my heart that it will survive when this beautiful romantic dream ends, but it's really of very little use. I can see what's coming, and it will be a soul-crushing, dignity-stealing event.

It's the seemingly insignificant moments like this one right now, that will disappear through my fingers, never to return, but for which I will always long. Arthur and I are in bed. It's late in the evening, and we are sitting side-by-side, propped up on our pillows, working. I'm on my laptop, editing and uploading a collection of photos of spring flowers with morning dew onto my photography site, and Arthur is working on a speech he is to give at the anniversary ball. Every once in a while, he tries out a line on me and watches me closely to gauge my reaction. Just now, he managed to bring tears to my eyes with his words.

"That was just so lovely." I nod and sniffle.

"I must be on the right track if I can make the Royal Watchdog cry." Arthur winks, then reaches over to his nightstand and grabs a tissue and dabs under my eyes.

"You really are, Arthur." I give him a quick kiss on the lips. "Can I say, I really feel like you've changed since I got here?"

"You may," he says in a particularly pompous voice.

I grin and match his tone. "Oh, well, thank you, kind sir." I bow my head. "But seriously, think of the words you would have written two months ago."

"To be completely honest, I wouldn't have written this myself. I would have had someone else do it. I *might* have read it over once before the ball, but more than likely I wouldn't even have done that much." He leans in and gives me a slow, sweet kiss on the lips. "You've been a very good influence on me, Ms. Sharpe, to help me change my tune in such a short time."

"I think we've both changed our tune. There's no way I would have considered helping you two months ago. But now—"

"Now you *want* to help me?" His eyes light up.

I nod, rewarded by the biggest smile I've seen from Arthur yet.

"*Really?* Are you actually saying I've managed to win you over then?" He goes from enthusiastic to cocky in a fraction of a second.

My pride kicks in, begging me to pretend I haven't changed my mind. "You haven't won me over. It was through careful observation that I have come to a new understanding of..."

He raises one eyebrow, and I stop talking for a second.

"Oh, God, this is so hard to say out loud...but I was...there are a few areas where...I may have made some assumptions." I sigh, then let the words tumble out of my mouth. "I was wrong."

Holding up one finger, I keep talking before he can start to gloat. "Not about all of it—I'll never change my mind about electing our leaders—but I may have underestimated what your family does for the nation and the other realms. In fact, I made up a list of all the areas in which my facts were...less than accurate. The right thing to do would be to go public with it."

Arthur claps his hands together. "And you're the type who does the right thing."

"Not really." I give him an evil grin. "I'm sleeping with you, aren't I?"

"Oh, but you couldn't help yourself where I'm concerned. You were overpowered by my hotness."

"Not really. I'm just using you for your Gord Ramsay perfectly scrambled eggs."

Arthur grabs both our laptops and sets them on the night table, then rolls on top of me, causing me to squeal with laughter. "That's it, Sharpe. Admit it. You want me for my body."

"Never! It's only for the breakfasts."

He pins my arms up over my head and says, "Last chance, Sharpe. Admit it."

"Okay, I also like the limo rides."

"I've never heard a lady refer to it as a limo ride, but I'll gladly take the compliment."

We both laugh, which turns into some kissing. After a moment, he lifts his head. "You're going to help me save the monarchy, aren't you?"

"Oh, damn, I think so."

Arthur beams down at me and gives me a solid kiss on the lips. "You have no idea how happy you've made me."

"But this means that *no one* can find out about us. Because if they do, nothing I say will have any merit."

"That's not a problem. No one here will say a word. They're all very good at keeping secrets." He kisses me again. "I can't believe I've convinced you. It's my oral skills, isn't it?"

"No! I mean, as wonderful as they are, it really was seeing what you do and finding out the truth."

"But come on, it has to be a little bit about that thing I do with my tongue when you're close to the end."

My body feels all tingly at the mention of it, but I'm not going to tell him that. "That has no bearing on my change of heart."

"Come on, it did," he teases. "Just admit it."

"Dear Lord, you're relentless."

"That's probably why I'm so good at it." He raises and lowers his eyebrows.

"You're nothing short of exasperating. It's a wonder I like you at all, really."

"But you do. Very much." He kisses my neck until I moan. "I can tell by that little sound you just made."

"All right. I like you."

As he works his way up to my earlobe, my words come out with a breathy quality. "Very much."

"Good. Because I like you, too," he says as he disappears under the sheets. "Especially this bit down here."

———

"Seriously?" Nikki asks. "You're just going to publicly apologize and say you were wrong about everything?"

"Not *everything*. But most of it." I sigh, feeling a mixture of relief and fear in admitting this it to her. I have purposely been avoiding calling Nikki for close to two weeks. We've texted and had one quick call, but the guilt of not telling her what I'm doing has been eating away at me.

"That's going to be really humiliating. Like Shock-Jogger-level of humiliation."

"I know."

"And you'll lose a *lot* of money that would have been yours, you know."

"I know. I've thought of that, too. I'll also be burning whatever bridge I could have possibly had with the Prime Minister...but I'm not sure I want to get in bed with the likes of him anyway—not literally, yuck—but figuratively. So, I think I'm better off in that way." I do my best to sound very confident, even though I'm terrified.

"I guess..." Nikki says, her voice full of concern. "But think of the *money*, Tessa. I mean, when you accepted the Prince's offer, it was so you could finally get ahead, and now just when you're about to do that, you're going to give up?"

"Oh, God. I know it sounds totally crazy, trust me. But maybe it'll prove my dedication to honest reporting over personal pride. Plus, I'll be able to look Tabitha in the eye, knowing I did the right thing."

"You can't buy those Bench boots with your niece's approval," she says. "But I suppose there are more important things than—holy crap! You're sleeping with him, aren't you?"

"What? Why would you think that?"

"Oh. My. God! You are! How long have you been sleeping with him?"

"What? Who said I was sleeping with him?" I ask, hoping to buy more time to come up with a reasonable explanation.

"I did. And you haven't denied it, so you very clearly are." Tried, convicted, and about to be sentenced. "Now it all makes sense. You won't leave even though you've been *claiming* to have a crappy time since the King got home." Nikki gasps. "How could you not tell me?"

"I couldn't. I'm so ashamed of myself. I'm being a *very bad, very stupid* woman. And now I'm willing to give up my career for him like some nineteen-fifties housewife."

"Wait? You're giving up your career for him? Is it because you're about to *become* some nineteen-fifties housewife? Only a very rich one who wears a crown and doesn't ever have to cook or clean or do laundry or wait for a sale to buy footwear?"

"No," I groan. "It's so much worse than you think. It's very clear that we have no future. This has all just been a mistake. A wonderful, sexy, orgasmic mistake that I've made over and over."

"And you kept it from me the whole time?"

"Please don't be hurt. I've been feeling horribly guilty about not telling you, but I was scared you'd talk me out of it. And I just couldn't let you do that. It's like…he's crack and I'm an addict, and the only thing that matters is getting more of him."

"You've got a serious cock addiction?"

"Not just the cock. The whole guy."

"If I weren't already in the tub, I think I'd collapse right now with shock."

"That's kind of how I feel each morning. Shocked at myself. Shocked at him for wanting to…do any of this. Then by evening, I can't think of anything but doing it all over again. I think I need a twelve-step program or something."

Nikki's voice goes quiet. "Are you in love with him?"

I swallow hard and let the truth squeak out. "I think so."

"Is he in love with you?"

"No, he can't be. I think he genuinely *likes* me, and he wants to have sex all the time, but there is no way he could be in love with me."

"And why the hell not?" She's offended on my behalf, and I love her for it.

"Because I'm the armpit-sniffing, potty-mouthed, Shock-Jogger-Blogger-slash-Royal Watchdog. I'm all wrong for him. This is just for fun. And pretty soon I'll come back home to reality and pretend it never happened. Or curl up in the fetal position and drink wine through a sippy cup for a few weeks, *then* pretend it never happened."

We talk for another twenty minutes, the conversation going back and forth between Nikki being hurt that I kept this all from her, worried about what I'm doing to myself, and giddy for me for what I've been letting Prince Arthur do to me. By the time we get off the phone, my mind is swirling with all of it. Somehow, talking about it brought all my fears to the forefront of my mind, right where I didn't want them. I wanted them tucked neatly at the back, like my collection of slightly-too-small knickers I'll wear when I lose those last ten pounds.

I stare out the window at the meadow and see Troy and Dexter out for a walk. The thought of leaving makes my heart ache. I can't let myself hope that things will go on, because I know they can't. I'm not queen material, and even though Arthur seems smitten with me, he hasn't said anything that would lead me to think we can have a future together.

I will never belong with these people. Take his sister, for example, whom Arthur is very close to. She despises me—for good reason, really. I represent everything that can hurt them, and even though Arthur forgives me, I know she can't, and won't. It's one thing when someone hurts you, but an entirely different thing when someone hurts someone you love. If only she knew I love him, too.

Oh, this is getting rather dramatic, isn't it? What am I doing? *Seri-*

ously? I never should have let him lure me to his room with the promise of crisps. I should have stayed away. Kept him at a distance. Because now it's too late. I'm not a Bram. I'm a Tessa, who has worm funerals and sobs uncontrollably over that commercial for Extra gum with the girl who saves all those little origami birds her dad makes for her. I've fallen for him, and it's too late to turn back now. I'm going to get crushed, because there is truly no way to make this work.

Oh, bugger.

29

A Girl's Best Friend

Arthur

I'm a bit of a brat when it comes to any type of big event. I don't want to go, so I tend to complain all through the leadup, then grit my teeth until it's over and I can go back to the solitude of my quarters. It doesn't even matter which type of event, really—balls, galas, ship-christenings—all are as excruciatingly dull as watching golf on TV.

But Arthur, what about the music, the dancing, and the beautiful women?

Yawn.

What about the food, the laughter, and the drinks?

Clear everyone else out of the room and leave me with the drinks —now we're talking.

But today I find myself not dreading the ball even one tiny bit. I didn't sneer once at the list of VIPs whom I must greet. I haven't used the term monkey suit even once since Vincent brought it to my apartment after having it pressed.

The ironic thing is that this particular ball *should be* the one I would dread the most. After the PM's announcement, the room will be divided into those who want to see our heads on platters (figuratively, most of them, I hope) and those who want to see our continued reign for the next millennium. It's going to be awkward as hell and will require the utmost delicacy in handling myself. Every expression, every choice of where to stand and with whom to speak will be analyzed relentlessly.

And yet, there is a spring in my step as I shower, shave, and dress. A good woman'll do that to you. Last night before I left Tessa's room, I asked her to go to the ball with me. It felt a little like some cheesy high school romance movie, but her reaction showed me why men bother with that type of romantic gesture in the first place. And that's nothing compared to what I have planned tonight.

A knock at my door has me grinning. Could it be one Ms. Sharpe coming back for more? Greedy little thing. I swing open the door with my best sexy grin and come face-to-face with my father. The expression he's wearing would soften any man's sceptre. I need to stop thinking it's her at my door, because the letdown is awful.

"I wanted to make sure you're ready to give the best speech of your useless life this evening."

"Well, thanks. I wasn't expecting a pep talk from dear old Dad."

He gives me a slow blink, then walks past me and heads straight for the liquor cabinet. "I'm doubting the decision to allow you to speak at all."

He's jealous. That's what's wrong. The advisory team held some stupid focus group, and apparently I'm more than five times as likable as my father, so they've suggested I increase my visibility and he decrease his. Even though it's just until the pending crisis has resolved itself, I have a feeling that the damage to our already strained relationship will last far beyond the vote. "If you'd rather make the speech, go ahead. It's not like I asked to be given the burden."

"Don't fuck this up." He slams back a whiskey and sets the glass down, then glares at Dexter, who is lying on the couch, watching *Monkey Thieves*. "Disgusting."

Dex glances at him and snorts. He never did take to my father. Like I told Tessa, he really is an excellent judge of character.

———

When Tessa opens the door, I am dumbstruck by her beauty. Seriously, I cannot make words form in my brain, let alone roll off my tongue. She's a vision. Her blonde hair is swept up in some sort of complicated twisty-bun thingy. The silver gown she's wearing has a hint of sparkle to it—not enough to be in any way gaudy, but enough to make a man believe that magic is real. It's cut tightly to her body, showing every luscious curve and dipping between her perfect ivory breasts just enough to give me a reminder of what the rest of them looks like, but not enough that she's showing anything I wouldn't want anyone else to see.

My eyes rake over her from head to toe and back up, and I'm not entirely sure I *wouldn't* go door to door through the kingdom to return one of the heels she's wearing. When I finally set my gaze on her face, I know the truth.

I would bloody well do it. With a smile on my foolish face.

"Nice tux," she says, then she reaches out and straightens my bow tie, giving me a whiff of her delicious perfume.

Excalibur wakes up and starts begging. "Christ, I want to mess up your hair right now."

She grins and raises one eyebrow. "And just how would you do that?"

"It would take me all night to explain it all. Instead, we should get this whole ridiculous ball business over with so we can come back here and I can show you." I trace her bare arms with my fingertips. Her skin may be the softest thing I've ever felt. Seriously, it's that soft. "Mind if I kiss you, or are you one of those girls who doesn't want to wreck her lipstick?"

She screws up her face as though she's really considering it, then shrugs. "Go ahead."

I pull her to me, and in the next few minutes we smear the hell out of her glossy pink lips. Finally, I pull back, trying to slow my breathing and get myself under control. Excalibur is going to be very, very disappointed. "We better go. We can't be late."

She smiles, and I see the anticipation in her eyes. "I'll go make myself presentable again."

"I'll stand here and stare at your beautiful bottom while you walk away."

———

"Hope you don't mind, we need to make one quick stop on the way to the ballroom." Her hand is resting on the crook of my arm in the most proper of fashions, but because it's her hand, I can only think very dirty thoughts, one of which is what I'd like to do to her when we get to the vault. But I better not allow my mind to wander too far down that road, or I'll be sporting a most visible hard-on by the time we arrive at the gala.

When we reach the vault room, there are two guards standing at the door. Normally there is just one, sitting on the inside, but for nights like tonight, there are a total of six. I nod, and one of them opens the door.

"Good evening, fellows," I say.

"Good evening, Your Highness."

Once inside the room, we go through the same routine with the other four men. I go to the keypad and press the code, then hold my face in front of the camera for a retina scan. When I look down at Tessa, she actually looks impressed.

"A little Bond-esque, no?" I ask.

"Very."

"Come on, Moneypenny, let's get you something for that beautiful neck of yours." I tug her hand and pull her in with me before she can say no.

She's already shaking her head, but I hold up one finger. "I can see those Sharpe family brains of yours going to work on ten different reasons why you won't borrow a necklace, but I have already prepared counterarguments, and since we are now twelve minutes behind schedule, please allow me. One, they're already paid for, some of them hundreds of years ago, so it's not coming out of anyone's taxes. Two, like the books in the library, they're going to waste in here. Three, for the first time in my life, I want to share something with someone else —someone who deserves to feel like a queen, even if she'll only allow herself that for one measly little evening. Four, I have this fantasy of seeing you in only the jewels. Maybe the heels could stay."

Tessa laughs, her cheeks turning pink. "All right. One necklace, but make it a cheap one."

I raise one eyebrow. "Define cheap."

"Less than a kitchen stool."

"How about less than a car?"

"Sofa."

"I said 'queen.' Would a queen really wear a sofa around her neck?" I reach up and run my fingertips along the base of her neck.

"Would she wear a car?"

"Good point." I lean down and kiss the crook of her neck. "How about this? You choose whichever one you like the best, and I won't tell you how much it's worth."

I continue to brush my lips along her skin, then move up to her earlobe. The other night, I discovered a little spot at the base of her ear that turns her to putty. After a moment of some careful work, I get what I want. A breathy little 'okay' escapes her lips.

She takes my hand as we move around the large room.

"You know what's funny?" she asks. "I feel a little scared to even be looking at them. Like I might somehow break something with my commoner's eyes."

I narrow my eyes at her. "Please don't call yourself that."

"Why not? It's what I am." She straightens her back, and I can see she's about to go into fight mode.

"You're anything but common. You're incredible." I pluck a tiara from a display case and set it on her head, then I smile and turn her to the mirror. "See? Look at you. Positively regal. This is how the world should see you."

She glances at herself in the mirror, blushes some more and looks at the floor.

"Don't look down. I want you to see yourself the way I see you." I stand behind her and lift her chin gently with one finger so she's looking at herself again. "This is how I see you. A vision of perfection."

She turns to me. "You talk a good game, Your Highness."

"I'm serious. No matter what happens, I want you to remember this moment, because I want you to know your worth." I lower my face so I can look her in the eye. "If I were to be really honest, I'd tell you that I want you to remember this moment as the beginning of something wonderful."

Her green eyes lock on mine, and it's as if she's looking directly into my soul. And for the first time in my entire life, I have just told the truth to a woman about how I feel, and it's fucking terrifying and absolutely wonderful at the same time.

One of the guards clears his throat. "Sorry, Your Highness. Mr. Hendriks is putting a call out to find you. I thought you should know."

I answer him without looking away from Tessa for even a second. "Tell him you've got eyes on me and that we'll be there in four minutes."

I hear him speaking into his mic as the door closes behind him.

"We should go," she says.

"I know everyone is waiting for us, but it would give me the greatest pleasure if you would choose something to wear first." I kiss her gently on the lips, careful not to smudge her lipstick. "Please let me do this for you, Tessa. I'm not a prince tonight. I'm a man who very much wants to spoil a woman, not for any other reason than because she deserves it." I pause, then kiss her again. "That's not entirely true. There's also that whole thing I've got running around in my head with you wearing nothing but the jewels."

"And my heels." She finally grins, and it's like the sun has come out after a storm. All rainbows and puppies and shit.

She glances down at the case of necklaces. "That one."

I lift the necklace and place it around her. It's a Harry Winston step-up cut emerald necklace, made in the nineteen-fifties for a Hollywood producer's wife. Each emerald is surrounded by brilliant-cut diamonds.

"Perfect choice." I turn her so she can see herself in the mirror again. She reaches up and touches the gems delicately, and the look on her face is worth every penny of the four million.

As we walk down the hall, she asks, "What if I lose it?"

"You won't." I slip my hand into hers, and it feels so natural there —like it's always been my hand to hold.

"But...what if I do?"

I shrug. "Then I'll be out the cost of a very nice house."

She starts doing that Lamaze breathing thingy again, and I'm glad I didn't tell her the truth.

When we arrive at the grand entrance to the ballroom, I look down at her. "You all right?"

She nods but looks terrified.

"You'll be fine. I promise." I squeeze her hand. "I'll be with you the entire time. Plus, you'll be by far the most stunning woman in the room."

30

Champagne Toasts & Cheaply-Made Expensive High Heels

Tessa

IS THIS REALLY HAPPENING? Am I walking into the ball on the arm of a crown prince? Wearing a necklace I'm sure would solve all my financial problems for life? Did he just say he's hoping I'll fall for him? Or is this some very strange, wonderful drug trip?

Perhaps it is. Oh, what if they've drugged me, and now they're actually leading me to the dungeon to chop off my head, but I think it's this wonderful, perfect, magical evening instead? But I don't feel drugged. I feel somehow more awake than I ever have. Everything about this is so vivid—the brightly lit grand ballroom filled with at least a thousand people in beautiful gowns and smart-looking tuxes. The scent of the huge flower arrangements on top of each of the round tables. The sea of ivory tablecloths and matching ivory chairs set against the enormous shiny black and white checked floor.

I hear our names being announced over the speakers. "His Royal Highness, Prince Arthur, and Ms. Tessa Sharpe."

Polite clapping comes from around the room. People are smiling at us. Well, some are scowling at me, mostly women, but some men, too. My heart pounds so loudly that the sounds of the room dull to the background. The music, the clink of glasses, people speaking in hushed tones. I've just been handed a glass of champagne, and it feels cool on my tongue. Bubbly and delicious.

"Drink up. You look like you could use it," Arthur says.

And when I look into his eyes, I relax completely. The sincerity on his face tells me everything will be okay. And I believe him.

Then the onslaught of greeters come forward, shaking the prince's hand and bowing. Wishing him well. Some greet me also; others either glance at me then move on, or they ignore me altogether. This goes on for quite a few minutes. I down the champagne. It's whisked away and another one appears in my hand without me being fully aware of how it happened. Then the music stops and the room goes silent. I look up to the stage where the small orchestra sits, waiting as the King stands before the microphone.

"I would like to welcome you all here tonight. We are here to cele-brate a great achievement, one that very few nations on this earth can boost. Eight hundred years of peace, eight hundred years of being one people with one purpose. I would like to invite my son to say a few words on behalf of our family. As the country's future king, it is only right that he speak on this auspicious occasion."

Applause fills the room, and Arthur whispers to me, "Sorry. Just a bit of business to attend to, then I'm all yours."

I watch him stride to the stage, and everything about him says leader. And he'd be a good one, at that. When he reaches the micro-phone, he finds me in the crowd and smiles, and I feel like I'm the only one in the room.

"Good evening, everyone. Thank you all for coming. It is our honour to welcome you all to our home to share in this event. Well, not everyone. I see the Prime Minister's turned up."

A burst of laughter fills the room, and Arthur gives them his 'hand in the cookie jar' grin.

"I only jest, of course, Jack. We're happy you would come to celebrate with us. As Prime Minister, your position is every bit as important as ours in ensuring a fair, just society in which the voices of the people are heard. I know there's been a lot of speculation in the past few days about how my family is managing the news of the referendum, and I'd like to fill you in, because as your sometimes-not-so-humble servants, we owe you the truth. I'm not going to stand here and tell you that we welcome the referendum. That would be a pile of horseshit, and you'd all know it.

"It's been a tough few days, but as a friend pointed out to me, change is always hard, and the threat of being downsized will always make one feel…well…threatened. We were shocked to learn of the Prime Minister's inexplicable desire to oust us after we backed his bid for leadership. The trust we once shared has not been honoured, and I would like you to think about that as you go to the polls in a few weeks. For once a man proves he will break trust in one situation, it is highly likely he will do so in other situations as well.

"But the referendum isn't what my father, my sister, and I should be focusing on right now. It's losing the faith of the people that should be—and is—more troubling, because our low approval ratings show we haven't been listening to you, and that is wrong. Were we in touch with the needs, wants, and problems of the very people who live and work here and make our nation what it is, you wouldn't be ready to kick us out. And that's on us. We've been closed off for a long time, carrying on with business as usual, while you have been growing and changing, and in a lot of cases, struggling.

"As you know, I have recently invited Tessa Sharpe to live in the palace and observe our every move. I was hoping I could convince her the nation needs us. But instead, she seems to have convinced me we haven't been acting in a way that warrants your continued support."

I look around and see the surprised faces around the room, including the King's. A sense of pride swells in my chest. Arthur finds me in the crowd again and smiles, then goes on.

"On this remarkable occasion, it is our duty to pause and reflect on Avonia's history. I have spent the last few days thinking about the original purpose of a monarch, you know, back eight hundred years ago, when it all began here. Yes, it was about power and money, of course, but there was also the aspect of offering protection for the nation and its people.

"King Edward's ability to raise a large military was a source of comfort for many, after years of both civil war and invasion. Having a king who could hold the line in the face of attack allowed the people to feel secure and get on with their lives without the constant worry of raids from neighbouring armies. By all accounts in history, he was a good ruler. Like a good father, Edward was fair, wise, and willing to fight for his people. Legend has it that he died on the battle field when the Scots tried to invade back in 1226. He didn't just send his men out, but went himself to hold the wall.

"He should be our inspiration today as we of the House Langdon consider our future. Wisdom, fairness, and bravery should be the cornerstone of this family, and I intend to make it so as we start our next century together. I stand before you today, committing to those principles, and promising to serve the people of Avonia through all the storms that may come our way. If, and when, I am given the privilege to take the throne, I promise you, I shall not only listen to you and be accountable to you, but I shall hold the wall."

The applause is nothing short of thunderous. I tear up as people all around the room rise to their feet. He grins down at me and nods at various people in the crowd until the ovation ends. "Now, let's get on the with the party. Drink up, eat up, and let's dance, because eight hundred years is a hell of an accomplishment."

Arthur bows, then walks past his father, off the stage, and makes his way to me, shaking hands the entire way down the aisle. When he finally gets to me, he holds out his hand. "May I have the pleasure of your company for the first dance?"

I blush like a school girl as he leads me out onto the center of the dance floor. The orchestra starts up. Arthur presses one hand to my back and holds my hand with the other one with a loose but firm grip. "Do you waltz?"

My heart is pounding, and I'm trying very hard not to notice the two thousand eyes trained on us as he starts to move. "Poorly."

"Well, I'm glad I spent all those years in Prince Charm School, then, because I can make anyone look good." He gives me a little wink, and I relax and let myself go as he glides us around the floor.

"You were amazing," I say. "Absolutely perfect."

"That's only because I've had the perfect woman to show me what the people needed to hear." He dips me, and my heart flutters. "One who helped me get my head out of my regal arse."

———

We dance together for two songs before an older woman in a bright pink gown cuts in. I step to the back of the room and pour myself a punch. I feel a little like a wallflower, standing alone at the punch table, drumming my fingers on my glass to the beat, but no one else is watching me now that I'm not with Arthur.

I feel a tap on my shoulder, and I turn to see two young men grinning at me. "You're the Shock Jogger girl, right?"

"That's me."

"Told you!" says the tall one. "Pay up, loser."

"Fine." The shorter one gives him a five, then grins at me. "How much did that hurt? Getting shocked like that? It looked bloody painful."

"I wouldn't recommend it."

They both laugh, then the short one says, "Can we get a picture with you?"

"Why not?" I smile politely.

When they've finished with me, they walk away and I make a beeline for the terrace. I suddenly feel very much out of place, and I can feel a thousand sets of eyes on me right now, and not one of them belongs to the man I need to see right now. He seems to have disappeared.

As I am passing the bar, I see a group of very regal-looking women pointing to me and whispering to each other. I give them a little nod. And then it happens. My left heel snaps off, and my foot slams against the floor. I watch helplessly as the heel spins out onto the dance floor.

Yup. That's what I needed right now. The humiliation of a heel-break. I lift my left foot onto my toes and try to walk out without doing the whole 'up-down' walk, but it's no use. My right heel is too high for me to remain level. I hear a burst of laughter behind me as I walk out the door. Can this night be done?

31

Shiny Crowns & Pinky Toes

Arthur

I AM outside walking through the garden with my grandmum, but in my mind, I'm back in the ballroom with Tessa.

"You're awfully quiet, Arthur. What's racing around in that brain of yours?" She pats my arm with her hand.

"Sorry, Grandmum, were you saying something?"

"Yes, I was starting to tell you how proud you've made me. You should really listen up, because I may not have many more chances to fill your head full of compliments."

I glance down at her, and my stomach drops. She looks so frail this evening, even though she's smiling. Her skin has become so crinkled and translucent, it's as though she might at any moment crack into dust. "Don't say that. You're going to be around for a long time."

"Yes, of course I am. I meant that you so seldom take the opportunity to impress me."

Ouch. I'm pretty sure the Dowager Countess Violet Crawley from

Downton Abbey was based on my grandmother. She has every bit as much snark. "You know what? You've never been the stereotypical grandmother. The type who bakes cookies and thinks your grandchildren can do no wrong."

"What would be the point of that?" she asks. "Besides, you've got the rest of the world to pump up your already sizable ego."

"Well, thank you."

"You're quite welcome. Now, I want to tell you something, and I need you to keep your mind on what I'm saying, rather than letting it wander back to that lovely young woman with whom you're so obviously sleeping."

"Grandmum, we're not—"

"Give me a little more credit than that, Arthur. I may be as old as Jesus, but I'm not thick in the head."

She stops at a stone bench and starts to sit down. I try to help her, but she waves my hand away.

"Stubborn old mule."

"Foolish young goat."

I flop down next to her and chuckle. "So, what do you need to tell me?"

"I made a number of mistakes in my life, Arthur. One of which was allowing your grandfather to raise your father with very little input from me." She sighs. "At the time, I believed it was just how things had to be. I didn't know the first thing about how to rule a nation. Back then, wives yielded to their husbands, not like today, when more often than not the men rarely have any say when it comes to their offspring.

"Anyway, had I been stronger, I would have followed my instincts and insisted on having an equal hand in your father's upbringing. Something more balanced, with a greater emphasis on the importance of human connection and what was once considered feminine —feelings, compassion, empathy—those types of things."

She stops and stares at the palace for a moment, and I'm not sure if she's forgotten why we're out here, or if she just needs a minute to think. Just when I'm sure she's got dementia, she turns back to me, her eyes watery. "We messed up, Arthur. We messed up very badly, and your father has wound up mistaking ruthlessness for strength. He's been a grave disappointment as a son, a king, and a father. Cutting himself—and the family—off from the people, disregarding their concerns. I'm afraid he's to go down as the Marie Antoinette of Avonia."

"I doubt that very much. In his entire life, I don't think he's ever offered anyone cake."

"Right you are. He's far too selfish to do even that, isn't he?" she asks. "He was awful to Cecily. Just awful. No wonder she..." She stops and shakes her head. "If I had realized how delicate your mother was, I never would have selected her."

"You couldn't have known she would—"

"But I should have been paying attention. She was so dreadfully unhappy." Her voice shakes. "He never looked at her, never spoke to her. Just pretended she wasn't there unless she gave him reason to berate her, which seemed to happen with an alarming regularity. It was a miracle that they even produced one heir, let alone two."

"It's okay, you don't have to explain." Because I do not want to think about my parents producing heirs, thank you very much.

"Yes, I bloody well do. The family is in trouble, and it's because of the piss poor job your grandfather and I did raising a king." She lets go of my hand and points to me. "But you, you, my dear boy, can save the monarchy. I saw it tonight when you were speaking. You won over that crowd, and believe me, before you got up on that stage, half that room was filled with enemies. You need to lead this family to victory."

"But I'm not the leader of this family."

"A title doesn't encourage others to follow. It's the things you spoke of tonight—wisdom, bravery, and a fair mind. You've got all three in spades, my boy. You just have to let people see it."

"I promise I'll do whatever I can."

"I know you will. I just wanted you to know that I believe in you."

I feel a lump in my throat and have to look up at the sky for a second to stop from becoming emotional. What the hell is wrong with me lately? First with Tessa, now with Grandmother.

"We may be facing an uphill battle, but at least we can be grateful your father didn't pay any attention to you when you were growing up. If he had, you may have ended up being a real horse's arse, too."

I burst out laughing.

"Are you offended?"

"Not in the least."

"Too bad. I was hoping to shock you. I've spent eighty-four years being prim and proper and bored out of my fucking mind. I intend to go out with a bang."

I lower my face and give her a light peck on the forehead. "Good for you. I hope the bang lasts a very long time."

"Me, too," she says. "But just in case I'm not here to guide you, I want you to continue what you started tonight. Let your heart lead you. Always find your humanity and look for it in others. If you and that Royal Watchdog can find yourselves in bed together, you can make peace with anyone. Including the Prime Minister. And the people."

My mouth drops to my knees. "How long have you known who Tessa was?"

"From the first night she was here. I have no idea why, but everybody seems to think I don't watch the news."

"Why didn't you say anything?"

"Because it's so much more fun to let you all think you can put one over on me. Easier, too. Do you know how many things I get out of by pretending to be feeble and confused?"

I laugh, and she joins in, resting her head on my shoulder. When it's over, she says, "We should get back. I'm sure your young lady is wishing you were with her."

I stand and offer her my hand. This time, she takes it and lets me help her up. We link arms and stroll back toward the castle in the warm early summer's evening.

"You'll be a wonderful king, Arthur. Fight for what's rightfully yours, and once you're wearing that crown, I promise it will have an entirely new sheen."

"Thank you, Grandmum. You know, you've always been my favourite in the family."

"I know."

"You're supposed to say I'm your favourite, too."

"You want me to lie?"

"Yes, I suppose I do."

"Too damn bad." She laughs. "Now, about your Tessa. You're going to have to fight for her, too, because in order for you to become the man I know you can be, you're going to need someone of her strength and intelligence by your side. Not to mention someone to laugh with..."

"Oh, I don't...I think...she's not——"

"Poppycock. She's perfect for you. She's precisely the one you need. Now, man-up and make her yours."

———

As we approach the palace, I see Tessa standing on the far side of the terrace alone, staring up at the sky. Even from this distance, she takes my breath away. I have to fight the urge to abandon my grandmother and run to her.

"Go. I'll be fine."

"No, I'll escort you inside."

"No offence, but I'd rather be on the arm of the handsome young Ollie, if you don't mind." She pats my arm, then slips hers away from me. "Come here, gorgeous."

Ollie's ears turn pink as he hurries over and holds her under the crook of her elbow.

As I watch them walk inside, I hear her say, "So, Ollie, dear, what are your thoughts on older ladies?"

I chuckle as I jog up the three steps to the terrace and make my way to Tessa. She turns and looks at me, then smiles, but her eyes don't light up the way they normally do when she sees me.

"What's wrong?" I ask as soon as I am close to her.

"I broke my shoe." She holds up one sparkly stiletto missing its heel.

"Oh, God, I've seen that happen to a woman once. It was both hilarious and cringeworthy at the same time."

She sets the shoe on the stone railing. "Well, I was cringing, and everyone who saw definitely found it hilarious."

She crosses her arms and rubs her upper arms with her fingers.

"Well, I wish I had been there to sweep you off your feet when it happened." I take off my jacket and wrap it around her shoulders.

"That would have shut them up." She smiles. "Thanks for the jacket. That's a pretty slick move, Your Highness."

"I'm famous for being slick. Now, what are we going to do about your shoe?"

"I think I'll limp back to my room. Those damn heels were giving me blisters anyway."

"Not on my watch." Reaching one hand under her knees, I lift her into my arms. She squeals out a laugh and wraps her arms around my neck. When we reach a stone table, I set her down carefully and take off her other shoe.

"You must have been at the top of your class in Prince Charming school."

I pick up one foot and rub it, and the funny thing is, it doesn't bother me at all to hold her warm foot. Normally, there is no way in hell I'd be touching someone's sweaty toes, but because they belong to her, they are lovely to me. "It was Prince *Charm* School, and yes, I was an A-plus student."

I rub the other foot for a moment and inspect her toes. Her pinky toes have horrible red blisters along the sides. "Good God. I don't think we've got one torture device in the dungeon that would outdo high heel shoes. And yet, you women put them on willingly."

"So, you *do* have a dungeon. I knew it!"

"It's used for storing wines now. They got rid of all the torture devices years ago." I pause and examine her foot again. "Would you like me to take you back to your room? We could spend the rest of the evening snuggled up watching TV or doing some of those things I had in mind earlier…"

"As completely perfect as that sounds, you're needed back inside. Show the people here those weren't just nice words before. They need to know you actually will follow through with the whole accessibility thing."

"In truth, the only person I really want to be accessible to right now is sitting in front of me."

"And she can't let you do it."

Her words warm my heart. As I stare at her, I realize she is the one whom I want by my side, win or lose. "Wait here. I'll be right back."

32

The Clock Strikes Twelve

Tessa

I sit on the table, under the stars, inhaling his scent from his jacket. God, he smells so freaking good. *Unforgettable* streams out onto the terrace through the open doors, and I hum along happily to the tune. It reminds me of dancing around the living room on my grandad's feet. I think of him and wish he were here to talk to right now because I don't have the first clue what I should do. I'm in love with a good man for the first time, but he's also a man I haven't been honest with. I've kept one foot in his world and one back in my old one, entertaining a job offer from his nemesis. I stare up the stars and whisper, feeling very silly, "Send me a sign, Grandad. Tell me what to do."

"Here we go." I turn and see Arthur striding toward me, carrying a small silk bag. "I figured out a way for me to stay at the party, and you to stay with me."

My face spreads into a wide grin. He looks so pleased with himself that it's like catching a rare glimpse of him as a little boy. I watch as he pulls out a pair of ballet slippers.

"They belong to my sister, but she's never worn them, so you don't have to be disgusted by the thought of wearing used shoes." He lifts my left foot and places it on his thigh, then retrieves a couple of Band-Aids from his jacket pocket. I watch as he wraps my toe, then picks up one of the slippers and slides it onto my foot. "Other one, please."

I switch feet and gaze at his face as he works. His eyebrows knit together as he carefully wraps my other toe. His hands are gentle. Loving, even. "If you show this side of yourself, you'll win."

He looks up at me for a moment, then slides the second slipper onto my foot. "You're saying if I spend the next few weeks fixing up booboos for the entire kingdom, I'll win?"

"I'm not kidding. Let them see who you really are. I promise, if they meet the real Arthur, they will love you."

"How can you possibly know that?"

"Because I quite possibly love you, and I am the worst of them."

He drops my foot and looks into my eyes. My heart pounds and my stomach flips, and I'm suddenly terrified that I've said too much. This wasn't supposed to be anything other than a bit of fun, and I sort of just told the Crown Prince I may be falling in love with him. His face is so serious, it frightens me.

Oh, God. I know he's going to dump me. Easy or hard, it won't really matter. All of this magic is about to come to a crashing end.

But it doesn't.

He moves closer to me, pressing himself up against the table where I sit. I watch as his mouth opens, waiting for him to say something. Anything. But he doesn't. He just leans down and kisses me like his life depends on it. His lips crush mine, and I taste champagne and smell his delicious cologne. I close my eyes and allow myself to fall even deeper.

I wrap my arms around his neck and feel his hands on my waist as our mouths continue to move together in the most passionate, perfect embrace. When we finally come to our senses, we're both panting from the heat of it.

"We should go inside," I say, regretting the words as soon as they roll off my tongue.

"Yes. We should." He lifts me off the table and sets me onto the patio.

I flex and point my right foot, then smile. "Very comfortable, Your Highness. Thank you."

"Don't thank me. You're the most exciting person here. I wouldn't have a moment's fun without you."

"I find that hard to believe. There are at least two hundred single girls in there who would happily see to it that you'd have a good time."

"Three hundred and twelve actually, but if they don't look exactly like you, or sound exactly like you, or think exactly like you, then they won't hold my interest for more than a minute." He kisses me again, then pulls back and says, "Let's go test out those dancing shoes."

Oh, God, I am in love. I am so very in love. The feeling bursts through my chest and excites every nerve ending. Then that pang of guilt flickers again and douses the happiness. If this relationship is going to have any chance at all, we have to start with a clean slate, and it must start with me meeting problems head-on rather than sweeping them under the rug. "Arthur, wait. I need to tell you something."

His face falls a little.

"Jack Janssen offered me a job...sort of. As a speech writer. He approached me at the ship christening, and I didn't want to tell you because I didn't know if I could trust you. Not until tonight." I let the words spill out quickly, my heart pounding in my chest.

"I see."

He does not look happy. Dammit. *Why did I lift the rug? Why?*

"And what were you to do in order to get the job?" His words are clipped in a way I have only heard him use with Damien. Bugger.

"I was to report anything useful I found to him before making it public. But I haven't found anything—"

"But you were looking."

"Yes. No. I mean, at the beginning I was, of course, but then things changed between us and I stopped, but I didn't tell him 'no.' I'm really sorry. I should have told you weeks ago. It's just that this entire time, I've had to allow for the possibility that you were just using me." I close my eyes, unable to face him.

"Because you were worried about falling for another arsehole like Richfield."

"Exactly," I say, feeling a surge of relief. "I have a bad habit of falling for the wrong—" I stop, and my head snaps back. "How would you know about Barrett?"

He swallows hard. "I had to have an extensive background check run. I'm sure you'd have expected that."

"Not really." My entire body feels numb. "But I suppose it makes sense. Even though it is a little jarring to find out someone you've been sleeping with for several weeks ran an extensive background check on you."

His eyes harden. "Yes, I suppose as jarring as finding out the woman who's been sharing your bed has been looking to get a job by screwing you over."

"Maybe more so, even?" I'm on the verge of sarcasm. We stare each other down for a moment, both of us intent on righteous indignation. "Wait? How extensive?"

He glances away for a second, and I know I'm about to get the upper hand, even though I'm sure I don't want it.

"Job history, educational background, previous addresses, financial status…"

I back up a few steps to put some distance between us. Nope. Don't want the upper hand.

Arthur takes one step toward me. "Tessa, the order was given before you even got here, when you were considered the biggest threat to my family's reputation. But I promise you, I've made sure the results of the report will be kept a secret."

I scoff at the word secret, which in his world extends to a circle of people no fewer than twenty-wide. "What else did you find out about me?"

"That you've had some exceptionally bad luck with men. I also may have seen and used some information from your old online dating profile, but that was *before* I really got to know you."

I suddenly feel sick. "Oh, my God. Do you even like Jelly Babies?"

"Not really. They're a little too sweet."

"Arthur! There you are." I turn my head and see an absolutely gorgeous redhead striding toward us, her black gown swaying along with her tiny hips.

"Brooke. I didn't think you were able to make it."

Brooke? Lady Doctor Brooke Frigging Beddingfield? *He didn't think she could make it?* Oh, Christ, I really don't have the first clue what this man has been up to when we're not in bed together.

"I wouldn't miss this. I flew in late this afternoon." Ignoring me, she kisses him right on the lips. A long one, too, not a little peck.

Arthur pulls back, looking more than a little uncomfortable. But who is he uncomfortable to be seen with? Me or her?

"Brooke, I'd like you to meet Tessa."

She glances me up and down, then says, "Charmed, I'm sure." The look in her eyes says she's anything but charmed to see me. "I hope you won't mind, but I need to steal the Prince away from you."

Clearly done with me, she turns to Arthur. "There are some very important people you'll want to meet, and I've managed to arrange a little sit down with them on your behalf."

"Oh, well, thank you. I'll be there in a minute. I just need to finish this conversation."

"I'm afraid they won't wait." She smiles sweetly, but underneath that smile is a very determined woman.

I give Arthur a meaningful look. "Don't waste the opportunity on my behalf. I'm pretty sure we're done here anyway."

He stares at me for a moment, then nods. "Very well."

Brooke links arms with Arthur and maneuvers him in the direction of the ballroom. I watch them walk away, my head swimming in the murky waters of our deceit.

I take a few minutes to collect myself, then set my shoulders back and walk into the ballroom, trying desperately not to notice the slippers hugging my feet. Trying not to think about what almost just happened between us or whom he's with at this exact moment. I walk quickly, hoping to get through the ballroom unnoticed. I'm almost at the doors when a hand is extended to me. I look up and find myself face-to-face with King Winston.

"Ms. Sharpe. May I have this dance?"

Well, why not? It's only the worst moment of my life. I curtsy, then follow him to the dance floor.

He turns to me, then places one hand on my waist and uses his other to guide me around the floor. "I apologize for not finding time to meet you sooner."

"No need. You've been in the middle of a crisis."

"Even more reason to maintain one's manners. It's by our conduct when in our worst moments that we are judged."

"So true." I smile but wonder if he's seen the report on me, too. He must have. My cheeks burn with humiliation. "I'm surprised you would want to talk to me at all, really, after everything I've written about your family."

He shrugs and gives me a friendly smile. "You were just doing your job. Besides, some of it you had right."

Well, that's not what I was expecting to hear—not after everything Arthur's said about him.

"My son certainly seems taken with you, and I can see the feeling is mutual."

"He's a wonderful person."

"That, he is. Do you love him?"

"I...umm..."

"It's a simple question." He smiles, but his words are curt. "You either do or you don't."

"I'm afraid we find ourselves in a rather complicated situation, so some words are best left unsaid."

"He told me you were intelligent. I must confess, I didn't quite believe him, but now I see it for myself."

"Thank you, Your Majesty." *Thank you? For assuming I'm an idiot?*

"If you *are* in love with him, you now find yourself in the unfortunate position of making a very difficult choice. You can declare your love for him, thus losing any shred of professional credibility you've managed to cling to and costing him his crown, or you can leave him, thereby saving both your own career and his."

He pauses, then gives me a smugly satisfied look before going on.

"As his loving father, which of those choices do you think I'd like to see you make?"

"The second one."

"Smart girl. I'm assuming smart enough to realize that were you and my son to get married, you'd only ruin him."

Ruin him? Nah-uh. I was just about to slink out of Arthur's life, but now I may have to change my mind, even if it's only to prove this arsehole wrong. "How exactly would I ruin your son?"

"By being you. Arthur can't marry some armpit-sniffing, breast-checking, accident-prone commoner. He needs someone graceful, accomplished, and well-born as his queen. Someone people will respect and admire."

"Someone like Lady Beddingfield."

"Precisely."

Ouch. Here's the King Winston that Arthur warned me about. It's like he somehow knew exactly what to say that would hurt the most. Everything I've said to myself. I am nothing, no matter what Arthur says.

The King goes on. "I know this must be difficult for you to hear, but I only want to do what's best for both of you. At some point, the fog of new passion will lift and Arthur will see he's made a terrible mistake. Better to know early on than when you're in too far."

My heart feels like it's being squeezed with every word. I want to tear away from this awful man and run from him, straight into Arthur's arms, but then I realize I don't want to run to him either, since he very likely has just been using me this entire time.

The song ends, and King Winston keeps hold of my hand. "You don't look well at all. I'll have my man Damien escort you to the vault to return that necklace."

I believe my carriage has just turned back into a pumpkin, hasn't it?

33

Ridiculous Hats & Bitter Disappointments

Arthur

IT'S NEARLY two o'clock in the morning. The guests have finally left, and I can't find Tessa anywhere, which has panic rising in my chest. Brooke's timing could not have been worse. If only I had a chance to explain to Tessa that it was all real. Everything I said to her, I meant. But then again, maybe it was only real on my end. She's the one who was looking for ammunition to hand over to Jack the Wanker Janssen. I'm angry and hurt, but I still hate like hell to know she's feeling the exact same way about me.

After Brooke showed up, I ended up stuck in a long, but vital discussion with some very powerful friends who are willing to pull out all the stops on our behalf. I could hardly leave them to go find Tessa, but now as I hurry to the private residences, I know in my gut that she's gone. I check her room first, letting myself in with the key that she gave me weeks ago. Her bed is made. The closet empty. She is gone. I hurry around the suite for any sign of her, then rush to my room.

When I open the door, I see them. The slippers are sitting neatly on the coffee table. Next to them is an envelope. I tear it open and see her handwriting.

Arthur,

We've been playing a horribly, stupidly dangerous game, and I've decided to end it. Even Michael Corleone wouldn't have dared to keep his enemies this close.

I am sorry for keeping the truth from you for so long, and were we to speak again, I imagine you would say the same thing to me. Whether you would mean it or not is another matter entirely.

The truth is, none of that matters. There's no point in trying to fix what has been broken beyond repair, because whatever we were to each other was built on lies and bad intentions, which means it was nothing from the start.

But even if we had been honest with each other, and even if we could trust each other, you and I could never have a future together. It became crystal clear tonight that I don't belong in your world, and I never have.

Don't worry, you'll still get what you want from me. I told you the other night that I wanted to help you, and I will keep my word.

You win,

Tessa

Oh, fuckity-fuck-fuck.

———

"Arthur, get up!" The shrill sound of my sister's voice wakes me from a dead sleep.

I open my eyes just in time for her to throw open the curtains and let the sun burn the corneas off my eyeballs. "Ahh! Shit."

"The parade is starting in fifteen minutes. Vincent has come by three times already to wake you." She whips off my covers, then screams and turns around. "Why are you naked?!"

"I sleep in the nude." I gather a sheet around me. "Why the hell are you tearing off my covers anyway?"

"I just told you! You are meant to be outside in your morning suit *right now*, looking more like a crown prince, and less like a vagabond."

"Can you dial back the shrill by about ten points? I have a splitting headache."

"Get. Up!" Her heels click across the floor. "The entire country is waiting for us. You will not keep them waiting, if you know what's good for you."

———

Exactly twenty-three minutes later, I climb into the gold and black open-air carriage, dressed in my ridiculous grey penguin suit and top hat. My father and grandmother sit across from me, and I sit next to Arabella, facing backwards as the horses begin to jostle us around for the unbearably long trek around the city. Grandmother is in a yellow dress with a large feathered matching hat that is so bright, it's like sitting across from the sun. Arabella is in a white dress with pink flowers and a tiny hat that looks like it belongs on a Chihuahua.

I burst out laughing. "Nice hat. Did your maid shrink it in the dryer?"

Arabella sighs. "So glad you could join us. It wouldn't be a parade without your snarky commentary."

"Finally up, I see," my father sneers.

"Who plans a bloody parade at ten in the morning the night after a ball?" I grumble.

"Well, maybe if you didn't get piss drunk and stay up all night, you would've had an easier time getting up at a respectable hour," Arabella says.

"You didn't seem drunk at the ball," my grandmother says.

"I wasn't. That was after."

"Why would you and Tessa start drinking so late at night?" she asks.

"She's gone." I take a flask out of my pocket. "I was drinking alone." I tip up the flask and let the liquid burn down my throat. I feel like I could vomit, but if I can keep it down, a little pick-me-up is exactly what the doctor ordered. Okay, so I'm not a doctor, but I did play one once in a fun little role-play thing with the Duchess of Funsville, so I figure I'm qualified to prescribe alcohol to fill the gaping hole in my soul.

"Put that away, you bloody idiot," my dad says, leaning forward to take it from me. I raise my hand so it's out of his reach and glare at him. Oh, it's good to be tall.

"I'll have it finished by the time we leave the palace gates." I tip it back and let the rest pour down my throat until the flask is empty.

"What do you mean, *she was gone?*" my grandmother asks.

"Just that."

"Good. So the girl can take a hint," my father says.

My gaze hardens. "What exactly is that supposed to mean?"

Arabella swats at me with her hand. "Put that away. We're about to cross the river."

I tuck the flask back in my pocket and hear the thrum of the television news helicopter that will follow us for the next three torturous hours. Oh, Christ. Where is a lone shooter when I need one? "No answer, Father?"

"I simply paid her the kindness of ensuring she was being realistic about the future."

As soon as we cross the river, the sound of people cheering joins the slapping of the helicopter blades. As if on cue, we all turn to look out the carriage and begin to smile and wave at the crowd.

None of us move our mouths, but we manage to hold an entire conversation through our teeth.

My father waves as he says, "Don't I get a thank you? I was doing your dirty work for you. I saw you with Brooke and knew you'd want to rid yourself of the blogger woman as quickly as possible."

"We've been over this before. I have no interest in marrying Brooke."

"Tell me you're not actually considering that little idiot to be queen."

I grin at a group of children waving miniature paper versions of our family's flag. "You're a total son of a bitch. No offence, Grandmother."

"None taken, darling."

"I may be a son of a bitch, but that's better than being an utter disappointment."

"Ha!" my grandmother says. "If anyone in this carriage is a disappointment, it's you, Winston. A bitter one."

"Shut up, you old bat."

"Don't speak to Gran that way!"

"I'll speak to her any way I like. I'm the bloody king."

"Not for long." My voice comes out sounding like Professor Snape. If I weren't so filled with rage, I'd find this almost amusing.

"What is that supposed to mean? Planning a regicide, are we?" he asks as he points at a little boy in the crowd and pretends to laugh.

"If I am, believe me, you won't know until it's too late." Neck getting sore. Smile and wave to the opposite side now.

"I could have you locked away for saying such things."

"Then *do it*. I'm sure the company would be an improvement. No offence, Arabella, Grandmother."

"None taken. Winston, did you really chase that lovely girl away?"

"What lovely girl? You can't be referring to that dumb bitch of a reporter."

"Say it again, and I swear to God, I'll punch your face right here." I don't know why I'm defending the woman who ran out on me last night, but somehow I can't stop myself.

My father snorts. "I honestly can't decide whether to hope for victory or defeat at the referendum. Victory will mean putting an absolute moron in charge when I die."

"Stop it. The both of you. You should both be ashamed of yourselves," Arabella hisses, her face frozen in a wide smile. "Neither of you deserves to rule so much as a sand castle, let alone a real kingdom."

My father lets out a strangled laugh. "Oh, and do you think you'd do a better job? With all your experience hosting tea parties and weeping over stray dogs?"

"I would do better than a man who gets caught evading his taxes, then flits about to get his jollies with women from every corner of the globe."

"The Earth is round, dear," Grandmum says.

"I know that. It's an expression."

"What did you say to her?" I growl at my father.

Arabella thinks I'm referring to her. "I said, it's an expression, which it is. I know the Earth is round. I'm the one who called it a globe!"

"I meant Father." The booze is kicking in finally, numbing my rage, but also my self-control. Hmm, not sure if this will be a good thing or a bad thing. "What did you tell Tessa?"

"I merely told her that you would require a more suitable woman as your wife, which you will."

Before I can respond, the carriage stops in front of the Abbey. Two footmen hurry around to open the half-doors for us and help the ladies down so we can shake hands with the people and accept flowers and cards. I seize the opportunity to hop over the barricades and stride straight into a pub on the corner with a crowd, as well as my security team, in tow.

"I'd like to buy a round for the house!" I call to the bartender, which earns me a cheer as I make my way up to the bar.

"I'll have a pint of Sheepshagger Gold, please." I take off my hat and lean my elbow on the bar. "Oh, can you make it fast? I'm in the middle of a parade," I say to the man behind the bar.

He gives me a shrug as he pulls on the tap. "I can pour fast, but I'm afraid drinking it down is the bit that takes all the time." He slides the glass to me.

"Leave that to me." I turn to the crowd. "Here's to our eight hundredth birthday! Even if I never sit my royal arse down on the throne, may we have another eight hundred more." I gulp down the beer in one go, which seems to be worthy of even more reverence than buying everyone a round.

I set down the glass and turn to the other patrons, who are all lining up to get their free drink. "All right. That's me. I have to get back to the parade."

Turning to Ollie, I mutter, "Forgot my wallet. Can you pay the man, and I'll square up with you later?"

Ollie, who already has his credit card out, just nods. We've been through this before.

Getting out is a lot harder than walking in. I am stopped every few feet to sign autographs and pose for photos. I make an arse of myself, doing the hang loose sign and making funny faces for the cameras. Give the people what they want, right? Know your audience, and all that bullshit.

When I get back to the carriage, my family sits waiting and glaring openly. I hop in and sit down. "Oh, don't look so sour. I was just doing some PR. You should try it sometime, Father. You know, *actually* spend a few minutes with the people of your nation. If you had bothered to do it even a little, we wouldn't be about to have all our stuff thrown out on the lawn."

"Is that what your little peasant girl told you?" my father asks.

Grandmum takes her turn now. "Oh, do shut up! The pair of you are like a couple of children badly in need of a smacked bottom!"

I open my mouth to speak, but she silences me with a finger pointed in my face. "Not one more word out of your bratty mouth. If the two of you want to go a round when we're back inside the castle walls, you have my blessing, but not here. Not when the vote is only weeks away. You will conduct yourselves with a sense of decorum, or I'll slap those stupid hats right off your heads."

When she's done, she turns and smiles out at the crowd and resumes her dainty waving, as though we've just been chatting about the weather. God, I love that woman.

34

So This Is Rock Bottom...

Tessa

I WAKE to the sound of the hair dryer down the hall. Oh, that's horribly loud. I open my eyes to find that I'm on the couch. My own couch. All at once, the events of the night before come tumbling down on me, crushing my heart and causing my stomach to lurch. The necklace, the dancing, the slippers, the lies, Brooke, the King, the running away, the champagne. "Oh, bollocks."

I slowly sit up and pull off the quilt to find I am still in my ball-gown. The boning is digging into my sides and back, reminding me never to go to a ball again. My ribs needn't worry, however, because my aching heart will make sure I never repeat such a mistake.

"Good morning, Cinderella." Nikki crosses the room and gives me a sympathetic smile.

"What time is it?"

"Almost noon. I wasn't sure if I should wake you or just let you sleep."

"I don't have anywhere to be." I catch a whiff of myself and recoil. "Except maybe the shower."

I watch as she walks to the sink. She comes back with a glass of water and a bottle of Advil. "Here."

"Thanks."

She sits on the armchair. "So, spill it first, or shower first?"

"Shower," I say, nodding firmly. Then my shoulders drop and I start to sob. Loud, pitiful, soul-shaking sobs.

"Oh, sweetie," Nikki plants herself next to me and puts her arm around my shoulder while I succumb to my sadness. "You fell hard, didn't you?"

"So hard. I'm such an idiot." I sob and sniffle. "He was just using me the whole time."

"What an arsehole." She pats my back as I cry. "What? Did he tell you last night after the ball or something?"

I sniffle. "It was all a lie. Sipping wine at sunset, his feelings for me. All of it. He doesn't even like Jelly Babies!"

"I'm not following, hon."

"I know, because I'm not making any sense. I'm too stupid to make sense!" I dissolve into tears while Nikki holds me.

"That's not true, sweetie. You're one of the smartest people I know. You just have terrible taste in men. No arsehole radar at all."

I nod. "You're right. You're always right. And you're such a good friend to help me when I stink so badly."

"Yes, I am," she says. "Tell you what. You go shower, I'll make you some tea and toast, and then you tell me everything."

I nod. "Okay." I stand and walk across the room. "Can you make my decisions for a while? I don't think I can be trusted."

"Sure, honey. First decision is that you go shower."

When I get to my tiny bathroom, I take a moment to look around. I'm home, where it's safe. No horrible princes who pretend to be in love with me. No fancy lady doctors. No nasty kings. I stare at myself in the mirror. Most of my eye makeup is mashed down onto my cheeks, and my skin is basically just a bunch of blotchy red patches.

The sight of it makes me cry pitifully.

Forty-five minutes later, I emerge in sweats and a hoodie. My hair drips onto my shoulders as I wander slowly back to the kitchen. Nikki is watching the news. There he is. Arthur walking out of a pub with a top hat and a huge grin. He looks devastatingly handsome. And happy. "Why he is so fucking happy? And why is he wearing that hat?"

"Shit." Nikki quickly shuts off the television. "Your toast is ready."

"Turn that back on."

"No."

"I'm serious, Nik, turn it back on! I want to see what he's doing."

"Remember you put me in charge of your life for now? First rule is no stalking, which in your case includes the news, unfortunately."

"What was he doing? Why isn't he at home in bed, crying his eyes out because I'm gone?"

"Second rule is that you can't spend all your time trying to figure out why he isn't devastated, because the only reasonable explanation is that he's a total son of a bitch who doesn't deserve you."

"But he's so wonderful." My face twitches, and I'm about to cry again. Oh, yes, here it goes…

————

I'm ashamed to say things went downhill from there. The rest of the afternoon and evening was pretty much a repeat of the same conversation over and over. So much for 'having a bit of fun and getting out before things get serious.' So much for 'maybe there *is* a good man for me, after all.' So much for true love *does* exist and my knight in shining armor actually wears a crown on special occasions. So much for incredible orgasms and melt-in-your-mouth blueberry scones. Oh, God, I forgot about the scones. I will miss them so…

I keep my phone off and don't turn on my computer for the next two days, mostly because as soon as Nikki leaves (she's going to stay at Dr. McPerfect's for a while), I break out the wine and spend the next forty-eight hours watching ABNC with the shades drawn, just in case I can get a glimpse of his gorgeous face again. And I do, because apparently now that we're through, he's turned into quite the man

234

about the town. He's at everything, smiling and laughing and joking with everyone who comes near him.

Each image is a dagger to my heart, even with the numbing effect of the wine. I'm now a disgusting mess, sweating out alcohol from my pores and eating handfuls of cereal straight from the carton at each meal. I sigh to myself. "At least things can't get any worse, right, Chester?"

Chester moves his gills to reassure me that it's all going to be okay.

"He's been dubbed the 'The PR Prince,'" Veronica Platt says into the camera. "The new, improved, fully accessible future monarch has vowed to be the eyes, ears, and voice of the people. He recently set up a Twitter account and has started posting pics on Instagram, but the past few days he's making appearances in the most surprising places. Giles Bigly has more on this."

"Thank you, Veronica. Yes, Prince Arthur has done an about-face, and quite frankly, it's *about time*. Since the ball, he's launched an all-out war on anti-royal sentiments, pulling out all the stops to prove that the monarchy belongs in Avonia."

I sit and watch as Arthur plucks a baby out of an adoring fan's arms. Even the baby adores him, laughing as he holds her up and makes little goo-goo sounds.

"I hate that baby," I tell Chester, who swims in his bowl as though to agree. "Oh, yes, she *is* a smug baby. You're exactly right."

The buzz of my intercom startles me, and I spill my wine on my hoodie. And yes, it is the same hoodie I've been wearing for two full days and nights. What? It's very comforting. I ignore the buzzing and go back to hating babies, but whoever is at the door is very persistent.

I get up and walk over to the intercom, press the button, and bark, "Go away."

The buzzing starts up again. I press the button again. "What?!"

"I have flowers for a Ms. Tessa Sharpe."

"From whom?"

"It doesn't say, Miss."

My heart skips a beat. Arthur! "Come up."

I open the door and wait impatiently for the lift door to open. When it does, I see a man in a suit walking toward me. He's holding the bouquet and a large yellow envelope. The envelope should set off alarm bells in my head, but I'm too focused on the flowers to notice.

"Tessa Sharpe?" he says.

"Yes." I smile. "I don't remember seeing you around the palace? Are you new?"

He gives me a confused look for a second, then hands me the flowers and the envelope. "You've been served."

———

So, turns out Chester was wrong. Things could get worse. And they did. I've just been served notice that the makers of the Shock Jogger are suing me for one million dollars for 'misrepresenting and thereby creating a hostile market for their product.'

I shouldn't blame Chester, though. His brain is the size of a grain of rice. No way I should be counting on his predictions to come true.

35

Dad Jokes & Finger Guns

Arthur

HAVE you ever had to become a version of yourself you despise? I mean *really* loathe with everything in you, and even standing under a scalding shower until you run the entire palace out of hot water doesn't make you feel clean? Maybe not, but that's how I've felt over the last two weeks. I've become the cheesy, dad-joke-making, finger-gun-pointing-while-clicking salesman for the Royal fucking Family. I've kissed so many babies my lips are going to stay in the pucker position if I don't stop.

At least it gives me something to focus on all day, rather than succumbing to the black void of despair that overtook me when Tessa ran out on me. Pathetic, I know. I'm fighting the urge to call and text her repeatedly until she gives me a chance to explain. Yes, I used the information from her dating profile to cheat a bit, but only at the beginning. The rest was real. Very real.

I should call her. I can't let things end this way. This is foolish. I pick up the phone yet again, but then I think about her plotting with the Slime Minister and set it back down. I go through this cycle about twenty times a day. The guilt, the wishing to explain, then the hurt, the anger, and the hopelessness.

Her words in the letter come to mind and slap me on the face again. If there's one thing about me, it's that I can take a hint. She's clearly through with me. Wham, bam, thank you, Arthur.

I hope she gets the job with Jack Janssen. I really do. They deserve each other. It was all a lie on her part. All those late-night confessions, and all that stupid staring into each other's eyes, and all those laugh-until-your-cheeks-hurt moments...all of it meant nothing to her.

Too bad I miss her so much, it actually hurts. I've been rather an idiot, haven't I? I kept my enemy so close that I can't seem to sleep or eat or even think without her near me. So, for now I'm in some weird sort of hell where I feel sick to my stomach all day and night—either from acting like a sodding politician or because, across the river, the only woman I've ever let even close to my heart is either very angry or very hurt or both. And I feel the exact same way. The irony of it is that the only person I want to talk to about this is the person who inflicted this horrible pain on me. She's the only one who will truly understand what I'm going through. Isn't that a kick in the neck?

I pace the room and check my phone for what must be the twelve millionth time, but still nothing. Just a few hundred notifications on my Instagram and Twitter accounts. Urgh. Dex has given up on me and gone to bed. He paced behind me for the first evening but then gave up around two a.m. Lazy, lazy pig.

A buzzing on my phone has me hurrying across the room. I pick it up, but it's not her. Instead, it's an article *about* her. "Royal Watchdog Sued for One Million Dollars."

Oh, bollocks. I sink onto my bed and quickly scan the article. I think about how she promised she'll still help me even though we're through, and a glimmer of hope comes over me. What if I can do something to help her? It would only be fair, really.

Besides, what if it worked and she would see that I meant every damn word I said to her? What if this is my one chance to prove to her I'll hold the wall?

36

Cures for the Commoner's Heartache

Tessa

"Oh, honey. I've never seen you this bad before." Nikki stands over me with a blend of disgust and sympathy on her face.

I am lying in the exact same spot I've been for a full day now. I reach under the coffee table and hold up the notice of civil litigation, and an eviction notice signed by Charles Porter for nonpayment of landscaping bills, plus disrupting the peace of my fellow residents. Nikki takes them and sighs. "Oh, no..."

"I have to move home with my parents. My *parents*, Nikki! *My* parents. I'm going to lose everything. I can't afford to pay for a lawyer." I sit up and scratch my head, which makes me cringe. "Ouch. My hair hurts."

"Yeah. It looks a little...crusty."

"I may or may not have spilled runny ice cream down the side of my head."

"How...? Never mind." She opens her mouth, then closes it again. "Nope."

"I'm totally screwed."

"Come on." Nikki takes me by the hand. "Let's go, lady. You're going to shower, then we're going to figure out what you're going to do about all of this."

One hour, three shampoos, and two cups of strong coffee later, I'm sitting at the table, eating a bowl of cheesy macaroni Nikki whipped up. She's on the phone with her dad, who is a retired barrister. My stomach tightens as I listen to her saying a whole lot of 'uh-huhs' and 'okays,' and 'is there any other way around its?'"

When she gets off the phone, she looks at me. "He doesn't think they have a case, but he said the worst thing you could have done is ignore it. You need to get someone to respond quickly, someone with a lot of experience in this type of thing. He said to tell you to hang in there, and that he'll make a few calls to see if he can find someone to help you out. Oh, and they want you to come around for dinner soon."

"Thanks, that's very kind of them. But maybe call him back and tell him not to bother calling around. I can't hire anyone anyway." I have a sip of tea and stare out the window at the palace in the distance. I feel a jab to my stomach and turn back to Nikki. My brain can only focus on something other than Arthur for about one minute at a time, which is utterly pathetic. You'd think that given the fact I'm about to be broke and homeless, I'd forget all about his royal liar pants. But I can't.

"Have you heard from him?"

I shake my head. "He's been too busy parading around town—literally—and having an absolutely wonderful time without me, while I've been lying stuck to the couch with ice cream in my hair." My voice rises with every word until I'm practically shouting. I slump down in my chair and tears stream down my cheeks. "I let myself get caught up believing it was something it wasn't, but the whole time he was just using me. I've been a total fool, Nikki. I fell in love with the wrong guy, *again*. But it's the last time. I'm done. Done with men for good. That's it. I surrender. I'm just going to grow old alone and wait for the chin hairs to start coming in."

"Other than the chin hairs, you might be on to something there, because men clearly don't work out for you."

I gasp, but she keeps talking before I can launch into an indignant rant.

"Now, I know you've just had your heart stomped on and handed to you, but you have to get your arse back to work. This is the *exact* time you should be capitalizing on everything, but you're not, and I'd hate to think you went through all of this for nothing."

"Me, too." I turn back to her, and my eyes fill up again.

Nikki slides a tissue box to me and sits back in her chair. "It's time to get it together, because you need to face your life. Like yesterday."

"I know. I will." My voice lacks any hint of enthusiasm, even though I know she's right.

I'm starting over. Again. And this time, I'm going to do things right. Face problems head-on, be honest, and use integrity as my guide. Unfortunately, I have to start with my final post about the Royal Family. I'll have to set aside my anger and pain and do my best to be objective for the first time since I've started writing about them. It's going to hurt like hell, but I know when it's over I'll have the satisfaction of knowing I did the right thing. Plus, I have another carton of Choco Loco ice cream in the freezer.

———

BLOG POST – May 12th

Tessa here. This will be my last post as The Royal Watchdog. I have spent the last few days reflecting on my time at the palace, and on my previously held beliefs and notions about the Royal Family.

I must admit publicly that my earlier posts were based, in large part, on 'educated guesses' as to what the Royals were doing and why. This is extremely difficult for me to admit, but I must, because it is the right thing to do. In my defense, had the Family been more forthcoming with their financial records, their values, beliefs, and duties all along, none of us would have had to guess. But, if their only crime is to have been private about such matters, this is not a good enough reason to oppose them.

I stand by my belief that a nation's people should elect their leaders, but other-

wise, I am no longer adamant that the Royal Family takes more than they give. The financial burden that they place on the taxpayers is far less than the money that they bring in through tourism and charity work.

I've spent time with dozens of recipients of the Family's patronage, and I must say, their lives have all been made better by the kindness and care they've received by Princess Arabella, Prince Arthur, and the Princess Dowager Florence. I've shared some of their stories on the blog recently, and it has been a truly touching experience to witness and would be a great loss to many, should the vote go against them.

More than that, we must pause to give thought to the fact that Avonia is a kingdom. It has been a kingdom for eight hundred years now, and there is something a little bit magical about that. Perhaps there is something to be said for magic to delight us and tradition to join us to our past in our busy, critical, modern world. Perhaps they serve as an important reminder of simpler times, and how we all just need to slow down a little bit and not let constant progress get in the way of having a rich life, whether you're in a small flat on Church Street or you're in a palace.

I had some tough questions for the Royal Family to answer when this whole thing started. I wanted to hold their regal feet to the fire, to force them to be accountable for their mistakes, but the truth is no one was holding me accountable for mine.

Did King Winston betray the people by dodging his taxes? Absolutely. Should he be held accountable for that? Yes, definitely. He has been made to pay back the money with a large fine, which is, by law, what would be required of anyone in this situation. Were his actions unforgivable? You'll be surprised to find that I don't believe that is for me to say.

You see, over the past few weeks, I've been thinking about my work as The Royal Watchdog, and what I bring to the world through it. And I've discovered that, although entertaining, and (I hope) thought-provoking, I'm not sure that there is value in someone spouting their hate-filled opinions into the world. In fact, I'm sure there is very little value in it. The world is filled with enough anger and judgement, without someone like me making a lot of assumptions and presenting them as facts.

I set out to be a respected journalist and have missed the mark in a way that is nothing short of outstanding. There is no room for passion in journalism—unless it is a passion for presenting the truth. Accurately, honestly, and unbiased.

Now, I know that The Royal Watchdog has never been an unbiased news source, but I can see that I'm not doing what makes me a better person.

Recently, my ten-year-old niece, Tabitha, asked me why it was okay for me to say such mean things about the Royal Family when she's always been told to be kind to others. I had no answer. So, my new rule in life is going to be, 'if I can't explain it to my niece, I shouldn't be doing it.'

(Well, maybe not in every way. I mean there are some grownup things I'd like to be doing that she doesn't need to know about, but otherwise, the rule works.)

For those of you who will be going to the polls, and I hope it will be every eligible citizen of Avonia because this is a vital referendum, and one that cannot be undone, I would like to share some of my observations about Prince Arthur, with whom I spent the most of my time. He may act like nothing could ever phase him, but in truth, he spends much of his time worrying. Worrying about doing the right thing, about the people he can't help, about whether he's done enough. And now, he's worrying about turning over our nation to Jack Janssen, a man who accepted his family's friendship when presented in good faith, but then turned on them as soon as the opportunity presented itself. We must ask ourselves why the Prime Minister would do that? Why does he need sole power over our country? Why should we trust a man who betrayed the very people who helped him in his climb to power?

I know, it is the very definition of patriarchal to have a leader decide he knows best for our country, but Prince Arthur doesn't see it that way. He sees it as his responsibility to hold the wall, as he put it. And to be completely honest, there's some comfort in having someone at the top who will care for and protect us all. (And please don't accuse me of being anti-feminist, because Prince Arthur could easily have a daughter and raise her to do the same.)

To be honest, I'm not sure which way I will vote, which is as shocking to me as it is to many of you. What I do know is that whatever decision is made, I think at the end of the day, we're all seeking the same thing. A fair, just, kinder world, one in which we don't feel judged or looked down on by others. And the only way to create that is to stop judging each other.

At the end of the day, the Royal Family are just people with hopes and dreams and pains and flaws, like the rest of us. They wake up each morning and do their best to get through the day. They need to sort out whether to do the right thing or the smart thing, when the choices aren't the same. Unlike us, they live a life of privilege that few can imagine, but this life comes with pressures and hardships that we can't fully understand, either. They have more critics than the rest of us.

But as of today, they have one less.

So, to the Royal Family, I apologize for my previous judgements and criticisms. For Prince Arthur, and Princess Dowager Florence especially, I thank you for welcoming me into your lives, and showing me who you really are. It has been an honour, one of which I am not worthy, but will strive to be.

———

When I finished the first draft, I spend an hour eating ice cream while tweaking the post before I hit post. My heart pounds as I wait for my confession to be uploaded for all the world to see. Part of me—the pathetic, lovesick part—hopes Arthur will read it and come rushing to me with his upper body poking out the sunroof of his limo, like Richard Gere in *Pretty Woman*. But that will never happen.

This isn't some Hollywood movie, and I'm not some beautiful prostitute who can give a billionaire a new lease on life. He's *never* going to marry someone like me. He's going to marry Lady Doctor Brooke Beddingfield, or…or someone else equally impressive and with the proper lineage. Not some failed reporter whose father is a mechanic and whose mother collects royal mugs for a hobby. I was just…someone willing to give him what he wants.

And now he has it.

I abandon the spoon and sip the Choco Loco straight from the carton.

Dignity? When has that ever mattered?

My thoughts turn to the serious backlash I'm about to face from my faithful fellow royal haters, but I don't even care. The only thing that matters is having this whole thing over with so I can move on and forget I've ever heard of Arthur Winston Phillip George Charles Edward Langdon.

———

Text from Noah: *Nina wanted me to say she loved your post, and she's glad you've finally come around from the dark side. She wants to invite you to her monthly book club. Hint: say no. They're an awful bunch.*

Voicemail from Mum: *Tessa? It's Mum. Finn was by earlier and showed me your blog post. Well done, sweetie! I always knew you'd come around and become a fan of our Royal Family again! Also, I'm surprised what a talented writer you are. Maybe that's your medium, more than being on screen, which tends not to work out for you. Are you coming by on Sund—BEEP.*

Text from Bram: *I take it you slept with him. Dumbass. If you need a job, I'll be hiring a new receptionist about three dates from now.*

Facebook Message from KingSlayer99: *I'm not sure I've ever felt so disappointed in another human being in my entire life. You've betrayed us all. I hope it was worth it, Tessa. Don't bother writing back, as I'm blocking you as soon as I hit send. BTW, I was just being nice this whole time. You're not smart or talented or beautiful. You've always been a loser and you always will be.*

37

I Was Mistaken. This Is Rock Bottom...

Tessa

I THOUGHT I had bottomed out the day after the ball, but that was only about three-quarters of the way down. It took another three weeks for me to *really* find the actual bottom. And let me tell you, it's dark down here.

I've been living with my parents for exactly twelve days, sixteen hours and forty-two minutes, and there is no end in sight to this current arrangement. I could do my own version of that Sinead O'Connor song, except in it, nothing would compare to my apartment. Once I paid off the landscaping fees and paid a five-thousand-dollar retainer to one of Nikki's dad's lawyer friends (a woman named Nancy Reagan—no relation to the former American president's wife, and whatever you do, do NOT bring that up unless you want to see her right eye start to twitch), and my income was cut by two-thirds by shutting down the Royal Watchdog blog, I am officially broke. Oh, and I almost forgot, I lost my damage deposit because the wallpaper

Nikki put up in the bathroom needed to be replaced. Nikki will pay me back for that at the end of the month.

My parents claim to be thrilled to have me home, but there are moments it's obvious I'm intruding on their privacy. I had no idea they had such an active sex life, and maybe they didn't when they had five children living here, but since we moved, they haven't become empty-nesters as much as *love* nesters. Yuck! The other evening, I came home from seeing a movie with Nikki, and when I walked into the TV room, it was clear they were up to something based on the guilty looks on their faces, and the fact that my father had a pillow across his lap. Also, my mum's blouse buttons were wildly mismatched, leaving a gaping hole where her bra should have been. So, now I've seen the future of my chest, and I can tell you, it's not a pretty sight.

Since then, I've taken to phoning ahead when I'm on my way home and calling loudly when I'm coming down the stairs. Or up the stairs, or in from the garden, or out *to* the garden. Really, now I'm just yelling wherever I go around here to avoid seeing that again.

The living arrangements themselves are less-than-pleasing. I'm not even in my old room. I'm in Finn's, because my old room is now a scrap booker's paradise since it had the best light of any of the upstairs bedrooms. Finn's room is a dark, dreary, tiny place that reminds me of the very back of a cave. I can tell Chester hates it in here, and I don't blame him. It smells of sports equipment and weed, even though I scrubbed it top to bottom before I moved in. But who am I to complain? At least I have a roof over my head while I sort out my mess of a life.

Almost all of my things have either been sold or are boxed up in a shed in the back garden, where I'm sure spiders are nesting at this very moment, since I'm sure that is what they do on Thursday mornings in June. They nest and lay eggs in your things while you lie in bed depressed, trying to force yourself to get up and get your arse moving again.

I stay perfectly still with my eyes wide open, listening for signs of life downstairs. Why is it one must open their eyes very wide in order to hear better? Hmm, I should Google that. Maybe I could start a site with all the answers to random questions like that. Oh, wait. That's Google, isn't it?

Anyway, it's very quiet, which means that Dad must be at work and Mum must be out. Or they're shagging. Ewww!

I throw off the covers and make my way down the hall, calling, "Who's up for some coffee? Anyone? Good morning!"

I get no reply. Ahhh. Silence.

There's a note on the kitchen table from Mum.

Tessa,

I've gone for my bridge game. Please clean up any crumbs after you make your breakfast, not like the other day when you ate half a loaf of bread with honey.

When I get back, let's chat about your career. Grace next door said that her niece is making a fortune selling something called Arbonne. You're definitely prettier than her, and if you learned how to properly apply makeup, you could be a real success!

Lars called earlier to tell you not to look at your royal website. Apparently, the comments have gotten worse, not better. Is there some way someone could delete them? Maybe Nikki would know how? I asked Lars to do it, but he said he would need your passcode, and he's also far too busy.

Anyway, I'll be back in time for lunch so we can sort out your future then.

Love, Mum

P.S. Please take the beef roast out of the freezer and scrub the potatoes on the counter if I'm not back by three. Noah and the family are coming for dinner. Won't that be nice?

No. It will *not* be nice. Worse than losing my flat, my money, and having to find a decent job is the fact that *my brothers know* I'm homeless, jobless and broke. And let me tell you, it really only took them about five minutes between them to figure out I was embellishing my previous earnings. So, no, Mum, having Noah over for dinner tonight does not sound very bloody nice!

I make four slices of honey toast (heavy on the honey) and take it to the TV room, where I turn on the television, only to see Veronica

Platt smiling back at me. My squished face is behind her, and across the bottom of the screen read the words "Lawsuit Dropped."

"What?" I jump up from the couch, letting toast fly off my lap, then stand motionless, listening to Veronica's smooth voice telling me about *my* lawsuit. Why does she always manage to scoop me?

"Wellbits, the makers of the Shock Jogger, have dropped their suit against Tessa Sharpe. On their website, it states that a deal has been struck on Ms. Sharpe's behalf but that they are not able to provide details at this time."

I grab the phone and dial my lawyer's office, where I reach her assistant, Rebecca, who puts me right through to Nancy Reagan.

"Tessa, what's happened? You haven't been brokering a deal behind my back, have you?" She sounds pissed, even though as far as I know, she's done basically nothing to earn my five thousand so far.

"I don't have the first clue what happened. I thought you would know."

"Hmm, very odd. I saw the news earlier and had Rebecca call the court clerk's office right when they opened. They confirmed that the suit has indeed been dropped and that some sort of settlement has been reached on behalf of the defendant—who is you."

I roll my eyes. Nancy Reagan seems to think I know nothing about the law, when in actual fact, I was a crime reporter for over a month. Plus, I used to watch *Is It Legal* every week with my grandad when I was a girl, thank you very much. "Well, that's amazing news, isn't it? I mean, we don't have to go to court or anything."

"Yes! Of course. You should go out and celebrate our victory."

Our victory? Really? "Since the case was settled independently of your office, I'm wondering if I could perhaps have my retainer back? I've recently hit some hard times, and that money would make a huge—"

"Oh, that's not really how a retainer works. You pay to book my time, which means it was set aside for you and therefore cannot be billed to someone else."

"Even though it is time in the future because you haven't actually started to work on my case yet? What if you find another client to fill that time?"

"Then *they'll* be paying for time further into the future than the time you paid for." She's speaking to me now like I'm a four-year-old who doesn't know how to poo on the toilet yet.

"No, but it would be the *same* days you were going to spend on my case, instead they're now freed up for someone else."

"But those days are already gone," Nancy says.

"Those days haven't happened yet."

"But they *will* happen, and when they do, they'll be gone."

"Yes, I understand how time works."

"I don't think you do. Not *legal* time anyway, but don't feel bad. Few people do. Now, you make sure you celebrate. Maybe go for a nice dinner with friends, or pop over to London to see a play or something."

"I can't."

"Why not?"

"Because *you* have all my savings."

"Well, if you didn't have any money, you shouldn't have gotten sued in the first place. I have to run now. I have clients waiting."

Click.

———

It takes me about ten minutes before I calm down enough to call Nikki so I can rant about what just happened. She's at the salon and has to step outside so she can hear me over the thumping beat of the dance music. I go through the entire story, even though she told me she's got a woman with highlights that are almost through processing.

When we finish deciding that Nancy Reagan is a level one bitch (the lawyer, not the former first lady), we move on to the topic of who is behind the settlement.

"Hang on." I hear the thumping music, and she shouts, "Tina! Can you rinse out Mrs. MacTaggart's hair, please?" Pause. *Thump. Thump. Thump.* "No, I'm afraid this can't wait! Can you just be a team player, Tina? Just this once?"

The music grows faint again. "There. I'm all yours. It's got to be Arthur. No one else could pull this off."

"No, can't be him. There must be some other reason."

"No, there isn't. It's *one hundred percent* him. No one else we know has that kind of money. Or connections."

"Yes, but he would never do this for me. Remember all the lying and the using? He's not one of the good ones." My tone is dangerously close to sounding like Nancy Reagan talking to me.

"When did you get so skeptical?"

"Oh, I don't know…maybe when Tommy-the-wanker stole all my money? Or maybe it was right around the time that giant arsehole Barrett dumped me and announced he was getting married to Helena Jones? I really can't say for sure." My voice drips with sarcasm.

"Fair enough. You may have a point there, but seriously, Tessa, you may have to allow for the possibility that he isn't as bad as he seems. Maybe Prince Arthur wanted to do something nice for you after he read your post?"

"Doubt it."

"Well, who do you think paid them out? Your fairy godmother?"

"I don't know, but it's not him."

———

I go for a long run, which is my form of celebrating my victory. I'm hoping that with each mile, I'll come closer to figuring out who came to my rescue. I can't let myself imagine that it was Arthur, because letting myself hope that he did it will only lead to me hoping we can have a life together. Which we can't. And I don't want it anyway. Because he's a lying user.

When I get back, I take a long shower, listening to the news as I scrub my face.

"In about an hour's time, the Prime Minister will be giving a press conference to answer questions about the upcoming referendum…"

"Grrr!" I reach out of the shower and shut off the radio, hoping to *never* hear about *anything* to do with Arthur ever again. I scrub my face, putting my full attention to maintaining a youthful, childlike glow. I miss the innocence of childhood. If only I could be ten again, with nothing more to worry about than how I was going to do on my upcoming spelling test. (I'd do very well, by the way. Spelling was my thing.)

My mind wanders to Tabitha's class tour and how sweet Arthur was with the kids. Oh, now my brain is just torturing me. I think of Tabitha asking about what would happen if the King doesn't call the election.

And then it hits me all in one fell swoop. I know what the Prime Minister is planning. And I know what I have to do to stop him.

I grab my phone and call Nikki. "I need your help! I have to get to the parliament building right away."

38

Latin Faux Pas & Donuts Causing Delays

Arthur

I\t's the day before the big vote. I am slumped in an armchair in the gold drawing room with Grandmum, watching the news. Even though it's just after lunch, I'm already exhausted from the past several weeks of campaigning. The Prime Minister is about to make a speech giving people the many reasons to oust us, and as soon as it's over I'll put my cheesy politician face back on and resume my final twenty-four hours of butt-smooching.

"Have you called her yet?" Grandmum asks, obviously trying to sound casual.

"No. And I'm not going to. She's made it very clear that she doesn't want a life with me, so if you don't mind, I think I'll salvage what's left of my pride."

"She'd change her mind if she knew you were the one to take care of that lawsuit for her."

"No, she wouldn't. And I'm not sure that I'd want her to anyway."

"Then why did you do it?"

"Because they made a faulty product, then tried to blame someone else for the fact that it failed."

Grandmum puts down her tea and gives me the one eyebrow. "Arthur..."

"What?" I turn back to the television, where the Prime Meanister is on the steps of the parliament building in front of a podium.

He opens his mealy mouth and speaks. "Good morning. We, the people of Avonia, have reached the eve of a landmark event. For the first time in eight hundred years, we have the power to take back our country from the family who swooped in and stole it so long ago. We no longer have to be beholden to the Langdons, no longer have to pay them reverence with our hard-earned tax money. We can simply say 'no'..."

"Arthur, you're an idiot if you're going to let your pride get in the way of a life with the woman you want."

"I'm trying to listen to this." I point to the television.

"Who cares what that wanker has to say? I'm talking about *love*."

Sighing, I turn to her. "Listen, it wasn't love. It was lust at best. And even if it *was* love, and even if it turned out that she wasn't just using me to get a job with..." I point to the television, "that *wanker,* I'd never want her to spend the rest of her days suffering in this family, with this," I wave my hand around in the air, "...so called life."

"You know, I just realized, you're either a chauvinist or a coward, but I can't decide which."

"What?" I scowl at her.

"You heard me. You either think you are entitled to make her decisions for her, which would make you a chauvinist, or you're too scared to go to her and put your heart on the line, in which case you are a coward. Very disappointing, either way."

"That's ridiculous." I jump up off the chair and walk to the window. "*She's* the coward. The first sign of trouble, she ran. She's not strong enough to do this. It would break her, like it did my mother and Arabella. So it's better that she's already gone—"

And then the most remarkable thing happens. I hear a familiar voice coming from the telly. "Tessa Sharpe, concerned citizen. Prime

Minister Janssen, currently our constitution requires the reigning monarch to call federal elections..."

I rush over to the television, and there she is, looking very nervous and absolutely lovely in a crisp white dress shirt. She has no microphone, so she has to practically shout to be heard.

"...you've made no move to change the constitution, which means that *if* the people vote to abolish the monarchy, you could legally install yourself as an *ipso facto* dictator."

Wince! "Not *ispo facto*, Tessa. *De facto*," I say to the screen.

Titters are heard from around the crowd, and I watch as a young woman with blue and purple hair whispers in her ear. Tessa turns bright pink, then says, "*De facto*. I meant *de facto* ruler."

The Slime Minister does a poor job of hiding his amusement. "I have no intention of installing myself as a dictator, *ispo facto* or otherwise. Next question."

Tessa's voice calls out again. This time, her tone says, 'Don't mess with me.' "I'm not finished with my question, sir. Why haven't you put forth a bill to have the proper changes to our election policy go into *immediate effect* should the monarchy be defeated?"

Jack rolls his eyes, but underneath the irritation, he's afraid. I can smell it from here. "This is irrelevant, and quite frankly, none of us have time for it. Why don't you go back to reviewing fitness equipment, sweetheart?"

A low 'ooooh' murmurs through the crowd.

The camera zooms in on Tessa, who now has her game face on. Shoulders back, chin up, jaw set. Yes! "I've seen that look before. He's in for it now," I say.

Tessa continues. "Do you recall a conversation you had with me on March twentieth, in which you stated that 'it's not right that our rulers are chosen simply by falling out of the right vagina'?"

The camera shift to Jack's face again. His eyes are dead cold. "Ridiculous. Next question, please." He looks around and points. "Giles, you're up. Let's make it important, please. After all, we are on the eve of a momentous referendum."

"I'd like you to answer her first question, sir. Why haven't you put a bill forward that would provide the people with the assurance they need?"

The Prime Weenister scoffs and shakes his head. "This is insanity. Does anyone have something else for me?"

A female reporter speaks up. "I do. Did you really say that comment about choosing our rulers simply by falling out of the right vagina?"

"Of course not. I would never say something so crass and insulting."

Tessa speaks up again. "But you did, sir. You said it to me at the christening of the ANS Viceroy. You then went on to say that 'if anyone is going to be a ruler until he dies, it should be someone the people elected in the first place.' Are you intending to install yourself as a *de facto* ruler? It's a yes or no question."

That's my girl!

"I'm not dignifying that with an answer. Unless anyone has anything else to ask, we're done here."

I turn to my grandmother. "I've got to go. I've got to go."

Spinning on my heel, I rush over to her, kiss her on the forehead and hurry out of the room. As I'm on my way, I hear her say, "Finally! Go get her, Arthur!"

———

One of the greatest things about the city of Valcourt is our exceptional traffic flow. Somehow, the city engineers of our nation have found a way to minimize delays, allowing a steady, smooth stream along every motorway. Unless it happens to be opening day of the first ever *Krispy Kreme* in Avonia. Then, apparently, traffic slows to the pace of an ancient wheelchair-bound poodle.

I tap my fingers on the seat arm as we sit, waiting for people to get their donut fix. "Come on, come on," I mutter.

Ollie, who is sitting next to me, says, "If I had a shot with the likes of her, I'd be making a run for it."

I glare for a second, feeling an unexpected surge of Neanderthal anger, but it doesn't phase Ollie, who says, "Relax. I'm just saying it's about bloody time."

I undo my seatbelt and open the door. "Agreed."

With that, I zig and zag my way through the vehicles, make my way to the sidewalk and sprint up the road that leads to Parliament Hill, my tie flying over my shoulder, the hot wind in my hair, the nerves in my gut tying themselves in knots.

There's absolutely no logic to what I'm doing, or to the fact that I feel that if I don't get there before the press conference ends, it'll somehow be too late. But I do. And I can't let that happen, because if it's too late with her, I'll never be happy again a day in my life.

My mind races as fast as my legs. What do I say when I see her? God, I didn't think this through. *You complete me?* No. Overused. *You're tough enough to be my queen?* Horrid. Shit. What the fuck do I say?

I turn and sprint up the long lawn that leads to the parliament buildings. The reporters are packing up, and I spot her in the parking lot, getting into the Citroën from the video. "Tessa!" I call, but she doesn't hear me. She gets in, and before I can make it to her, she's gone.

39

Truly, Madly, Completely

Tessa

"Oh, my God. I'm such an idiot!" I hide my face in my hands.

"Stop that. You were the only one in the entire country to even *think* of asking him about why he hasn't put forth that bill. You're *brilliant*." Nikki pulls out onto the road and turns toward home. "Look at all the cars going to Krispy Kreme. I wonder how long it would take for us to get a box of donuts?"

"Quit trying to distract me. I'm busy being a loser." I turn to her and lean my head against the seat rest. "*Ipso facto?*"

"Easy mistake. Anyone could make that mistake." She cranes her neck to the right. "How long will it take before the line-up dies down?"

"Months. It took, like, six months for the lines to die down in Scotland." I sigh, glad that we're heading in the opposite direction of the throngs of vehicles. "But seriously, why do *I* always have to be the one to publicly humiliate myself?"

"Because you're brave enough to put yourself out there. Most people are total wimps, but your desire to do the right thing is stronger than your desire to not look like a total arse. That's what makes you so great."

"No, that's what makes me a total arse."

"Most people see the wrong in the world and they do nothing about it, Tess. Nothing. You have courage, and you're tough as gel nails. You didn't shrink in front of that rat bastard when most people would. You're kind of my hero."

"Thanks." I blink back tears.

My cell buzzes in my purse. I reach down and pick it up, seeing two texts.

Awesome.

Text from Bram: *Ipso facto? Oh, Christ, you certainly know how to keep the country entertained.*

Text from Lars: *Good God, how is it that we are we related? Nice try, though. I could see where you were going with that. Nina was thrilled that you tried to help the Royal Family.*

The ringer sounds, and my mum's face appears on the screen. I groan and answer. "Hi, Mum."

"Tessa!" she shouts into the phone. "We watched your news conference. Well done, you! Although, I do think you really should stick to writing, my darling. It just goes better for you when you have time to check all your words over."

"Thanks, Mum. I have to go. I'm just with Nikki. She's…driving, and I don't want to distract her."

"Oh! You're with her. Perfect. Then you don't need to take the bus to get home."

"I'm not on my way home, actually."

"Of course you are, Twinkle. Remember? It's a school holiday, and you said you'd help Dad watch the grandkids while I go to get my hair coloured. Bring Nikki. We haven't seen her in ages."

Grrr. "I'll see if she can drive me." I ring off and toss my phone back in my purse.

"You need a ride so you can go help your dad babysit?"

"You heard all that?"

"How could I not?" she asks. "Do you want me to take you there, or do you need an excuse? I could run out of gas if you like."

"No, I should go. I've promised myself I'm going to stop avoiding things I don't want to deal with, remember?"

"The new, improved Tessa?"

"Exactly." I groan. "Not that it won't be just dreadful when my brothers arrive to pick up the kids. You're invited, by the way."

"Do you think your mum'll have made a batch of lemon custard tarts?"

———

Twelve minutes. That's how long it takes to get from downtown Valcourt to Abbott Lane in a car driven by Danica Patrick, a.k.a. Nikki, when lemon custard tarts are waiting. Not exactly a nice man in a hybrid with heated leather seats, but it was fast, my clothes are mud-free, and it's really hot out today, so I don't actually need my tush warmed for me. Take what you can get, right?

When we pull up, my dad is in the front garden with the kids, most of whom are drawing on the sidewalk with chalk while the twins are racing down the sidewalk on the scooters Arthur bought them, which honestly guts me, even though I tell myself it doesn't. My dad is sipping beer and admiring his peonies that are in full bloom.

He turns, looking delighted to see me as I unfold myself from the tiny car. "There's my girl. Well done, you."

He reaches out and gives me a huge bear hug, and I laugh, feeling like a little kid, just like I always do when he hugs me. It's kind of nice to be home, even if my brothers will take the piss out of me when they get here. Fuck 'em. "Thanks, Dad."

The screeching of tires down the road interrupts the moment. A black SUV with red and yellow flags comes barreling down the street.

"Slow down, you wanker!" my dad shouts, letting go of me and stepping off the curb with his hand out.

The car comes to a quick halt. "Oh, bugger. Dad, I think that's the Royal Family."

"I don't give a dead rat's arse who it is. I'm not going to stand here and watch them hit one of my grandkids." The kids are safely on the sidewalk, mind you, and now they're snickering and repeating the phrase 'dead rat's arse.' He's going to hear about that later.

The back door swings open, and Arthur gets out. He glances at my father. "Sorry about that, sir. We've been chasing your daughter all the way from Parliament Hill."

He looks at Nikki. "You're very fast."

She gives him a come-hither look. "I certainly am."

I clear my throat, and she jumps a little. "Sorry, that was purely reflex. Won't happen again," she murmurs.

Then Arthur's eyes land on me. I fix him with a look of steel. "Shouldn't you be out campaigning?"

"I should be." He takes two steps toward me. "But the thing is, I don't give a good Goddamn if we win or lose." He glances at the children, who are giggling. "Sorry, kids, you should never swear. Not very regal behaviour."

He turns back to me and swallows, his face filled with worry. "I've come to the realization that none of it matters if I won't have you by my side for the next sixty years or so."

"Nope. You do not get to say that. What we had wasn't real. It was all just a bunch of lies. Sipping wine at sunset, and the Jelly Babies! And...and the world is spinning too fast thing? Yeah, you probably thought I wouldn't have figured that out, but I've spent the past few weeks going over every conversation we had and comparing it to my old dating profile, so I know exactly which parts were bullshit! Sorry, kids!"

"All right, you got me. At the beginning, I did use ill-gotten information to try to persuade you to like me. But I stopped as soon as I really got to see the woman underneath this tough-girl mask you wear all the time."

"Just stop. I can't, Arthur. It's over, and we both have to accept that."

"No, we bloody well don't. We may have started out on the wrong foot, and we may have taken too long to trust each other, but what we felt for each other was real. *Very real.* More real than anything I've felt in my life."

I shake my head and shut my eyes tightly so I don't have to look at his gorgeous face. "You were using me, and I was using you, and even if we weren't, we still can't be together because I'll just ruin you."

"Bollocks. You're the only one who can *save* me."

"Didn't you see me at the press conference? I was a disaster. I'm *always* a disaster. I'm not the right woman for you."

"I'll be the judge of that, thank you."

Another vehicle rounds the corner. This time, it's a fast-approaching news van. I watch in shock as my father steps out into the middle of the road and holds his arms out to stop them. What the hell is going on today?

Giles Bigly jumps out, along with a cameraman. Ollie positions himself next to my father and holds up his hands as well. "Please keep a respectful distance. This is a private matter."

The man hurries over to the sidewalk and aims the camera at us but doesn't dare step past Ollie.

"This is why." I point to the news crew. "I'm not cut out for any of it. You need to marry someone sophisticated and accomplished and… and regal. Not someone who's likely to step in horseshit getting out of the carriage and come reeking down the aisle at the Abbey."

His face grows serious as he closes the distance between us. "No, you're probably right. It would probably be an unmitigated disaster. Comedic fodder for talk shows for years to come."

I give him a big nod, trying to ignore how my heart has just sunk to my feet. "Exactly. Now, I appreciate the whole romantic chasing me through town—very flattering—but I think we both know we should just say goodbye now so we can each start the lives we're meant to lead."

"Nope."

"Nope?" I purse my lips together.

"You heard me. Nope. I chased you through town for a reason. The life I'm meant to lead is with you. Crown or no crown. *You're* my purpose, Tessa."

My eyes fill with tears. "Oh, bugger. You're not going to make it very easy to walk away, are you?"

Arthur smiles, his face full of emotion. "In case you couldn't tell, I'm trying to make it impossible for you to walk away." He reaches up and holds my cheeks in his hands. The feeling of his skin on mine cracks open my hardened heart, spilling molten lava of love all through my body. I know it's cheesy, but it's true.

He smiles down at me. "Because, the thing is, if I'm going to marry anyone, it's going to be you, broken, horseshit-covered heels and all. There's no other woman on this planet I want to watch limping her way up the aisle toward me. I never thought I'd find someone I would love—truly, madly, completely like this—but I did. I found you. And you're the only woman who can keep me from turning into a completely arrogant disaster. I need you, Tessa. And I don't need anyone. More than that, I love you with every beat of my foolish heart. And if all of that doesn't convince you, you need to know I have a cupboard filled with bags of crisps back at the palace."

I laugh through my tears and reach up and put my hands over his. "You really should have led with that."

"Would that have saved me some time in getting to kiss you again?" He grins and lowers his mouth over mine.

"Definitely."

"Damn." He closes the distance between our mouths and kisses me deeply, waking every ounce of hope, and love, and lust that I tried to bury away. He wraps his arms around my waist and lifts me up off my feet, our lips staying locked together through the jeers and cheers of my nieces and nephews, through the loud throat clearing of my father, through Ollie firmly reminding us there are cameras filming us, through Nikki telling him to mind his own damn business.

None of that matters, because it's really just Arthur and me now.

And, with any luck, forever...

40

Poll-Predicting Betta Fish

Arthur

IT'S LATE on Friday night. The past thirty hours have been both the most terrifying and wonderful of my life. Case in point, the press conference I held last night to make a final plea on behalf of my family. Terrifying, but also wonderful because Tessa stood next to me, holding my hand through the entire thing, and the press loved it. They got all caught up in asking questions about our relationship and seemed to forget about the vote—for a few minutes, anyway. Wonderful when Tessa realized I was the one who put a grinding halt to the lawsuit from those horrid Shock Jogger people. She was *really, really, really* grateful, if you get my drift. Especially since she found out how I settled the case. Instead of paying them out, I've agreed to shoot a video for them, testing out the product myself. But don't worry about me. I'm a seasoned runner, and I'm sure I'll manage without getting zapped.

And now it's just the two of us snuggled up on the couch in my room, watching the polls come in (well, actually four, if you count Dex and Chester). My grandmother sat with us for the first four hours, then went to bed after saying she had no doubt in her mind that we'd win. After all, we've given the people the very real possibility of a royal wedding, and there is nothing more irresistible.

Arabella has flown to Turkey with some friends to go to a spa and have her nails done rather than sit around chewing them off like the rest of us. My father has gone to our castle on the north shore, but don't feel bad for him. He's not-so-alone. Dexter is curled up on the other side of Tessa with his snout on her lap, staring up at her.

"Look at him, he's an absolutely smitten pig," I say.

She gives me a wicked grin. "Just like his owner."

I laugh and kiss her hard on the mouth, grateful she's here during what would have been, without a doubt, the most stressful night of my life. If it weren't for her, I'd be stinking drunk by now. But she's here, and I'm not, because win or lose, I'll have a reason to go on. The polls are far too close for me to feel at all relaxed, though. We're up by less than two percent, but the western province still hasn't completed their count. The experts on ABNC are predicting a win for us, but unless they have time machines, I'm not going to trust that they know any more than Chester the betta fish, who is fast asleep on his ridiculous little fish hammock. Chester has decided to move in with me, since he doesn't like Finn's stinky bedroom, and Tessa will be spending much of her time here anyway. She can't officially move in, not without creating quite the scandal, which, for the moment, we would like to avoid.

Veronica Platt wraps up an interview with one of the polling experts, then footage of me and Tessa reuniting comes onto the screen, again. "Aww, look, pumpkin," I say, and I don't even hate myself for saying it. "There we are declaring our love for each other."

"It's right there on the national news. This is going to be quite the life, isn't it?" she asks, shaking her head a little.

"Yes, but I have no doubt you can handle it." I kiss her on the forehead. "Thank God your parents raised you with four horrible brothers."

"Thank God for that."

An hour later, we hurry to my grandmother's room and knock

gently on the door. When she doesn't answer, I open it and we walk in and are greeted by the sound of her snoring.

"Maybe we should just let her sleep," Tessa whispers.

I shake my head. "No, she'll want to know."

"Know what?" she croaks.

I walk over to her bed and hold a glass of champagne out to her. "That we won!"

She opens one eye. "Your girlfriend was right. Not worth waking me for." Rolling over onto her side, she says, "You'll really need to trust her judgement if you're going to be king someday. She's much smarter than you."

Epilogue

AUTO-TUNE THE PRINCE

Arthur

"Oh, darling, it's not that bad." Tessa kisses me on the cheek as the video plays on her parents' telly. Isa has cleared the room of children by sending them out to the garden with popsicles and is happily getting her revenge on me for the whole 'come out, little baby' mistake.

I watch from the back of the room with my arms folded across my chest. Finn grins back at me every few seconds, proud to be the first to show the family the auto-tuned version of the damn video.

On the screen, my entire body folds up on itself and I shout, "Fuckity-Fucking Hell!"

I glance at Tessa's mum, who is the only one not laughing. "It's not funny at all, is it?"

"Thank you, Evi. Glad somebody gets it." Even Tessa's laughing so hard, she's crying. But she, at least, has the sense to apologize between bouts of giggles.

"It was rather painful, actually. I feel like *I* should sue *them*."

The Shock Jogger people wanted to shoot the video live, going for massive exposure over the safety of being able to splice out any problems. No wonder Wellbits is going under. "Until that moment right there," I point to the screen, "I couldn't for the life of me figure out that whole, 'not my hair' business."

Tessa stops laughing and turns to me. "Feels like it'll all fall out, right?"

"Exactly." I smile down at her, glad to have her to commiserate with. "I once read about a woman who got shocked so hard, all her hair fell out."

"*Weekly World News*?" she asks, setting her attention on the screen again.

"Probably fake, right?"

"Probably."

"Although they were right about that man who had a baby..."

When the video ends, Tessa turns to me, clearly holding in another bout of laughter. "My knight in shining armor."

"Oh, stop it."

She wraps her arms around me. "No, you are. You did that to save me."

"And you'd think you would be a little more sympathetic to me for that very reason."

"I'm sorry, Arthur, it's just...so fucking funny." She kisses me on the lips, and I find my bruised ego being soothed, but just a smidge.

Reaching up on her tiptoes, she whispers in my ear, "I promise I'll make it up to you later."

Totally worth it.

The Royal Wedding

(A CROWN JEWELS ROMANCE, BOOK 2)

Irresistibly Funny. Wildly Romantic.

When most girls get engaged, at most they face a disapproving mother-in-law, but in Tessa Sharpe's case, it's a disapproving nation. No one in Avonia wants the former anti-royal blogger to wed Prince Arthur. The anti-royals haven't forgiven her for abandoning ship and swimming over to the Prince's yacht, and the royal watchers won't ever forget all the horrible things she wrote about their beloved Royal Family.

Up against all odds, Tessa has only six months to prove herself worthy of the title of Princess. Her scheming future father-in-law is going to throw every obstacle in her way, including the beautiful, poised, and highly accomplished Lady Doctor Brooke Beddingfield. But Tessa is determined to make this work *and* keep her fledgling career as a reporter intact.

Will Tessa manage to fight her way down the aisle and find her Prince Charming waiting? Or will one of them succumb to mounting pressure and run the other way before they can say I do?

Don't miss the must-read second installment in the

Crown Jewels Romance trilogy! Get your copy today and be part of Tessa and Arthur's continuing crazy romance...

The Honeymooner

(PARADISE BAY, BOOK 1)

**From bestselling author Melanie Summers comes the
wickedly funny, ridiculously romantic spinoff of her
highly-acclaimed Crown Jewels Series...**

Twenty-nine-year-old workaholic Libby Dewitt lives by the motto 'if
you fail to plan, you plan to fail.' She's finally about to start her dream
life with her steady-as-a-rock fiancé, Richard Tomy. Together, they're
the perfect power couple—right down to the fact that he's agreed to
use their honeymoon to help further her career in mergers and acqui-
sitions. But ten minutes before the wedding, her dreams dissolve via
text message.

Devastated and humiliated, Libby escapes to Paradise Bay alone.
She's got two goals for her trip: to devise a plan to get Richard back
and to convince resort owner Harrison Banks to sell his property to
her company. Unfortunately, when she arrives, she discovers that tall,
dark, and built, Harrison is not about to make anything easy for her.

Instead, he derails her plans while at the same time, bringing out a
side of Libby she's kept carefully tucked away—a carefree, adrenaline
junkie. After a few days together, Harrison's got her wondering if the

life she always wanted was meant for some other girl. Suddenly, Libby must decide which version of herself she wants to be.

Will she go back to her comfortable, safe life, or risk everything to be with the only man who's ever made her feel truly alive?

About the Author

Melanie Summers lives in Edmonton, Canada, with her husband, three kiddos, and two cuddly dogs. When she's not writing, she loves reading (obviously), snuggling up on the couch with her family for movie night (which would not be complete without lots of popcorn and milkshakes), and long walks in the woods near her house. Melanie also spends a lot more time thinking about doing yoga than actually doing yoga, which is why most of her photos are taken 'from above'. She also loves shutting down restaurants with her girlfriends. Well, not literally shutting them down, like calling the health inspector or something. More like just staying until they turn the lights off.

She's written fourteen novels (and counting), and has won one silver and two bronze medals in the Reader's Favourite Awards.

If you'd like to find out about her upcoming releases, sign up for her newsletter on www.melaniesummersbooks.com.